Country Bunch

Country Bunch

A COLLECTION BY MISS READ

ILLUSTRATED BY ANDREW DODDS

LONDON
MICHAEL JOSEPH

First published by
MICHAEL JOSEPH LTD
26 Bloomsbury Street
*London, W.C.*1
NOVEMBER 1963
SECOND IMPRESSION FEBRUARY 1964

Set and printed in Great Britain by Tonbridge Printers
Ltd, Peach Hall Works, Tonbridge, Kent, in Bell eleven on
thirteen point, and bound by James Burn at Esher, Surrey

To
MARY ELLEN CHASE
with love

ACKNOWLEDGEMENTS

Acknowledgement is gratefully made for permission to include the following works or extracts from them:

Hodgson, Ralph: *The Gypsy Girl* (from COLLECTED POEMS, published by Macmillan & Co. Ltd., London, and the Macmillan Company of Canada, Ltd.). Frost, Robert: *Stopping by Woods on a Snowy Evening, The Runaway* (from THE COMPLETE POEMS OF ROBERT FROST. Copyright 1923 by Holt, Rinehart and Winston, Inc. Copyright renewed 1951 by Robert Frost. Reprinted by permission of Holt, Rinehart & Winston, Inc., Publishers, N.Y.). Bridges, Robert: *Spring Goeth All in White* (from MODERN VERSE FOR LITTLE CHILDREN, published by The Clarendon Press, Oxford). Davies, W. H.: *The Rain* (from THE COMPLETE POEMS OF W. H. DAVIES, published by Jonathan Cape Ltd., by permission of Mrs. H. M. Davies). Hardy, Thomas: *The Field of Waterloo* (from THE DYNASTS, published by Macmillan and Co. Ltd.), UNDER THE GREENWOOD TREE (published by Macmillan & Co. Ltd.), *The Darkling Thrush* (from THE COLLECTED POEMS OF THOMAS HARDY, published by Macmillan & Co. Ltd.). Thomas, Edward: *The Gallows, The Owl* (from COLLECTED POEMS, published by Faber & Faber Ltd., reprinted by permission of Mrs Helen Thomas). Sitwell, Sacheverell: *Outside Dunsandle* (from SELECTED POEMS, published by Gerald Duckworth & Co. Ltd.). Bell, Julian: *Pluviose* (from ESSAYS, POEMS AND LETTERS, published by The Hogarth Press). Thomas, R. S.: *Farm Child* (from SONG AT YEAR'S TURNING, published by Rupert Hart-Davis Ltd.). Lee, Laurie: *The Milkmaid* (from THE SUN, MY MONUMENT, published by The Hogarth Press, and by Doubleday & Co. Inc., N.Y.). Cornford, Frances: *The Coast: Norfolk, Country Bedroom, Bickers Cottage* (from COLLECTED POEMS, published by the Cresset Press). Coatsworth, Elizabeth: *On a Night of Snow* (from THE NIGHT AND THE CAT, published by the Macmillan Company, N.Y. Copyright, 1950 by the Macmillan Company). Blunden, Edmund: *Country Sale, Old Remedies, Poor Man's Pig, The Yellowhammer, Solutions* (reprinted by permission of Edmund Blunden). Cane, Melville: *Snow Towards Evening* (from AND PASTURES NEW. Copyright, 1926 by Harcourt, Brace & World, Inc.; copyright, 1954 by Melville Cane. Reprinted by permission of the publishers). Macneice, Louis: *Glass Falling* (from COLLECTED POEMS, published by Faber & Faber Ltd.). De la Mare, Walter: *Rain* (by permission of The Literary Trustees of Walter de la Mare and the Society of Authors as their representative). Kirkup,

James: *The Virtuoso* (from SPRING JOURNEY, published by Oxford University Press). Mew, Charlotte: *Arracombe Wood* (from COLLECTED POEMS, published by Gerald Duckworth & Co. Ltd.). Bates, H. E.: *The Little Fishes* (from SUGAR FOR THE HORSE, published by Michael Joseph Ltd., reprinted by permission of the author). Aumonier, Stacey: *Octave of Jealousy* (from UPS AND DOWNS, published by William Heinemann Ltd., reprinted by permission of Mrs Stacey Aumonier). Dolci, Danilo: TO FEED THE HUNGRY (published by MacGibbon & Kee Ltd.). Thompson, Flora: LARK RISE TO CANDLEFORD (published by Oxford University Press). Horace: extract tr. by Janet Maclean Todd (from VOICES OF THE PAST, published by Phoenix House Ltd.). Holdsworth, Geoffrey: *The Old Gardener* (reprinted by permission of Country Life Ltd.). Mitford, Mary Russell: *Our Village*, and Walton, Izaak, *The Compleat Angler* (from TWO PROSE IDYLLS, edited by J. Edward Mason, published by Thomas Nelson & Sons Ltd.). Farjeon, Eleanor: EDWARD THOMAS: THE LAST FOUR YEARS (published by Oxford University Press, reprinted by permission of the author). Uttley, Alison: COUNTRY THINGS (published by Faber & Faber Ltd.). Osborne, Dorothy: Letters (published by The Clarendon Press, Oxford). Lee, Charles: *Mr Sampson* (from ENGLISH SHORT STORIES xvth-xxth CENTURIES, published by J. M. Dent & Sons Ltd.). Jerome, Jerome K.: THREE MEN IN A BOAT (published by J. M. Dent & Sons Ltd.). Thomas, Dylan: UNDER MILK WOOD (published by J. M. Dent & Sons Ltd.). Scovell, E. J.: *The Boy Fishing* (from THE RIVER STEAMER, published by The Cresset Press). Fleming, Marjorie: *Three Turkeys* (from THIS WAY DELIGHT, edited by Herbert Read, published by Faber & Faber Ltd.). Bell, Adrian: CORDUROY (published by the Bodley Head Ltd.). *83 Years in Aldermaston* (reprinted by permission of Newbury Weekly News). Grattan and Singer: ANGLO-SAXON MAGIC AND MEDICINE (published by Oxford University Press, reprinted by permission of Wellcome Historical Medical Library). Chaucer, Geoffrey: CANTERBURY TALES (edited by F. N. Robinson, published by Houghton Mifflin Co.). The poster on page 206 is reproduced by permission of the Cambridge and County Folk Museum; that on page 232 by permission of the *Newbury Weekly News*.

8

CONTENTS

Acknowledgements   7
Foreword   15

COUNTRY PEOPLE

The Old Gardener: PALATINE ANTHOLOGY   19
The Plowman: GEOFFREY CHAUCER   20
A Beggar at Grasmere: DOROTHY WORDSWORTH   21
Queenie and Twister: FLORA THOMPSON   22
Bessie Bighead and the Cows: DYLAN THOMAS   25
A Poet at Work: DOROTHY WORDSWORTH   26
The Schoolmaster: OLIVER GOLDSMITH   27
The Night School: GEORGE ELIOT   28
A Victorian Village Schoolmaster: ALISON UTTLEY   32
Milkmaid: LAURIE LEE   34
A Squire of Somerset Returns Home: HENRY FIELDING   35
A Country Doctor: HENRY FIELDING   38
Dorothy Osborne's Ideas of a Husband: DOROTHY OSBORNE   40
Roderick Random Lies Wounded: TOBIAS SMOLLETT   42
Another Aspect of Aldermaston:
    THE NEWBURY WEEKLY NEWS   43
Old Postie: FLORA THOMPSON   43
Dorothy Osborne's Day at Chicksands: DOROTHY OSBORNE   44
Two Old Men of Wessex: THOMAS HARDY   46
The Shepherd: WILLIAM BLAKE   48
Lucy: MARY RUSSELL MITFORD   49
Lucy's Husband: MARY RUSSELL MITFORD   51
Farm Child: R. S. THOMAS   52
Gertie with the Wasp Waist: FLORA THOMPSON   53
Living in the Country: TOBIAS SMOLLETT   55
Meg Merrilies: JOHN KEATS   57
The Gipsy Girl: RALPH HODGSON   58
Outside Dunsandle: SACHEVERELL SITWELL   58
Gipsies at Candleford Green: FLORA THOMPSON   59
Edward Thomas: ELEANOR FARJEON   61
Mr Sampson: CHARLES LEE   63

COUNTRY PLACES

A Thanksgiving to God: ROBERT HERRICK   85
The Country Bedroom: FRANCES CORNFORD   86
Some Dwellings: MARY RUSSELL MITFORD   87
An Ancient English Country Seat: ALEXANDER POPE   89
Bickers Cottage: FRANCES CORNFORD   90
Tea Break at Dorcas Lane's Smithy: FLORA THOMPSON   91
Night: DYLAN THOMAS   92
Morning: DYLAN THOMAS   93
The Coast: Norfolk: FRANCES CORNFORD   94
A North Country Kitchen in Winter: ALISON UTTLEY   95
Arracombe Wood: CHARLOTTE MEW   96
The Hall Farm: GEORGE ELIOT   97
The Field of Waterloo: THOMAS HARDY   99

BIRD, BEAST AND FISH

Parson Woodforde's Pigs: JAMES WOODFORDE   104
The Poor Man's Pig: EDMUND BLUNDEN   104
Parson Woodforde's Cat: JAMES WOODFORDE   105
Miss Betsy Barker's Alderney: ELIZABETH GASKELL   106
Aubade: WILLIAM SHAKESPEARE   106
Mr Jorrocks and the Grouse: R. S. SURTEES   107
The Town and Country Mouse: HORACE   109
Field Mice and House Mice: GILBERT WHITE   111
Boys by a Stream: BERTRAM SMITH   112
The Runaway: ROBERT FROST   113
Instruction on Frogs: IZAAK WALTON   114
The Boy Fishing: E. J. SCOVELL   115
White Owls: GILBERT WHITE   116
The Tortoise: GILBERT WHITE   116
The Grasshopper and the Cricket: JOHN KEATS   118
Parson Woodforde's Bees: JAMES WOODFORDE   119
Bird Watching: DOROTHY WORDSWORTH   119
Bevis Watches Swallows: RICHARD JEFFERIES   120
Three Turkeys: MARJORIE FLEMING   120
Swan Battle: JEROME K. JEROME   121
Vincenzo C. A Story told in Prison: DANILO DOLCI   122
The Cuckoo: WILLIAM SHAKESPEARE   123

The Red Robin: JOHN CLARE 124
The Owl: EDWARD THOMAS 125
The Yellowhammer: EDMUND BLUNDEN 125
The Darkling Thrush: THOMAS HARDY 126
Magpies: OLD RHYME 127
Solutions: EDMUND BLUNDEN 127
The Gallows: EDWARD THOMAS 128
The Octave of Jealousy: STACEY AUMONIER 131

THE CHANGING SEASONS

Description of Spring: HENRY HOWARD 155
April Morning: DOROTHY WORDSWORTH 156
A May Morning: GEOFFREY CHAUCER 157
Spring Goeth all in White: ROBERT BRIDGES 157
Perdita's Speech: WILLIAM SHAKESPEARE 158
Leaving the World: JOHN KEATS 158
Dorothy's Daffodils . . .: DOROTHY WORDSWORTH 159
. . . And Her Brother's: WILLIAM WORDSWORTH 160
From You Have I been Absent: WILLIAM SHAKESPEARE 160
An October Day: DOROTHY WORDSWORTH 161
Glass Falling: LOUIS MACNEICE 162
The Rain: W. H. DAVIES 162
After the Storm: WILLIAM WORDSWORTH 163
Rain: WALTER DE LA MARE 163
Pluviose: JULIAN BELL 164
The True Tale of Elizabeth Woodcock:
    THE CAMBRIDGE CHRONICLE 165
On a Night of Snow: ELIZABETH J. COATSWORTH 167
When Icicles Hang by the Wall: WILLIAM SHAKESPEARE 168
The Virtuoso: JAMES KIRKUP 168
Snow Toward Evening: MELVILLE CANE 169
That Time of Year: WILLIAM SHAKESPEARE 170
Stopping by Woods on a Snowy Evening: ROBERT FROST 170
Bright Morning: JOHN KEATS 171

REMEDIES AND RECIPES

Old Remedies: EDMUND BLUNDEN 175
Dorothy Osborne's Medicine: DOROTHY OSBORNE 176
Miss Lane's Wine Jelly: FLORA THOMPSON 177

Salamandering: FLORA THOMPSON 178
Parson Woodforde has Earache . . . : JAMES WOODFORDE 179
. . . And Toothache: JAMES WOODFORDE 180
Toothache Again: JAMES WOODFORDE 180
Cure for Ague: JAMES WOODFORDE 181
Parson Woodforde's Cow Polly: JAMES WOODFORDE 181
Parson Woodforde's Stye: JAMES WOODFORDE 182
To Cure a Stye: ALISON UTTLEY 182
Bad Colds: ALISON UTTLEY 183
Homely Cures: ALISON UTTLEY 183
The Power of Plants: WILLIAM SHAKESPEARE 184
Anglo-Saxon Medicine:
    J. H. G. GRATTAN AND CHARLES SINGER 185
Quince Tree: NICHOLAS CULPEPER 187
Parsley (Common): NICHOLAS CULPEPER 189
Garden Mint: NICHOLAS CULPEPER 190
Burdock: NICHOLAS CULPEPER 192
How to Make Eel a Most Excellent Dish: IZAAK WALTON 193
Of Clownes Wound-Wort: JOHN GERARD 194
Of Teasels: JOHN GERARD 198
Of African Marigold: JOHN GERARD 199
Of Lily in the Valley: JOHN GERARD 200
Of Daffodils: JOHN GERARD 201
Of the English Jacinth: JOHN GERARD 202
Parson Woodforde's Antidote: JAMES WOODFORDE 203

COUNTRY OCCASIONS AND JUNKETINGS

Cambridge Coronation Festival 207
Country Frolic: JAMES WOODFORDE 210
Pilgrimage in Spring: GEOFFREY CHAUCER 211
A Great Fair at Reading: DOROTHY OSBORNE 212
Washing Clothes: JEROME K. JEROME 214
Harvest Time in the '80s: FLORA THOMPSON 215
Country Funeral: DOROTHY WORDSWORTH 218
Country Dancing in Cumberland: JOHN KEATS 219
After Honey-Taking: THOMAS HARDY 220
A Cheerful Party: JAMES WOODFORDE 223
The Cricket Match: MARY RUSSELL MITFORD 223
Country Sale: EDMUND BLUNDEN 227

Laura and the Pig-Killing: FLORA THOMPSON   229
Thetford Assizes 1785: JAMES WOODFORDE   231
The Fabulous Coat:
   THE READING MERCURY AND OXFORD GAZETTE   231
The Cheap-Jack Calls at Lark Rise: FLORA THOMPSON   234
Mr Jorrocks at Newmarket: R. S. SURTEES   237
Mr Jorrocks's Phaeton Ride: R. S. SURTEES   237
Towing and Being Towed: JEROME K. JEROME   239
A Suffolk Meet: ADRIAN BELL   240
Mr Jorrocks's Dinner Party: R. S. SURTEES   246
The Little Fishes: H. E. BATES   249

Index of Authors   256

FOREWORD

I have chosen the following passages for the best reason of all – I like them, and hope that you will too. They deal, as the headings show, with the vital stuff of country living; people, places, weather, wild and domestic animals, trees, flowers and crops, herbal remedies, and country pursuits and pleasures of divers kinds.

For good measure I have included three country stories which are particular favourites of mine, and in every case you will find the source of each extract if you want to read more yourself from the original.

Now, more than ever, we need the countryside. It is being covered at an alarming rate by bricks and mortar, and what is left to us is doubly dear. Walter de la Mare once said: 'Even a Cockney's starven roots may thirst for the soil,' and there are few Englishmen who are not countrymen at heart.

You will find in these pages comment on country living from the time of Horace to the present day. The writers vary in time, temperament and talent, but they have in common a relish of country things and the ability to transmit their pleasure in them.

I hope that you will find here as much colour and refreshment as in any good mixed country bunch from a market stall.

COUNTRY PEOPLE

Those of us who are lucky enough to live in the country have a proper appreciation of the importance of our neighbours. We know each one, where he lives, why he lives there, what he does for a living (with luck even what he earns!), his pastimes and his general behaviour. We probably know something of his forbears too. And he, we can be sure, knows just as much about us.

For we are sparsely enough scattered within the parish bounds to welcome the sight of another living soul, and to take an active interest in him. We are spared the ignominy of semi-suffocation amidst strangers in tubes and buses. We are not squashed in shops and offices, or edged from pavements crowded with anonymous hordes. We are blessed with room to breathe and time to dally. When we meet each other we exchange gossip and glee, sorrow and sympathy, and continue on our way with food for thought. It is not surprising that we also develop an uncanny eye for details of dress and personal appearance. As you will see in many of the following passages, the country dweller who writes (I am thinking particularly of Dorothy Wordsworth and Thomas Hardy) does so with a wealth of minute detail born of loving observation – itself the outcome of acute interest and the benison of unhurried time.

Here are a few country people from all ages. I find their portraits as vivid as the living figures who call at my cottage, the postman, my neighbour, or the dark-eyed gipsy with pegs in a basket. Some will be old friends already, I have no doubt, but there may be new acquaintances here whom I hope you will relish as heartily as I do.

THE OLD GARDENER

Dear earth, embosom here a gardener old
Who toiled for thee, and not for greed of gold;
Vine and grey olive planted he nearby
And channelled water, thee to fructify.

Lie gently on his body then, and bring
Peace to his bones; and glow with flow'rs in spring.

From the Palatine Anthology
translated by Geoffrey Holdsworth

THE PLOWMAN

With hym ther was a Plowman, was his brother,
That hadde ylad of dong ful many of fother;
A trewe swynkere and a good was he,
Lyvynge in pees and parfit charitee.
God loved he best with al his hoole herte
At alle tymes, thogh him gamed or smerte,
And thanne his neighebore right as hymselve.
He wolde thresshe, and therto dyke and delve,
For Cristes sake, for every povre wight,
Withouten hire, if it lay in his myght.
His tithes payde he ful faire and wel,
Bothe of his propre swynk and his catel.
In a tabard he rood upon a mere.

Geoffrey Chaucer:
Prologue to the Canterbury Tales

*When we were embroiled with the Romantic Revival at school I
remember that one of our notes on William Wordsworth read:*
*'His almost photographic accuracy' – a resounding phrase which
has echoed down the years for me in company with:*
*'Jeremiah had often to suffer the opprobrium of anti-patriotism,'
which, as you might expect, was encountered in another subject and
was quite a different kettle of fish.*
*I think you will agree that William's sister Dorothy shared with
him this gift of observing details ignored by less astute eyes. How
many of us, I wonder, would notice 'three bell-shaped patches of*

*darker blue behind, where the Buttons had been' on a passing
beggar's coat?*

*You will find other extracts from Dorothy Wordsworth's Journal
later on. Surely she is one of the most lovable of women, happy in
serving others, possessed of acute sensibility, and, above all, love for
her fellows. 'He said nothing, and my heart smote me' is typical of
the keen sympathy which enlivens all her writings.*

*She was born at Cockermouth, Cumberland, on Christmas Day
1771, and died in her well-loved Lake District in 1855, at Grasmere, after suffering years of mental and physical ill-health.*

A BEGGAR AT GRASMERE

December 22nd, Tuesday, 1801

. . . As we came up the White Moss, we met an old man, who
I saw was a beggar by his two bags hanging over his shoulder;
but, from a half laziness, half indifference, and a wanting to *try*
him, if he would speak, I let him pass. He said nothing, and my
heart smote me. I turned back, and said, 'You are begging?'
'Ay,' says he. I gave him a halfpenny. William, judging from
his appearance, joined in, 'I suppose you were a sailor?' 'Ay,'
he replied, 'I have been 57 years at sea, 12 of them on board a
man-of-war under Sir Hugh Palmer.' 'Why have you not a
pension?' 'I have no pension, but I could have got into Green-
wich hospital, but all my officers are dead.' He was 75 years of
age, had a freshish colour in his cheeks, grey hair, a decent hat
with a binding round the edge, the hat worn brown and glossy,
his shoes were small thin shoes low in the quarters, pretty good.
They had belonged to a gentleman. His coat was blue, frock
shaped, coming over his thighs, it had been joined up at the
seams behind with paler blue, to let it out, and there were three
bell-shaped patches of darker blue behind, where the Buttons
had been. His breeches were either of fustian, or grey cloth,
with strings hanging down, whole and tight; he had a checked

shirt on, and a small coloured handkerchief tied round his neck. His bags were hung over each shoulder, and lay on each side of him, below his breast. One was brownish and of coarse stuff, the other was white with meal on the outside, and his blue waistcoat was whitened with meal. In the coarse bag I guess he put his scraps of meat etc. He walked with a slender stick – decently stout, but his legs bowed outwards.

Dorothy Wordsworth: *Grasmere Journal*

Flora Thompson's three books about Lark Rise and Candleford describe life in rural Oxfordshire at the end of the last century and the beginning of the present one. She writes with beautiful lucidity and a complete lack of sentimentality about those hard times, and her characters are etched with the clarity of a fine engraving.

The country labourer has never been blessed with much money, and Queenie's longing in Victoria's reign for a pound a week is understandable.

An old lady of my acquaintance, who began work at the age of twelve, some time in the '90s, told me that she was employed as a nursemaid at a shilling a week.

When I asked her what she did with the money she laughed, and said:

' I saved up for a month and bought a pair of shoes for three and eleven!'

I can only hope that she spent the penny change on something more frivolous.

QUEENIE AND TWISTER

Queenie's ideal of happiness was to have a pound a week coming in. 'If I had a pound a week,' she would say, 'I 'udn't care if it rained hatchets and hammers.' Laura's mother longed for thirty shillings a week, and would say, 'If I could depend on thirty shillings, regular, I could keep you all so nice and tidy, and keep *such* a table!'.

Queenie's income fell far short of even half of the pound a week she dreamed of, for her husband, Twister, was what was known in the hamlet as 'a slack-twisted sort o' chap,' one who 'whatever he died on, 'uldn't kill hisself wi' hard work.' He was fond of a bit of sport and always managed to get taken on as a beater at shoots, and took care never to have a job on hand when hounds were meeting in the neighbourhood. Best of all, he liked to go round with one of the brewers' travellers, perched precariously on the back seat of the high dogcart, to open and shut the gates they had to pass through and to hold the horse outside public-houses. But, although he had retired from regular farm labour on account of age and chronic rheumatism, he still went to the farm and lent a hand when he had nothing more exciting to do. The farmer must have liked him, for he had given orders that whenever Twister was working about the farmstead he was to have a daily half-pint on demand. That half-pint was the salvation of Queenie's house-keeping, for, in spite of his varied interests, there were many days when Twister must either work or thirst.

He was a small, thin-legged, jackdaw-eyed old fellow, and dressed in an old velveteen coat that had once belonged to a gamekeeper, with a peacock's feather stuck in the band of his battered old bowler and a red-and-yellow neckerchief knotted under one ear. The neckerchief was a relic of the days when he had taken baskets of nuts to fairs, and, taking up his stand among the booths and roundabouts, had shouted 'Bassalonies big as ponies!' until his throat felt dry. Then he had adjourned to the nearest public-house and spent his takings and distributed the rest of his stock, gratis. That venture soon came to an end for want of capital.

To serve his own purposes, Twister would sometimes pose as a half-wit; but, as the children's father said, he was no fool where his own interests were concerned. He was ready at any time to clown in public for the sake of a pint of beer; but at home he was morose – one of those people who 'hang up their fiddle at the door when they go home' as the saying went there.

But in old age Queenie had him well in hand. He knew that he had to produce at least a few shillings on Saturday night, or, when Sunday dinner-time came, Queenie would spread the bare cloth on the table and they would just have to sit down and look at each other; there would be no food.

Forty-five years before she had served him with a dish even less to his taste. He had got drunk and beaten her cruelly with the strap with which he used to keep up his trousers. Poor Queenie had gone to bed sobbing; but she was not too overcome to think, and she decided to try an old country cure for such offences.

The next morning when he came to dress, his strap was missing. Probably already ashamed of himself, he said nothing, but hitched up his trousers with string and slunk off to work, leaving Queenie apparently still asleep.

At night, when he came home to tea, a handsome pie was placed before him, baked a beautiful golden-brown and with a pastry tulip on the top; such a pie as must have seemed to him to illustrate the old saying 'A woman, a dog and a walnut tree, the more you beat 'em the better they be.'

'You cut it, Tom,' said a smiling Queenie. 'I made it a-purpose for you. Come, don't 'ee be afraid on it. 'Tis all for you.' And she turned her back and pretended to be hunting for something in the cupboard.

Tom cut it; then recoiled, for, curled up inside, was the leather strap with which he had beaten his wife. 'A just went as white as a ghoo-ost, an' got up an' went out,' said Queenie all those years later. 'But it cured 'en, it cured 'en, for's not so much as laid a finger on me from that day to this!'

Flora Thompson: *Lark Rise*

I think that Bessie Bighead is the most moving of the throng of characters that emerge from Under Milk Wood.
This 'Play for Voices' was finished only a month before Dylan

Thomas's death in New York in 1953, after he had worked intermittently upon it for ten years.

BESSIE BIGHEAD AND THE COWS

The coming of the end of the Spring day is already reflected in the lakes of their great eyes. Bessie Bighead greets them by the names she gave them when they were maidens.

> Peg, Meg, Buttercup, Moll,
> Fan from the Castle,
> Theodosia and Daisy.

They bow their heads.

Look up Bessie Bighead in the White Book of Llaregyb and you will find the few haggard rags and the one poor glittering thread of her history laid out in pages there with as much love and care as the lock of hair of a first lost love. Conceived in Milk Wood, born in a barn, wrapped in paper, left on a doorstep, big-headed and bass-voiced, she grew in the dark until long-dead Gomer Owen kissed her when she wasn't looking because he was dared. Now in the light she'll work, sing, milk, say the cows' sweet names and sleep until the night sucks out her soul and spits it into the sky. In her life-long love light, holily Bessie milks the fond lake-eyed cows as dusk showers slowly down over byre, sea and town.

Dylan Thomas: *Under Milk Wood*

25

A POET AT WORK

May 7th, Friday, 1802

William had slept uncommonly well, so, feeling himself strong, he fell to work at *The Leech Gatherer;* he wrote hard at it till dinner-time, then he gave over, tired to death – he had finished the poem. I was making Derwent's frocks. After dinner we sate in the orchard. It was a thick, hazy, dull air. The thrush sang almost continually; the little Birds were more than usually busy with their voices. The sparrows are now full fledged. The nest is so full that they lie upon one another, they sit quietly in their nest with closed mouths. I walked to Rydale after tea, which we drank by the kitchen Fire. The Evening very dull – a terrible kind of threatening brightness at sunset above Easedale. The Sloe-thorn beautiful in the hedges, and in the wild spots higher up among the hawthorns. No letters. William met me. He had been digging in my absence, and cleaning the well. We walked up beyond Lewthwaites. A very dull sky; coolish; crescent moon now and then. I had a letter brought me from Mrs Clarkson while we were walking in the orchard. I observed the sorrel leaves opening at about 9 o'clock. William went to bed tired with thinking about a poem.

Dorothy Wordsworth: *Grasmere Journal*

There have been many famous village schoolmasters whose teachings and example have influenced many lives. I remember with affection the schoolmaster who ruled the village school in Kent where I spent three blissful years.

He was a thick-set dark-haired man with a great sense of humour and a fine bass voice. With a certain amount of judicious persuasion he could be encouraged to abandon a lesson to lead us in song instead. This pleased us all mightily. And why not?

We shared tattered copies of The National Song Book, and sang 'I'll Go No More A-Roving' and 'Shenandoah,' our childish trebles fluttering around that sonorous glorious bass like minnows round a salmon. But our favourite song was 'Charlie is my Darling,' for though we were as far as we could be from the Highlands in these islands, we were romantically inclined, and as staunch as Oxford in our adherence to lost causes. With 'Charlie' we fairly raised the pitch-pine roof high above us.

Here are a few portraits of more famous, but no less loved, schoolmasters.

THE SCHOOLMASTER

Beside yon straggling fence that skirts the way
With blossomed furze unprofitably gay,
There, in his noisy mansion, skilled to rule,
The village master taught his little school:
A man severe he was, and stern to view,
I knew him well, and every truant knew;
Well had the boding tremblers learned to trace
The day's disasters in his morning face;
Full well they laughed with counterfeited glee
At all his jokes, for many a joke had he;
Full well the busy whisper, circling round,
Conveyed the dismal tidings when he frowned;
Yet he was kind, or if severe in aught,
The love he bore to learning was in fault;
The village all declared how much he knew;
'Twas certain he could write and cypher too;
Lands he could measure, terms and tides presage,
And even the story ran that he could gauge;
In arguing too, the parson owned his skill,
For e'en though vanquished, he could argue still;
While words of learned length and thundering sound
Amazed the gazing rustics ranged around,
And still they gazed, and still the wonder grew,
That one small head could carry all he knew.

Oliver Goldsmith: *The Deserted Village*

George Eliot (1819–1880) was the name under which Mary Ann Evans wrote. This passage from Adam Bede *gives not only a fine description of the schoolmaster, but absorbingly detailed sketches of his three elderly pupils.*

George Eliot was in her forties when she wrote her powerful and often tragic country novels. Her strong evangelical upbringing, against which she later rebelled, coloured her writing. A deep note of compassion sounds through her work, and can be distinguished very clearly in the following passage.

THE NIGHT SCHOOL

Bartle Massey's was one of a few scattered houses on the edge of a common, which was divided by the road to Treddleston. Adam reached it in a quarter of an hour after leaving the Hall Farm; and when he had his hand on the door-latch, he could see, through the curtainless window, that there were eight or nine heads bending over the desks, lighted by thin dips.

When he entered, a reading lesson was going forward, and Bartle Massey merely nodded, leaving him to take his place where he pleased. He had not come for the sake of a lesson tonight, and his mind was too full of personal matters, too full of the last two hours he had passed in Hetty's presence, for him to amuse himself with a book till school was over; so he sat down in a corner, and looked on with an absent mind. It was a sort of scene which Adam had beheld almost weekly for years; he knew by heart every arabesque flourish in the framed specimen of Bartle Massey's handwriting which hung over the schoolmaster's head, by way of keeping a lofty ideal before the minds of his pupils; he knew the backs of all the books on the shelf running along the whitewashed wall above the pegs for the slates; he knew exactly how many grains were gone out of the ear of Indian-corn that hung from one of the rafters; he had long ago exhausted the resources of his imagination in trying to think how the bunch of leathery sea-weed had looked and grown

28

in its native element; and from the place where he sat, he could make nothing of the old map of England that hung against the opposite wall, for age had turned it of a fine yellow brown, something like that of a well-seasoned meerschaum. The drama that was going on was almost as familiar as the scene, nevertheless habit had not made him indifferent to it, and even in his present self-absorbed mood, Adam felt a momentary stirring of the old fellow-feeling, as he looked at the rough men painfully holding pen or pencil with their cramped hands, or humbly labouring through their reading lesson.

The reading class now seated on the form in front of the schoolmaster's desk, consisted of the three most backward pupils. Adam would have known it, only by seeing Bartle Massey's face as he looked over his spectacles, which he had shifted to the ridge of his nose, not requiring them for present purposes. The face wore its mildest expression: the grizzled bushy eyebrows had taken their more acute angle of compassionate kindness, and the mouth, habitually compressed with a pout of the lower lip, was relaxed so as to be ready to speak a helpful word or syllable in a moment. This gentle expression was the more interesting because the schoolmaster's nose, an irregular aquiline twisted a little on one side, had rather a formidable character; and his brow, moreover, had that peculiar tension which always impresses one as a sign of a keen impatient temperament: the blue veins stood out like cords under the transparent yellow skin, and this intimidating brow was softened by no tendency to baldness, for the grey bristly hair, cut down to about an inch in length, stood round it in as close ranks as ever.

'Nay, Bill, nay,' Bartle was saying in a kind tone, as he nodded to Adam, 'begin that again, and then perhaps it'll come to you, what d, r, y, spells. It's the same lesson you read last week, you know.'

'Bill' was a sturdy fellow, aged four-and-twenty, an excellent stone-sawyer, who could get as good wages as any man in the trade of his years; but he found a reading lesson in words of one syllable a harder matter to deal with than the hardest stone he had ever had to saw. The letters, he complained, were so 'uncommon alike, there was no tellin' 'em one from another,' the sawyer's business not being concerned with minute differences such as exist between a letter with its tail turned up and a letter with its tail turned down. But Bill had a firm determination that he would learn to read, founded chiefly on two reasons: first that Tom Hazelow, his cousin, could read anything 'right off,' whether it was print or writing, and Tom had sent him a letter from twenty miles off, saying how he was prospering in the world, and had got an overlooker's place; secondly, that Sam Phillips, who sawed with him, had learned to read when he was turned twenty; and what could be done by a little fellow like Sam Phillips, Bill considered, could be done by himself, seeing that he could pound Sam into wet clay if circumstances required it. So here he was, pointing his big finger towards three words at once, and turning his head on one side that he might keep better hold with his eye of the one word which was to be discriminated out of the group. The amount of knowledge Bartle Massey must possess was something so dim and vast that Bill's imagination recoiled before it: he would hardly have ventured to deny that the schoolmaster might have something to do in bringing about the regular return of daylight and the changes in the weather.

The man seated next to Bill was of a very different type: he was a Methodist brickmaker, who, after spending thirty years of his life in perfect satisfaction with his ignorance, had lately 'got religion,' and along with it the desire to read the Bible. But with him, too, learning was a heavy business, and on his way out tonight he had offered as usual a special prayer for help, seeing that he had undertaken this hard task with a single eye to the nourishment of his soul – that he might have a greater abundance of texts and hymns wherewith to banish evil memories and the temptations of old habit; or, in brief language, the devil. For the brickmaker had been a notorious poacher, and was suspected, though there was no good evidence against him, of being the man who had shot a neighbouring gamekeeper in the leg. However that might be, it is certain that shortly after the accident referred to, which was coincident with the arrival of an awakening Methodist preacher at Treddleston, a great change had been observed in the brickmaker; and though he was still known in the neighbourhood by his old sobriquet of 'Brimstone,' there was nothing he held in so much horror as any further transactions with that evil-smelling element. He was a broad-chested fellow, with a fervid temperament, which helped him better in imbibing religious ideas than in the dry process of acquiring the mere human knowledge of the alphabet. Indeed, he had been already a little shaken in his resolution by a brother Methodist, who assured him that the letter was a mere obstruction to the Spirit, and expressed a fear that Brimstone was too eager for the knowledge that puffeth up.

The third beginner was a much more promising pupil. He was a tall but thin and wiry man, nearly as old as Brimstone, with a very pale face, and hands stained a deep blue. He was a dyer who, in the course of dipping homespun wool and old women's petticoats, had got fired with the ambition to learn a great deal more about the strange secrets of colour. He had already a high reputation in the district for his dyes, and he was bent on discovering some method by which he could reduce the expense of crimsons and scarlets. The druggist at Treddleston had given him a notion that he might save himself a great deal of labour and expense if he could learn to read, and so he had begun to give his spare hours to the night-school, resolving that his 'little chap' should lose no time in coming to Mr Massey's day-school as soon as he was old enough.

It was touching to see these three big men, with the marks of their hard labour about them, anxiously bending over the worn books, and painfully making out, 'The grass is green,' 'The sticks are dry,' 'The corn is ripe' – a very hard lesson to pass to after columns of single words all alike except in the first letter. It was almost as if three rough animals were making humble efforts to learn how they might become human. And it touched the tenderest fibre in Bartle Massey's nature, for such full-grown children as these were the only pupils for whom he had no severe epithets, and no impatient tones. He was not gifted with an imperturbable temper, and on music-nights it was apparent that patience could never be an easy virtue to him; but this evening, as he glances over his spectacles at Bill Downes, the sawyer, who is turning his head on one side with a desperate sense of blankness before the letters d, r, y, his eyes shed their mildest and most encouraging light.

George Eliot: *Adam Bede*

Alison Uttley is still writing her delightful country books with the same sharp observation and affection which distinguishes so many country writers.

This portrait of a north country schoolmaster, who taught her in the 'nineties, is a fine example of many wise men who strove – and still strive – to open the eyes of their pupils to the wealth around them.

A VICTORIAN VILLAGE SCHOOLMASTER

The schoolmaster gave us a general education, the country schooling of the late 'nineties, with reading, writing, arithmetic, and religious teaching as the foundation, but so strong was his personality, and so original his mind that every child received an excellent and diverse training in music and science and country life, such as a modern school might envy.

In the top class we read from a school newspaper, a weekly periodical for which we paid twopence, with excellent coloured pictures and extracts from famous books and notes on current affairs. There I first met Gulliver and Rip Van Winkle and Don Quixote, characters who shared my life, for they were as real as the children around me. At the end of each week I proudly took my newspaper home for the family to share.

We carried little blue spelling-books, with lists of words which we learned each night. I learned my column as I walked through the wood, and the words were tangled with thoughts about bluebells and cuckoos and nut trees. There are many worse things than learning lists of words, and I enjoyed making new acquaintances.

In the summer the girls sewed with the sewing mistress, who often talked about her home farm as she arranged our work. We learned to put on a patch and to make buttonholes in pink and blue cotton, which showed up our bad stitches. In winter we knitted garters and stockings and gloves. It was the lesson I disliked.

While we sewed and whispered and dropped our needles on the dusty floor and pricked our fingers so that the blood dabbled the work, the boys had practical gardening with the headmaster. How we envied them! They went clumping and running to their own small gardens, cut out from among the bracken on the lower slopes of the hill. They took spades and forks and a wheelbarrow. They dug the soil and planted vegetables. When they returned, flinging wide the schoolroom door and bringing in a breath of that cold hilly air in their jackets and the smell of manure on their boots, we longed for that freedom. Later we had it, and girls too possessed their own gardens, for the headmaster believed in equality between boys and girls.

The boys sat down in their class and wrote gardening notes in real paper note-books at the headmaster's dictation, and I, behind the curtain, with all the little girls in the school sewing together, listened, and remembered, and told my father when I got home. There was great interest at our farm in the school gardening, and the schoolmaster's methods were tried out in our own kitchen garden. He was a famous horticulturalist in our district.

He was a keen field geologist, and he communicated his enthusiasm for his hobby to the children in the school; we had lessons in geology several times a week. Sometimes we passed a magnifying-glass along the row as we examined fossils and the delicate structure of crystals; we each had our own specimen to identify and describe. Sometimes we went out to the deserted quarries and gazed in wonder at the strata in those exposed faces of rock. We walked with him by the stone walls, looking for what we could find in the blocks of rough sandstone, spying the tiny glitter of quartz and mica.

We stood on a hill and gazed across the valleys, and he told us of other days, long ages past, when mammoths roamed. There was a cave a few miles away where their bones had been found. He pointed out a hill that had glacier markings. Our mountain-limestone cliffs had once been at the bottom of the sea, but few of us had ever seen the sea. We watched our own river and saw its rushing waters breaking down the banks. He took us to the little brook and told us of its work.

We were all country children and he opened a wide world of time and space to our imaginations, and every child had a vision. We were attentive to the magical property the earth possessed. We each held a stone in our grubby hot little fist and we gazed at it, and who can tell what our thoughts were, as we went back through time to those far ages, what world cataclysms and prehistoric monsters we imagined!

Alison Uttley: *Country Things*

MILKMAID

The girl's far treble, muted to the heat,
calls like a fainting bird across the fields
to where her flock lies panting for her voice,
their black horns buried deep in marigolds.

They climb awake, like drowsy butterflies,
and press their red flanks through the tall branched grass,
and as they go their wandering tongues embrace
the vacant summer mirrored in their eyes.

Led to the limestone shadows of a barn
they snuff their past embalmed in the hay,
while her cool hand, cupped to the udder's fount,
distils the brimming harvest of their day.

Look what a cloudy cream the earth gives out,
fat juice of buttercups and meadow-rye;
the girl dreams milk within her body's field
and hears, far off, her muted children cry.

Laurie Lee

Henry Fielding was born in 1707. He was of good family, spent three years at Eton and finished his education at Leyden University. Later he became a barrister and principal magistrate for Westminster. His wisdom and courage helped to put down the appalling flood of crime at this time, and to check corruption in administration.

These two passages reflect his humanity and sound good sense. Tom Jones was his most famous novel, published in 1749. He died five years later, in 1754, at the early age of 47.

A SQUIRE OF SOMERSET RETURNS HOME

Mr Allworthy had been absent a full quarter of a year in London, on some very particular business, though I know not what it was; but judge of its importance by its having detained him so long from home, whence he had not been absent a month at a time during the space of many years. He came to his house very late in the evening, and after a short supper with his sister, retired much fatigued to his chamber. Here, having spent some minutes on his knees – a custom which he never broke through on any account – he was preparing to step into bed, when, upon opening the cloathes, to his great surprise he beheld an infant, wrapt up in some coarse linen, in a sweet and profound sleep, between his sheets. He stood some time lost in astonishment at this sight; but, as good nature had always the ascendant in his mind, he soon began to be touched with sentiments of compassion for the little wretch before him. He then rang his bell, and ordered an elderly woman-servant to rise immediately, and come to him; and in the meantime was so eager in contemplating the beauty of innocence, appearing in those lively colours with which infancy and sleep always display it, that his thoughts were too much engaged to reflect that he was in his shirt when the matron came in. She had indeed given her master sufficient time to dress himself; for out of respect to him, and regard to decency, she had spent many minutes in adjusting her hair at the looking-glass, notwithstanding all the hurry in which she had been summoned by the servant, and though her master, for aught she knew, lay expiring in an apoplexy, or in some other fit.

It will not be wondered at that a creature who had so strict a regard to decency in her own person, should be shocked at the least deviation from it in another. She therefore no sooner opened the door, and saw her master standing by the bedside in his shirt, with a candle in his hand, than she started back in a most terrible fright, and might perhaps have swooned away, had he not now recollected his being undrest, and put an end to her terrors by desiring her to stay without the door till he had thrown some cloathes over his back, and was become incapable of shocking the pure eyes of Mrs Deborah Wilkins, who, though in the fifty-second year of her age, vowed she had never beheld a man without his coat. Sneerers and prophane wits may perhaps laugh at her first fright; yet my graver reader, when he considers the time of night, the summons from her bed, and the situation in which she found her master, will highly justify and applaud her conduct, unless the prudence which must be supposed to attend maidens at that period of life at which Mrs Deborah had arrived, should a little lessen his admiration.

When Mrs Deborah returned into the room, and was acquainted by her master with the finding the little infant, her consternation was rather greater than his had been; nor could she refrain from crying out, with great horror of accent as well as look, 'My good sir! what's to be done?' Mr Allworthy answered, she must take care of the child that evening, and in the morning he would give orders to provide it a nurse. 'Yes, sir,' says she; 'and I hope your worship will send out your warrant to take up the hussy its mother, for she must be one of the neighbourhood; and I should be glad to see her committed to Bridewell, and whipt at the cart's tail. Indeed, such wicked sluts cannot be too severely punished. I'll warrant 'tis not her first, by her impudence in laying it to your worship.' 'In laying it to me, Deborah!' answered Allworthy: 'I can't think she hath any such design. I suppose she hath only taken this method to provide for her child; and truly I am glad she hath not done worse.' 'I don't know what is worse,' cries Deborah, 'than for such wicked strumpets to lay their sins at honest men's doors; and though your worship knows your own innocence, yet the world is censorious; and it hath been many an honest man's hap to pass for the father of children he never begot; and if your worship should provide for the child, it may make the people the apter to believe; besides, why should your worship provide for what the parish is obliged to maintain? For my own part, if it was an honest man's child, indeed – but for my own part, it goes against me to touch these misbegotten wretches, whom I don't look upon as my fellow-creatures. Faugh! how it stinks! It doth not smell like a Christian. If I might be so bold as to give my advice, I would have it put in a basket, and sent out and laid at the churchwarden's door. It is a good night, only a little rainy and windy; and if it was well wrapt up, and put in a warm basket, it is two to one but it lives till it is found in the morning. But if it should not, we have discharged our duty in taking proper care of it; and it is, perhaps, better for such creatures to die in a state of innocence, than to grow up and imitate their mothers; for nothing better can be expected of them.'

There were some strokes in this speech which perhaps would have offended Mr Allworthy, had he strictly attended to it; but he had now got one of his fingers into the infant's hand, which, by its gentle pressure, seeming to implore his assistance, had certainly out-pleaded the eloquence of Mrs Deborah, had it been ten times greater than it was. He now gave Mrs Deborah positive orders to take the child to her own bed, and to call up a maid-servant to provide it pap, and other things, against it waked. He likewise ordered that proper cloathes should be pro- cured for it early in the morning, and that it should be brought to himself as soon as he was stirring.

Such was the discernment of Mrs Wilkins, and such the respect she bore her master, under whom she enjoyed a most excellent place, that her scruples gave way to his peremptory commands; and she took the child under her arms, without any apparent disgust at the illegality of its birth; and declaring it was a sweet little infant, walked off with it to her own chamber.

Henry Fielding: *The History of Tom Jones*

A COUNTRY DOCTOR

In this situation the surgeon found Tom Jones, when he came to dress his wound. The doctor perceiving, upon examination, that his pulse was disordered, and hearing that he had not slept, declared that he was in great danger, for he apprehended a fever was coming on, which he would have prevented by bleeding, but Jones would not submit, declaring he would lose no more blood; 'and, doctor,' says he, 'if you will be so kind only to dress my head, I have no doubt of being well in a day or two.'

'I wish,' answered the surgeon, 'I could assure your being well in a month or two. Well, indeed! No, no, people are not so soon well of such contusions; but, sir, I am not at this time of day to be instructed in my operations by a patient, and I insist on making a revulsion before I dress you.'

Jones persisted obstinately in his refusal, and the doctor at last yielded; telling him at the same time that he would not be answerable for the ill consequence, and hoped he would do him the justice to acknowledge that he had given him a contrary advice; which the patient promised he would.

The doctor retired into the kitchen, where, addressing himself to the landlady, he complained bitterly of the undutiful behaviour of his patient, who would not be blooded, though he was in a fever. 'It is an eating fever then,' says the landlady; 'for he hath devoured two swinging buttered toasts this morning for breakfast.'

'Very likely,' says the doctor; 'I have known people eat in a fever; and it is very easily accounted for; because the acidity occasioned by the febrile matter may stimulate the nerves of the diaphragm, and thereby occasion a craving which will not be easily distinguishable from a natural appetite; but the ailment will not be corrected, nor assimilated into chyle, and so will corrode the vascular orifices, and thus will aggravate the febrific symptoms. Indeed, I think the gentleman in a very dangerous way, and, if he is not blooded, I am afraid will die.'

'Every man must die some time or other,' answered the good woman; 'it is no business of mine. I hope, doctor, you would not have me hold him while you bleed him. But, hark'ee, a word in your ear; I would advise you, before you proceed too far, to take care who is to be your paymaster.'

'Paymaster!' said the doctor, staring; 'why, I've a gentleman under my hands, have I not?'

'I imagined so as well as you,' said the landlady; 'but as my first husband used to say, everything is not what it looks to be. He is an arrant scrub, I assure you. However, take no notice that I mentioned anything to you of the matter; but I think people in business oft always to let one another know such things.'

'And have I suffered such a fellow as this,' cries the doctor, in a passion, 'to instruct me? Shall I hear my practice insulted by one who will not pay me? I am glad I have made this discovery in time. I will see now whether he will be blooded or no.' He then immediately went upstairs, and flinging open the door of the chamber with much violence, awaked poor Jones from a very sound nap, into which he was fallen, and, what was still worse, from a delicious dream concerning Sophia.

'Will you be blooded or no?' cries the doctor, in a rage. 'I have told you my resolution already,' answered Jones, 'and I wish with all my heart you had taken my answer; for you have awaked me out of the sweetest sleep which I ever had in my life.'

'Ay, ay,' cries the doctor; 'many a man hath dozed away his life. Sleep is not always good, no more than food; but remember, I demand of you for the last time, will you be blooded?'

– 'I answer you for the last time,' said Jones, 'I will not.' – 'Then I wash my hands of you,' cries the doctor; 'and I desire you to pay me for the trouble I have had already. Two journeys at 5s. each, two dressings at 5s. more, and half a crown for phlebotomy.' – 'I hope,' said Jones, 'you don't intend to leave me in this condition.' – 'Indeed but I shall,' said the other.

'Then,' said Jones, 'you have used me rascally, and I will not pay you a farthing.' – 'Very well,' cries the doctor; 'the first loss is the best. What a pox did my landlady mean by sending for me to such vagabonds!' At which words he flung out of the room, and his patient turning himself about soon recovered his sleep; but his dream was unfortunately gone.

Henry Fielding: *The History of Tom Jones*

Dorothy Osborne came of an illustrious family. Her father, Sir Peter Osborne, was appointed Lieutenant Governor of Guernsey, Alderney and Sark in 1621, and at the time of the Civil War held Castle Cornet, the fort in Guernsey, for Charles I, with outstanding bravery. His home and estate were at Chicksands in Bedfordshire.

Dorothy, the youngest child of eight, was born in 1627. The letters by which she is remembered were written between 1652 and 1654 to William Temple who became her husband in the latter year. He was to be a wise statesman, a man of great courage and patriotism, whose honesty and outspokenness matched his gifted wife's.

She lived all her life in country places, and her description of a suitable husband reflects her likes and dislikes in the men she met there. Few writers have her wit and common sense. Few women have been more constant in love.

DOROTHY OSBORNE'S IDEAS OF A HUSBAND

There are a great many ingredients must goe to the makeing mee happy in a husband, first, as my Cousin Fr: say's, our humors must agree, and to be that hee must have that kinde of breeding that I have had and used that kinde of company, that is hee must not bee soe much a Country Gentleman as to understand Nothing but hawks and dog's and bee fonder of Either then of his wife, nor of the next sort of them whose aime reaches noe further then to bee Justice of peace and once in his life high Sheriff, who read noe book but Statut's and study's nothing but how to make a speech interlarded with Latin that may amaze his disagreeing poore Neighbours and fright them rather then perswade them into quietnesse; hee must not bee a thing that began the world in a fre scoole, was sent from thence to the University, and is at his farthest when hee reaches the Inn's of Court, has noe acquaintance but those of his forme in these places, speaks the french hee has pickt out of Old Law's, and admires nothing but the Storry's hee has heard of the Revells that were kept there before his time; hee must not bee a Towne Gallant neither that lives in a Tavern and an Ordinary, that cannot imagin how an hower should bee spent without company unlesse it bee in sleeping, that makes court to all the Women hee sees, thinks they beleeve him and Laughs and is Laught at Equaly; Nor a Traveld Mounsieur whose head is all feather inside and outside, that can talk of nothing but dances and Duells, and has Courage Enough to were slashes when every body else dy's with cold to see him; hee must not bee a foole of noe sort, nor peevish nor ill Natur'd nor proude nor Covetous and to all this must bee added that he must Love mee and I him as much as wee are capable of Loveing. Without all this his fortune though never soe great would not sattisfye mee, and with it a very moderat one would keep mee from ever repenting my disposall.

Letters of Dorothy Osborne to William Temple

This vivid sketch of two affrighted countrymen comes from Tobias Smollett's first and best known novel Roderick Random. Peregrine Pickle *and* Humphrey Clinker *were to follow in good time.*
Smollett was born in Dunbartonshire in 1721, and sailed as

41

surgeon's mate on one of the ships of the Cartagena Expedition. This naval experience gave him much of the material for Roderick Random. *Smollett died in 1771 at the age of 51.*

RODERICK RANDOM LIES WOUNDED IN THE BARN

I had not lain here many minutes, when I saw a countryman come in with a pitchfork in his hand, which he was upon the point of thrusting into the straw that concealed me, and, in all probability, would have done my business, had I not uttered a dreadful groan, after having essayed in vain to speak. This melancholy note alarmed the clown, who started back, and discovering a body all besmeared with blood, stood trembling, with the pitchfork extended before him, his hair bristling up, his eyes staring, his nostrils dilated, and his mouth wide open. At another time I should have been much diverted by this figure, which preserved the same attitude very near ten minutes; during which time I made many unsuccessful efforts to implore his compassion and assistance, but my tongue failed me, and my language was only a repetition of groans. At length an old man arrived, who, seeing the other in such a posture, cried, 'Mercy upon en! the leaad's bewitched! why, Dick, beest thou besayd thyself?' Dick, without moving his eyes from the object that terrified him, replied, 'O vather! vather! here be either the devil or a dead mon! I doan't know which o' en, but a groans woundily.' The father, whose eyesight was none of the best, pulled out his spectacles, and having applied them to his nose, reconnoitred me over his son's shoulder; but no sooner did he behold me, than he was seized with a fit of shaking even more violent than Dick's, and, with a broken accent, addressed me thus: 'In the name of the Vather, Zun, and Holy Ghost, I charge you, an you been Satan, to be gone to the Red Zea; but an you be a murdered man, speak, that you may have a christom burial.'

Tobias Smollett: *The Adventures of Roderick Random*

ANOTHER ASPECT OF ALDERMASTON

Miss Ellen Nash, Aldermaston Parish Church cleaner for 34 years, died on Thursday in the house in which she was born. She had lived in The Street all her life, and in her 83 years spent only three weeks away from the village.

Miss Nash's father was sexton at the Parish Church for over half a century. She could recall the time when he helped to bury Maria Hale, the notorious Aldermaston witch, who was said to be able to turn herself into a hare. One day the hare was shot in the leg – and ever after this, Maria Hale walked with a limp.

When the witch died, Mr Nash and other villagers piled stones on the grave to ensure that she would not come up again.

Having lived continuously in the village longer than anyone else, Miss Nash also remembered playing truant from school when the giant maypole was taken from Aldermaston's village green.

The Newbury Weekly News, 21 February, 1963

OLD POSTIE

There was one postal delivery a day, and towards ten o'clock, the heads of the women beating their mats would be turned towards the allotment path to watch for 'Old Postie.' Some days there were two, or even three, letters for Lark Rise; quite as often there were none; but there were few women who did not gaze longingly. This longing for letters was called 'yearning' (pronounced 'yarnin' '); 'No, I be-ant expectin' nothing', but I be so yarnin',' one woman would say to another as they watched the old postman dawdle over the stile and between the allotment plots. On wet days he carried an old green gig umbrella with whalebone ribs, and beneath its immense circumference he seemed to make no more progress than an overgrown mushroom. But at last he would reach and usually pass the spot where the watchers were standing.

'No, I ain't got nothin' for you, Mrs Parish,' he would call. 'Your young Annie wrote to you only last week. She's got summat else to do beside sittin' down on her arse writing home all the time.' Or, waving his arm for some woman to meet him, for he did not intend to go a step further than he was obliged: 'One for you Mrs Knowles, and, my! ain't it a thin-roes 'un! Not much time to write to her mother these days. I took a good fat 'un from her to young Chad Gubbins.'

So he went on, always leaving a sting behind, a gloomy, grumpy old man who seemed to resent having to serve such humble people. He had been a postman forty years and had walked an incredible number of miles in all weathers, so perhaps the resulting flat feet and rheumaticky limbs were to blame; but the whole hamlet rejoiced when at last he was pensioned off and a smart, obliging young postman took his place on the Lark Rise round.

Flora Thompson: Lark Rise

DOROTHY OSBORNE'S DAY AT CHICKSANDS

You aske mee how I passe my time heer, I can give you a perfect accounte not only of what I doe for the present, but what I am likely to doe this seven yeare if I stay heer soe long. I rise in the morning reasonably Early, and before I am redy I goe rounde the house till I am weary of that, and then into the garden till it grows to hott for mee. About ten a clock I think of makeing mee redy, and when that's don I goe into my fathers Chamber, from thence to dinner, where my Cousin Molle and I sitt in great State, in a Roome and at a table that would hold a great many more. After dinner wee sitt and talk till Mr B. com's in question and then I am gon. the heat of the day is spent in reading or working and about sixe or seven a Clock, I walke out into a Common that lyes hard by the house where a great many young wenches keep Sheep and Cow's and sitt in the shade singing of Ballads; I goe to them and compare theire voyces and Beauty's to some Ancient Shepherdesses that I have read of and finde a vaste difference there, but trust mee I think these are as innocent as those could bee. I talke to them, and finde they want nothing to make them the happiest People in the world, but the knoledge that they are so. most commonly when wee are in the middest of our discourse one looks aboute her and spyes her Cow's goeing into the Corne and then away they all run, as if they had wing's at theire heels. I that am not soe nimble stay behinde, & when I see them driveing home theire Cattle I think tis time for mee to retyre too. when I have supped I goe into the Garden and soe to the syde of a small River that runs by it where I sitt downe and wish you with mee, (You had best say this is not kinde neither) in Earnest tis a pleasant place and would bee much more soe to mee if I had your company. I sitt there somtimes till I am lost with thinking, and were it not for some cruell thoughts of the Crossenesse of our fortun's that will not lett mee sleep there, I should forgett there were such a thing to bee don as goeing to bed.

Letters of Dorothy Osborne to William Temple

Thomas Hardy was born in 1840 in Dorset where his forbears had lived for generations. This passage is taken from Under the Greenwood Tree, *in which the vivid characters of the Mellstock choir are described. As a boy Hardy went carol singing with his father in the Stinsford church choir, and these early impressions bore fruit later.*

He died in 1928.

TWO OLD MEN OF WESSEX

William Dewy – otherwise grandfather William – was now about seventy; yet an ardent vitality still preserved a warm and roughened bloom upon his face, which reminded gardeners of the sunny side of a ripe ribstone-pippin; though a narrow strip of forehead, that was protected from the weather by lying above the line of his hat-brim, seemed to belong to some town man, so gentlemanly was its whiteness. His was a humorous and kindly nature, not unmixed with a frequent melancholy; and he had a firm religious faith. But to his neighbours he had no character in particular. If they saw him pass by their windows when they had been bottling off old mead, or when they had just been called long-headed men who might do anything in the world if they chose, they thought concerning him, 'Ah, there's that good-hearted man – open as a child!' If they saw him just after losing a shilling or half-a-crown, or accidentally letting fall a piece of crockery, they thought, 'There's that poor weak-minded man Dewy again! Ah, he's never done much in the world either!' If he passed when fortune neither smiled nor frowned on them, they merely thought him old William Dewy.

'Ah, so's – here you be! Ah, Michael and Joseph and John – and you too, Leaf! a merry Christmas all! We shall have a rare log-wood fire directly, Reub, to reckon by the toughness of the job I had in cleaving 'em.' As he spoke he threw down an armful of logs which fell in the chimney-corner with a rumble, and looked at them with something of the admiring enmity he would have bestowed on living people who had been very obstinate in holding their own. 'Come in, grandfather James.'

Old James (grandfather on the maternal side) had simply called as a visitor. He lived in a cottage by himself, and many people considered him a miser; some, rather slovenly in his habits. He now came forward from behind grandfather William, and his stooping figure formed a well-illuminated picture as he passed towards the fire-place. Being by trade a mason, he wore a long linen apron reaching almost to his toes, corduroy breeches and gaiters, which, together with his boots, graduated in tints of whitish-brown by constant friction against lime and stone. He also wore a very stiff fustian coat, having folds at the elbows and shoulders as unvarying in their arrangement as those in a pair of bellows: the ridges and the projecting parts of the coat collectively exhibiting a shade different from that of the hollows, which were lined with small ditch-like accumulations of stone and mortar-dust. The extremely large side-pockets, sheltered beneath wide flaps, bulged out convexly whether empty or full; and as he was often engaged to work at buildings far away – his breakfasts and dinners being eaten in a strange chimney-corner, by a garden wall, on a heap of stones, or walking along the road – he carried in these pockets a small tin canister of butter, a small canister of sugar, a small canister of tea, a paper of salt, and a paper of pepper; the bread, cheese, and meat, forming the substance of his meals, hanging up behind him in his basket among the hammers and chisels. If a passer-by looked hard at him when he was drawing forth any of these, 'My buttery,' he said, with a pinched smile.

Thomas Hardy: *Under the Greenwood Tree*

THE SHEPHERD

How sweet is the Shepherd's sweet lot!
From the morn to the evening he strays;
He shall follow his sheep all the day,
And his tongue shall be filled with praise.

For he hears the lambs' innocent call,
And he hears the ewes' tender reply;
He is watchful while they are in peace,
For they know when their Shepherd is nigh.

William Blake

Mary Russell Mitford (1786–1855) was the daughter of a doctor who could not cure himself of gambling. The family fortunes alternated between wealth and poverty, and for the last years of his life it was Mary who kept the family afloat by her writings.

She is remembered chiefly for the charming pastoral essays which compose Our Village, *and from which* Lucy *and* Lucy's Husband *are taken; but she also wrote poetry and one or two tragedies which enjoyed short runs on the London stage.*

She was born at Alresford in Hampshire, but Our Village *describes the Berkshire village of Three Mile Cross where she spent much of her life.*

Her style is artfully artless. She appears to prattle effortlessly, but there is a balanced rhythm about the structure of her prose which denotes a musical ear and much practice in her craft. She is a good example of a prose writer who has disciplined herself by writing verse.

LUCY

About a twelvemonth ago we had the misfortune to lose a very faithful and favourite female servant; one who has spoiled us for all others. Nobody can expect to meet with two Lucys. We all loved Lucy, – poor Lucy! She did not die, – she only married; but we were so sorry to part with her, that her wedding, which was kept at our house, was almost as tragical as a funeral, and from pure regret and affection we sum up her merits and bemoan our loss, just as if she had really departed this life.

Lucy's praise is a most fertile theme; she united the pleasant and amusing qualities of a French soubrette, with the solid excellence of an Englishwoman of the old school, and was good by contraries. In the first place, she was exceedingly agreeable to look at; remarkably pretty. She lived in our family eleven years, but having come to us very young, was still under thirty, just in full bloom, and a very brilliant bloom it was. Her figure was rather tall and rather large, with delicate hands and feet, and a remarkable ease and vigour in her motions; I never saw any woman walk so fast or so well. Her face was round and dimpled, with sparkling grey eyes, black eyebrows and eye-lashes, a profusion of dark hair, very red lips, very white teeth, and a complexion that entirely took away the look of vulgarity which the breadth and flatness of her face might otherwise have given. Such a complexion, so pure, so finely grained, so healthily fair, with such a sweet rosiness, brightening and varying like

49

her dancing eyes whenever she spoke or smiled! When silent, she was almost pale; but, to confess the truth, she was not often silent. Lucy liked talking, and everybody liked to hear her talk. There is always great freshness and originality in an uneducated and quick-witted person, who surprises one continually by unsuspected knowledge or amusing ignorance; and Lucy had a real talent for conversation. Her light and pleasant temper, her cleverness, her universal kindness, and the admirable address, or, rather the excellent feeling, with which she contrived to unite the most perfect respect with the most cordial and affectionate interest, gave a singular charm to her prattle. No confidence or indulgence – and she was well tried with both – ever made her forget herself for a moment. All our friends used to loiter at the door or in the hall to speak to Lucy, and they miss her, and ask for her, as if she were really one of the family. She was not the less liked by her equals. Her constant simplicity and right-mindedness kept her always in her place with them as with us; and her gaiety and good humour made her a most welcome visitor in every shop and cottage round. She had another qualification for village society – she was an incomparable gossip, had a rare genius for picking up news, and great liberality in its diffusion. Births, deaths, marriages, casualties, quarrels, battles, scandal – nothing came amiss to her. She could have furnished a weekly paper from her own stores of facts, without once resorting for assistance to the courts of law or the two houses of parliament. She was a very charitable reporter too; threw her own sunshine into the shady places, and would hope and doubt as long as either was possible. Her fertility of intelligence was wonderful; and so early! Her news had always the bloom on it: there was no being beforehand with Lucy . . .

. . . Scattered amongst her great merits Lucy had a few small faults, as all persons should have. She had occasionally an aptness to take offence where none was intended, and then the whole house bore testimony to her displeasure: she used to scour through half-a-dozen doors in a minute, for the mere purpose of banging them after her. She had rather more fears than were quite convenient of ghosts and witches, and thunder, and earwigs, and various other real and unreal sights and sounds, and thought nothing of rousing half the family, in the middle of the night, at the first symptom of a thunderstorm, or an apparition. She had a terrible genius for music, and a tremendously powerful shrill, high voice. Oh! her door-clapping was nothing to her singing! it ran through one's head like the screams of a peacock. Lastly, she was a sad flirt; she had about twenty lovers whilst she lived with us, probably more, but upwards of twenty she acknowledged.

Mary Russell Mitford: Our Village

LUCY'S HUSBAND

Poor dear Lucy! her spouse is the greatest possible contrast to herself; ten years younger at the very least; well-looking, but with no expression good or bad; – I don't think he could smile if he would, – assuredly he never tries; well-made, but as stiff as a poker; I dare say he never ran three yards in his life; perfectly steady, sober, honest, and industrious; but so young, so grave, so dull; one of your 'demure boys' as Falstaff calls them, 'that never come to proof.' You might guess a mile off that he was a school-master from the swelling pomposity of gait, the solemn decorum of manner, the affectation of age and wisdom, which contrast so oddly with his young unmeaning face. The moment he speaks you are certain. Nobody but a village pedagogue ever did or ever could talk like Mr Brown, ever displayed such elaborate politeness, such a study of phrases, such choice words and long words, and fine words, and hard words. He speaks by the book – the spelling-book – and is civil after the fashion of the Polite Letter-Writer. He is so entirely without tact, that he does not in the least understand the impression produced by his wife's delightful manners, and interrupts her perpetually, to speechify and apologise, and explain and amend. He is fond of her, nevertheless, in his own cold, slow way, and proud of her, and grateful to her friends, and a very good kind of young man altogether; only that I cannot quite forgive him for taking Lucy away in the first place, and making her a school-mistress in the second. She a school-mistress, a keeper of silence, a maintainer of discipline, a scolder, a punisher! Ah! she would rather be scolded herself; it would be a far lighter punishment.

Mary Russell Mitford: *Our Village*

FARM CHILD

Look at this village boy, his head is stuffed
With all the nests he knows, his pockets with flowers,
Snail-shells and bits of glass, the fruit of hours
Spent in the fields by thorn and thistle tuft.
Look at his eyes, see the harebell hiding there;

Mark how the sun has freckled his smooth face
Like a finch's egg under that bush of hair
That dares the wind, and in the mixen now
Notice his poise; from such unconscious grace
Earth breeds and beckons to the stubborn plough.

R. S. Thomas

GERTIE WITH THE WASP WAIST

There was a young married woman named Gertie who passed as a beauty, entirely on the strength of a tiny waist and a simpering smile. She was a great reader of novelettes and had romantic ideas. Before her marriage she had been a housemaid at one of the country mansions where men-servants were kept, and their company and compliments had spoiled her for her kind, honest great carthorse of a husband. She loved to talk about her conquests, telling of the time Mr Pratt, the butler, had danced with her four times at the servants' ball, and how jealous her John had been. He had been invited for her sake, but could not dance, and had sat there all the evening, like a great gowk, in his light-grey Sunday suit, with his great red hands hanging down between his knees, and a chrysanthemum in his buttonhole as big as a pancake.

She had worn her white silk, the one she was afterwards married in, and her hair had been curled by a real hairdresser – the maids had clubbed together to pay for his attendance, and he had afterwards stayed for the dancing and paid special attention to Gertrude. 'And you should've seen our John, his eyes simply rolling with jealousy . . .' But, if she managed to get so far, she was then interrupted. No one wanted to hear about her conquests, but they were willing to hear about the dresses. What did the cook wear? Black lace over a red silk underslip. That sounded handsome. And the head housemaid and the stillroom maid, and so on, down to the tweeny, who, it had to be confessed, could afford nothing more exciting than her best frock of grey cloth.

Gertie was the only one of them all who discussed her relations with her husband. 'I don't think our Johnny loves me any more,' she would sigh, 'he went off to work this morning without kissing me.' Or, 'Our John's getting a regular chaw-bacon. He went to sleep and snored in his chair after tea last night. I felt that lonely I could have cried me eyes out.' And the more robust characters would laugh and ask her what more she expected of a man who had been at work in the fields all day, or say, 'Times is changed, my gal. You ain't courtin' no longer.'

Gertie was a fool and the hamlet laughing-stock for a year or so; then young John arrived and the white silk was cut up to make him a christening robe and Gertie forgot her past triumphs in the more recent one of producing such a paragon. 'Isn't he lovely?' she would say, exhibiting her red, shapeless lump of a son, and those who had been most unsympathetic with her former outpourings would be the first to declare him a marvellous boy. 'He's the very spit of his dad; but he's got your eyes, Gertie. My word! He's going to break some hearts when the time comes, you'll see.' As time went on, Gertie grew red and lumpy herself. Gone were the wasp waist and the waxen pallor she had thought so genteel. But she still managed to keep her romantic ideas, and the last time Laura saw her, by that time a middle-aged woman, she assured her that her daughter's recent marriage to a stable-boy was 'a regular romance in real life,' although, as far as her listener could gather, it was what the hamlet people of the preceding generation would have called 'a pushed-on, hugger-mugger sort of affair.'

Flora Thompson: *Over to Candleford*

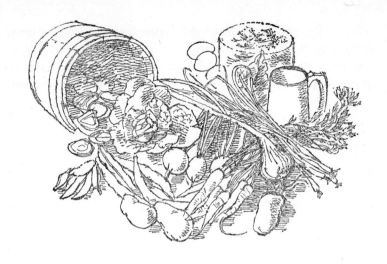

LIVING IN THE COUNTRY

Shall I state the difference between my town grievances, and my country comforts? At Brambleton Hall I have elbow-room within doors, and breathe a clear, elastic, salutary air – I enjoy refreshing sleep, which is never disturbed by horrid noise, nor interrupted, but in a-morning, by the sweet twitter of the martlet at my window – I drink the virgin lymph, pure and crystalline as it gushes from the rock, or the sparkling beveridge, home-brewed from malt of my own making; or I indulge with cyder, which my own orchard affords; or with claret of the best growth, imported for my own use, by a corre-spondent on whose integrity I can depend; my bread is sweet and nourishing, made from my own wheat, ground in my own mill, and baked in my own oven; my table is, in a great measure, furnished from my own ground; my five-year-old mutton, fed on the fragrant herbage of the mountains, that might vie with venison in juice and flavour; my delicious veal, fattened with nothing but the mother's milk, that fills the dish with gravy; my poultry from the barn-door, that never knew confinement, but when they were at roost; my rabbits panting from the warren; my game fresh from the moors; my trout and salmon struggling from the stream; oysters from their native banks; and herrings, with other sea-fish, I can eat in four hours after they are taken – My salads, roots, and pot-herbs, my own garden yields in plenty and perfection; the produce of the natural soil, prepared by moderate cultivation. The same soil affords all the different fruits which England may call her own, so that my dessert is every day fresh-gathered from the tree; my dairy flows with nectarious tides of milk and cream, from whence we derive abundance of excellent butter, curds, and cheese; and the refuse fattens my pigs, that are destined for hams and bacon – I go to bed betimes, and rise with the sun – I make shift to pass the hours without weariness or regret . . .

Tobias Smollett: *Humphrey Clinker*

The most colourful and mysterious of all country people are gipsies. They are viewed with suspicion, dislike and even disgust by their settled neighbours, but who can fail to feel a lift of the heart when they see the painted caravans, the swarthy foreign faces, and the raggle-taggle gaudy clothes passing by?

I probably have more gipsy clothes pegs, made from hazel boughs, than any other woman in Berkshire, for I cannot resist the tales they tell me at the porch, and their monkey-sad eyes. Not that I believe them, but one should pay cheerfully for entertainment, and this I willingly do. It is a pity in some ways, for I really prefer spring pegs.

Here are other people's reactions to gipsies. I have put John Keats' Meg Merrilies first. He has caught exactly the tough open-air quality which all gipsies have.

You will find many extracts, one way or another, from John Keats's writings. It is incredible to realise that this mature-minded and wise poet, who saw the nature of man and his surroundings so clearly and compassionately, despite being wracked with physical fevers and ardent unrequited love, was only twenty-six when he died in Rome in 1821.

MEG MERRILIES

Old Meg she was a gipsy;
And lived upon the moors:
Her bed it was the brown heath turf,
And her house was out of doors.
Her apples were swart blackberries,
Her currants, pods o' broom;
Her wine was dew of the wild white rose,
Her book a church-yard tomb.

Her brothers were the craggy hills,
Her sisters larchen trees;
Alone with her great family
She lived as she did please.
No breakfast had she many a morn,
No dinner many a noon,
And, 'stead of supper, she would stare
Full hard against the moon.

But every morn, of woodbine fresh
She made her garlanding,
And, every night, the dark glen yew
She wove, and she would sing.
And with her fingers, old and brown,
She plaited mats of rushes,
And gave them to the cottagers
She met among the bushes.

Old Meg was brave as Margaret Queen,
And tall as Amazon;
An old red blanket cloak she wore,
A chip-hat had she on:
God rest her aged bones somewhere!
She died full long agone!

John Keats

THE GIPSY GIRL

'Come, try your skill, kind gentlemen,
A penny for three tries!'
Some threw and lost, some threw and won
A ten-a-penny prize.

She was a tawny gipsy girl,
A girl of twenty years,
I liked her for the lumps of gold
That jingled from her ears;

I liked the flaring yellow scarf
Bound loose about her throat,
I liked her showy purple gown
And flashy velvet coat.

                                        Ralph Hodgson

OUTSIDE DUNSANDLE

What a liar
Was the tinker woman whom we met
Under the long stone wall!
But what a creature of mystery
With her tousled terrible child,
Eating bread,
And her veiled eyes.

She told us the wrong way to go,
Only for a few coppers,
Knowing we should come back again.
She watched, while the boy
With frayed sleeves and groundsel hair
Munched away.

She would have sent us over the edge of the world
For a few pennies,
Far away there out in the west.
I see her in the long rags of rain
Gathering wet sticks
For the turf fire,
Waiting for lost travellers to come by.

Sacheverell Sitwell

GIPSIES AT CANDLEFORD GREEN

Many gipsies frequented the neighbourhood, where there were
certain roadside dells which they used as camping-grounds.
These, for weeks together, would be silent and deserted, with
only circles of black ash to show where fires had been and scraps
of coloured rag fluttering from bushes. Then one day, towards
evening, tents would be raised and fires lighted, horses would
be hobbled and turned out to graze, and men with lurchers at
their heels would explore the field hedgerows (not after rabbits.
Oh, no! Only to cut a nice ash stick with which to make their old
pony go), while the women and children around the cooking-
pots in the dell shouted and squabbled and called out to the men
in a different language from that they used for business purposes
at cottage doors.

'There's them ole gipos back again,' the villagers would
say when they saw blue smoke drifting over the tree-tops.
'Time they was routed out o' them places, the ole stinkin'
lot of 'em. If a poor man so much as looks at a rabbit he soon
finds hisself in quod, but their pot's never empty. Says they
eats hedgehogs! Hedgehogs! He! He! Hedgehogs wi' soft
prickles!'

Laura liked the gipsies, though she did sometimes wish they
would not push with their baskets into the office, three or four
at a time. If a village woman happened to be there before them

she would sidle out of the door holding her nose, and their atmosphere was, indeed, overpowering, though charged as much with the odours of wood-smoke and wet earth as with that of actual uncleanliness.

There was no delivery of letters at their tents or caravans. For those they had to call at the Post Office. 'Any letters for Maria Lee?' or for Mrs Eli Stanley, or for Christina Boswell, they would say, and, if there were none, and there very often were not, they would say: 'Are you quite sure now, dearie? Do just look again. I've left my youngest in Oxford Infirmary,' or 'My daughter's expecting an increase,' or 'My boy's walking up from Winchester to join us and he ought to be here by now.'

All this seemed surprisingly human to Laura, who had hitherto looked upon gipsies as outcasts, robbers of hen-roosts, stealers of children, and wheedlers of pennies from pockets even poorer than their own. Now she met them on a business footing, and they never begged from her and very seldom tried to sell her a comb or a length of lace from their baskets, but one day an old woman for whom she had written a letter offered to tell her fortune. She was perhaps the most striking-looking person Laura ever saw in her life: tall for a gipsy, with flashing black eyes and black hair without a fleck of grey in it, although her cheeks were deeply wrinkled and leathery. Someone had given her a man's brightly-coloured, paisley-patterned dressing-gown, which she wore as an outdoor garment with a soft billycock hat. Her name was Cinderella Doe, and her letters came so addressed, without a prefix.

The fortune was pleasing. Whoever heard of one that was not? There was no fair man or dark man or enemy to beware of in it, and though she promised Laura love, it was not love of the usual kind. 'You're going to be loved,' she said, 'loved by people you've never seen and never will see.' A graceful way of thanking one for writing a letter.

Flora Thompson: Candleford Green

I feel that this brief and vivid portrait of a great countryman should be included in this section on country people.

Edward Thomas came late to poetry, but was soon recognised as a fresh lyrical poet in the English tradition. His death in 1917 at the age of thirty-nine left a sad gap in contemporary poetry.

Eleanor Farjeon, who is still writing poetry and prose for children as well as adults, was one of his many friends.

EDWARD THOMAS

'I like what I see,' said W. J. Ibbett on his deathbed. This old poet and scholar, of whom I shall write something more one day, uttered these words when he was lying bedridden, past writing and reading, facing a window filled with the branches of a tree. Birds came and went in it, weather moved in it, it changed with the seasons.

'Keep your senses fresh,' was Professor John Earle's first advice to his children in the nursery of his Somerset rectory. One of them took, remembered, and lived by it for seventy-nine years.

Edward lived thirty-nine years. In all of them he kept his senses fresh, and liked what he saw. He saw more than anybody I ever knew, and he saw it day and night. The seasons and the weather never failed him. It made him wonderful to walk with, and to talk with, and not to talk with. And when he was alone – as I think he loved best to be, except when Robert Frost increased what he saw and smelt and heard and felt and tasted – he walked with *himself*, with his eyes and his ears and his nostrils, and his long legs, and his big hands, in shape so strong, in touch so sensitive. These things were the continuous life of his thirty-nine years. The years might have numbered more, but soldiering did not rob him of what he liked. He could not live a day in the open air without being given something to 'enjoy enormously'; clear weather, flat shingle, a line of trees, the tallness of a church tower on a marsh, even a row of huts – he liked what he saw. And knew that nobody else liked it as much as he did.

Eleanor Farjeon: *Edward Thomas: The Last Four Years*

Charles Lee was born in 1870 and wrote tales about Cornish people. One collection of them was called Our Little Town, *from which* Mr Sampson *is taken.*

MR SAMPSON

On a moorland by-road two cottages stood under one roof. One had four rooms, the other only two – a kitchen below and a bedroom above. It was a lonely spot; the nearest house was a mile away, the nearest village twice as far. Catherine and Caroline Stevens occupied the larger dwelling; the other had been vacant for many years. The sisters owned both houses, and had a modest little income besides, which they supplemented by the sale of the produce of their poultry-yard. Catherine was fifty-five, Caroline fifty-three, and they had dwelt in this solitary place all their lives. Seniority, and a shade of difference in their temperaments, gave Catherine the rule. She was the more active of the two, and had what she humbly called a temper. Speaking in parables, she drank weak tea, while milk and water sufficed for the gentle Caroline. Catherine was the business woman. Eight o'clock on every Thursday morning saw her trudging down the road on her way to a neighbouring market town, with a basket on her arm containing eggs and perhaps a chicken or two, while Caroline, who seldom stirred abroad, stood at the gate and watched her out of sight. Caroline was on the watch again at five in the evening, to greet her on her return with the week's supply of groceries and gossip.

One Thursday she was back a full half-hour before her time. She panted as she sat down, and her eyes were bright with excitement. Caroline's pulse began to flutter.

'Sister,' she said faintly, 'what is 'a?'

Catherine pointed to the fireplace.

'There's somebody want to take it,' she said.

'The house? Never!'

'Ess, the house. A man.'

'Sister! A single man!'

'Ess. A stranger from up the country.'

'Aw, Cath'rine! You didn'—'

'Ess, I did. Why not? Trust me. I know better from worse. A staid man, and his name's Isaac Sampson, and that's a good respectable name – took out of Scripture, both ends of it. And he's to work 'pon the roads, breaking stones, and there an't no solider trade than that, I should think. And he'll pay a shilling a week, and I've took the arnest-money for the first week, and him and the furniture's coming up to-morrow. There!'

Caroline gasped.

'Cath'rine! A single man, and a foreigner! And us all alone!'

'You'm talking foolish, sister. A staid, respectable man, I tell 'e, and sixty if he's a day. You've see'd en too, and spoke to en. He passed o' Tuesday and give us the time o' day.'

'There was two people passed o' Tuesday.'

'This one passed in the morning.'

Caroline reflected.

'Grey whiskers all round, soft black hat up to'm, stooped a bit, and said " 'Marnen' ", broad-like?'

'That's the chap. I reco'nised him to once when 'a spoke to me. A civiller-spoken man I never look to meet. Recommended by the butcher, too. Ess, I asked Mr Pearse about him, and 'a said 'a was honest enough for all he knowed – and that's a deal for a man to say that kill his own meat. I'll tell 'e how 'twas.'

With all its ramifications of detail and comment, the telling of the five minutes' interview in the market-place took half an hour at least. By that time the idea which at first had so terrified Caroline had grown familiar and accepted.

'P'raps if we ask him,' said she, 'he'll kill the chickens for us. I shan't never get over wringing the poor dear mortals' necks, not if I live to be a hundred.'

It was late next evening when Mr Sampson arrived with his possessions in a farm-cart. The sisters watched, peeping from behind the geraniums into the rainy April twilight, while the furniture was being unloaded. Evidently Mr Sampson was no

Sybarite. When a chair, a table, a bed, a box, and a miscellaneous bundle had been carried in, the empty cart drove off, and the new tenant went in and shut the door.

'My life! did 'e see?' exclaimed Catherine. 'No carpet, no mats, no ornyments, not so much as a li'll picksher! A rough sort, I seem. I do 'most wish I hadn' took his shilling.'

'Poor soul!' murmured Caroline. 'At his age, and nobody to look after him! I'm glad we laid the fire. He'll be looking for a bit o' comfort in a strange house, and there an't no better comp'ny than a good fire, nor no worse than a black grate this wisht malincholy weather. I hope he'll light the fire.'

'He'll be biling the water for his tay, I reckon,' said Catherine, 'so he's bound to light en.'

'Cath'rine! I didn' see no kettle carr'd in!'

'Nor I nuther, come to think. P'raps 'twas in his box.'

'With his Sunday clo'es! A dirty black kettle! Aw, Cath'rine!'

'Well, must be somewheres. The man must have his tay. 'Tidn' in nature for a mortal to go without tay.'

'Well, I do hope he've lighted the fire. That kitchen's like a bird-cage for draughts . . . Aw, my dear life! what was that?'

They were sitting by the fire, and out of the back of the grate came a sudden sound, a sharp double tap, twice repeated. They looked at each other in some alarm, for it seemed to be in the room with them. Then Catherine's face cleared.

'I know,' she said confidently. 'He's knocking his pipe agin the bars of the grate. He's a-setting there, close up to we, smoking away 'front of the fire.'

'Like father used,' said Caroline. 'Nice and comfor'ble, with his boots off, I shouldn' wonder. There! now he's raking the fire. 'Tis 'most as if 'a was in the same room with us.'

They kept silence for a while, trying to realise their new neighbour's proximity through the party wall, straining their eyes after the shadow of his company. Presently Catherine had an idea.

'How if we should rattle the fire-showl a bit?' she suggested. ' 'Twill seem more sociable, like.'

Caroline stretched out her hand, and drew it back, reddening.

'I don't like to, somehow. It seem so – so forward, like-a-thing.'

'Aw, nonsense! How's going to know we done it a-purpose? And the grate wants righting up, anyhow. Here, give it me.'

She scraped up the ashes with defiant vigour, and let the shovel fall clattering.

'There! Now call your sister all the bold 'uzzies you can think for!'

Caroline smiled faintly, holding up her finger. But even if Mr Sampson heard the signal, he was not imaginative enough to interpret its kindly meaning, and respond. It was ten minutes before they heard another sound –the double tap again.

'One more pipe, and then to bed,' commented Catherine. 'That was father's way.'

They remained over the fire, talking a little in discreet tones, their ears ready to seize the slightest sound through the wall, their imaginations busy with the man who sat unconscious within a few feet of them. Once he coughed, and they speculated on the sound. Was it an ordinary clearing of the throat, as Catherine maintained, or was Caroline right in detecting a hollow ring, and arguing a weakness of the chest? Once he whistled a few slow notes; they recognised a fragment of a revival hymn, and drew favourable deductions. If it had been a low pothouse song—! At last they heard once more the tap-tap of the pipe-bowl, followed immediately by the scraping of chair-legs on the bare floor.

'Just like I said!' exclaimed Catherine. 'He's going to bed now. La me! 'tis nine o'clock! How quick the time have gone, to be sure!'

'I'm glad we took him in, good man,' said Caroline. 'It make a bit o' comp'ny don't 'a?'

Sleep was long in coming to them after the social excitements of the evening. They awoke later than usual next morning, and were only down in time to see Mr Sampson go past on his way to work. They hurried to the gate.

'He don't stoopy so much as I thought,' said Caroline. 'A

clever man for his age, I seem. Idn' his left-hand coat pocket plummed out, like?'

'So 'tis. Got his dinner inside, I reckon. Wonder what 'a is.'

'Cath'rine! How's going to manage for his meals?'

'Dunnaw. Cook 'em himself, s'pose, same as we. And a wisht poor job 'a'll make of it, I seem.'

'Poor chap! We – we couldn' offer to cooky for 'm, s'pose?'

'Wouldn' be fitty – not till we do know him better. Pretty and foolish we'd look if 'a was to say "No, thank 'e." '

'P'raps he'll ask us to,' said Caroline as they turned to go in. 'Aw, Catherine! If 'a haven' gone and left the door all abroad!'

'So 'a have, the careless chap! I've a mind—'

She turned about, looked warily down the road, and then marched resolutely out of the one gate and in at the other.

'What be doing, sister? Cath'rine, what be about?'

Catherine's face was set. 'I'm going to geek in,' she said, and went straight up to the door. A fearful fascination drew Caroline after her. Together they peeped into the room.

'There's his mug and tay-pot on the table,' whispered Catherine. 'I don't see no plate.'

'Nor no kettle,' murmured Caroline. 'I'd a jealous thought 'a hadn' got no kettle. Look, he've a-bilet the water for his tay in that dinky saucepan.'

'I'm going inside,' Catherine announced, and stepped boldly forward. Caroline cast a nervous glance behind her, and followed.

'Here's a frying-pan all cagged with gress; haven' been claned, not since 'twas bought, by the looks of it. He've had bacon for his brukfas'.'

'Here's the piece in the cupboard – half a pound of streaky; and nothing else but the heel of a loaf.'

'I claned up the floor yes'day, and now look to en! Such a muck you never behold.'

'Cath'rine! We can't leave en go on this-a-way! It go to my heart to see en so.'

'No more we won't. We'll come in after brukfas' and do up the place.'

67

'But he'll know. He might be vexed.'

'Don't care,' said Catherine recklessly. 'If he's vexed, he can take himself off. This room have got to be clane and fitty agin Sunday, and clane and fitty we'm going to make it.'

One thing led to another. On his return Mr Sampson found the house swept and garnished. The grate was polished, the fire laid; a strip of old carpet was spread before the hearth, another strip guarded the entry. A piece of muslin had been nailed across the window, and on the window-shelf stood two geranium plants, gay with scarlet blossom. The table was set for a meal, with knife, fork, mug and plate, and on the plate was an inviting brown pasty. He went upstairs, and found his bed neatly made, and a bright-coloured text pinned on the wall where it would meet his waking eyes. Mr Sampson pondered on these things while he ate the pasty to the last crumb. Presently he went out and knocked at his neighbours' door. Catherine opened it; the other conspirator trembled in the background.

'Thank 'e, marm,' said Mr Sampson, shortly.

'You'm welcome, Mr Sampson. Anything we can do to make 'e comfor'ble—'

Mr Sampson shifted his feet, spat respectfully behind his hand, and said nothing. Catherine gained courage.

'Won't 'e step inside?' she asked, and immediately bobbed backwards, uttering an odd little squeak, as her skirt was tugged from behind by the alarmed Caroline. Mr Sampson stared at her in mild astonishment.

'No, thank 'e – do very well here,' he said. 'Patsy was capital,' he added after a pause.

'Sister made it. She's gen'rally reckoned a good hand.'

'Thank 'e, marm,' said Mr Sampson, raising his voice and addressing the obscure interior over Catherine's shoulder. The vague figure within responded with a flutter and an inarticulate twitter. 'If you'll leave me know what's to pay—'

'We won't say nothing 'bout that, Mr Sampson. But I was going to say – sister and me have been talking things over – and I was going to ask 'e—'

With many hesitations Catherine expounded a plan of mutual accommodation, by which she and Caroline were to cook his food and keep his rooms tidy in return for the heavier outdoor work – digging the garden, gathering fuel from the moor, and the like. A special clause stipulated for the wringing of the chickens' necks. Mr Sampson agreed readily, and grew spasmodically confidential. Lived with a widowed sister till last year. Sister married again, and gone to live in the shires. Doing for himself ever since, and making a terrible poor job of it. Knew no more about cooking than a cow did about handling a musket. Could make shift to fry a rasher, and that was about all. Reckoned he'd do very well now, and was properly grateful to the ladies for their proposal.

'Aw, you'm kindly welcome, Mr Sampson!' It was Caroline who spoke, close up to her sister's elbow.

'Thank 'e, marm,' he replied, and Caroline shrank back into the shadows.

The arrangement worked capitally. Every evening on returning from work, Mr Sampson found his house in order, his table laid, and something savoury warming at the fire – a broth of leeks and turnips, maybe, or maybe a potato pie. The pasty for tomorrow's 'crowst' was ready in the cupboard. Having supped and digested, he would go forth and work in the garden till dusk, when he would come round to the door for a few good-night words with the sisters. Bit by bit, Caroline's maidenly tremors subsided. She gathered confidence before this mild, slow-spoken old man, and when at the end of the second week he came to pay his rent, and was invited once more by Catherine to step inside, and was politely demurring, it was the younger sister's soft 'Do 'e, now, Mr Sampson,' that decided him to enter.

When he had gone, they agreed that his company manners were unexceptionable. Thrice he had to be pressed to light his pipe before he would consent, and then – what touched them most – every few minutes he bestirred his stiff joints, went to the door, and put his head outside like a real gentleman, instead of making a spittoon of their spotless fireplace. They felt safe in repeating the invitation. Soon no invitation was needed. He dropped in as a matter of course every evening at the accustomed hour, sat for the accustomed period in his accustomed chair, and bore his part in the accustomed talk. It was a wonder to Caroline that she had ever been afraid of him, now that he had come to be as much a part of the natural scheme of things as the grandfather clock that ticked in the corner by the staircase. Indeed, with his round moon-face, his slow and weighty speech, and his undeviating regularity of habits, he bore no small resemblance to that venerable timepiece. The comparison does him great honour; for 'Grandf'er,' as the sisters affectionately called it, held a deservedly high place in their esteem. Those who dwell in crowded marts may regard their clocks and watches as mere mechanical contrivances, but to two lone women in a solitary place, the household clock, especially if it be such a clock as Grandf'er, with his imposing seven foot of stature and his solemn visage of shining brass, is something more than a mere nest of cogs and pulleys. Such a clock is the real master of the house; he orders the comings and goings, the downsittings and uprisings of his votaries; his ponderous ticking pervades every room; when he huskily clears his throat, voices are hushed and respectful silence is kept till he has delivered his hourly message to transient mortality; the operation of winding him up is an affair of solemn ritual. It was not long before Mr Sampson heard the history of the two outstanding events in Grandf'er's otherwise untroubled existence – the vain and impious attempt of a misguided stranger to carry him off in exchange for a paltry twenty pounds in gold, and that other episode of his frenzy, when, in the dead of night, he had a false alarm of Eternity, and struck a hundred and seventeen on end, while the sisters, called from their beds by the dread summons, hovered about him, white-robed and tearful.

The four made a comfortable and well-balanced *partie carree*. Catherine led the talk; Mr Sampson seconded her bravely; Caroline was the best of listeners; while Grandf'er filled the gaps, when gaps occurred, with his well-conned discourse, soothing to hear with a clear conscience at the end of a well-spent day. There was no more harmonious and happy a fireside company in all the countryside.

Then came the catastrophe. One evening – it was a Thursday, about three months after Mr Sampson's arrival – he knocked at the door as usual. It remained shut. He tried the latch. It would not open. He called out, and Catherine's voice made answer:

'Grieved to say it, Mr Sampson, but you can't come in.'

'How? What's up with 'e?'

'I can't tell 'e, but you mustn't come in. Will 'e plaise to go away, Mr Sampson?'

He thought it over slowly. 'No,' he said at last. 'Not till I do know what's the matter.'

'Aw dear!' There were tears in her voice. 'I beg of 'e, go!'

'Not till I hear what's up,' he repeated.

A murmur of agitated talk came to his ears.

'If you'll open door,' he said, 'you can tell me comfor'ble. I won't come in if you don't wish, but I'm bound to know what's up.'

More whispering. Then a bolt was withdrawn, and the door opened an inch or two.

'Come,' he said, and pushed gently. The door resisted.

'I can't look 'e in the face. If I must tell 'e, I must, but I die of shame if I look 'e in the face.'

'So bad as that?'

'Worse. Worse'n anything you could think for. Aw dear! How be I to tell 'e?'

The door threatened to close again. Mr Sampson said nothing, but quietly set his foot in the gap between door and door-post. It was a substantial foot, substantially shod. The mere toe of it, which alone was visible within, was eloquent of masculine determination. Catherine made a desperate plunge.

'Mr Sampson, they'm a-talking about us.'

'How *us*?'

'You and we. 'Tis all over the country – scand'lous talk. Aw, that I should live to see the day!'

'If you'll kindly give me the p'tic'lars, marm,' he said patiently, after a pause.

71

'We never thought no harm,' she sobbed. ' 'Twas only neighbourly to offer to do for 'e, and you all alone and so helpless. I'm sure the notion never come into our heads. 'Tis a sin and shame to say such things.'

'Say *what* things?'

'Say – we – we'm a-trying to catch 'e!'

The terrible word was out. The pair within awaited the result with trembling expectation. It came – first a long low whistle; then – could they believe their ears? – an unmistakable chuckle. Catherine shrank back as from the hiss of an adder. The door swung open and Mr Sampson confronted them, his eyes a-twinkle with sober enjoyment.

'That's a stale old yarn,' he said. 'Heard en weeks ago. Only 'twas told *me* 'tother way about. Don't mind telling 'e I mightn' have thought of it else.'

'Thought of what, Mr Sampson?'

'Why, courting of 'e, to be sure,' said the gentleman placidly.

The ladies gasped in unison.

'You don't mane to say you you – you'm—' stammered Catherine at last.

'Ess, I be, though. This fortnit, come Sunday. If you'll kindly take it so, and no offence.'

'But – but we never noticed nothing.'

'No, s'pose. 'Tis like the cooking, you see – I'm a terrible poor hand at it. Now 'tis out. Ben't vexed, I hope.'

'Aw, no! But—'

'There!' he hurried on. 'Think it over, will 'e? There's the saving to consider of, you see, money and trouble both. And I've put by a pound or two. Not so young as I was, but we an't none of us that. And not so dreadful old, nuther. Wouldn' think of parting of 'e; reckon we could be pretty and comfor'ble together, the three of us, though I can't marry but one of 'e, 'course. So talk it over, will 'e? I'll be round agin tomorrow evening. Good night.'

He had reached the gate before Catherine found voice to recall him.

'Mr Sampson! Plaise, Mr Sampson!'

72

'Well, marm?' he said, slowly returning.

'Ascuse my asking, but – would 'e mind telling – telling *whichy* one you was thinking of – of courting?'

Mr Sampson's fingers went to the back of his head.

'Now you'll be laughing upon me,' he said. 'Whichy one? Well, I don't know whichy one, and that's the truth. But it don't make no odds,' he added cheerfully. 'Settle it between yourselfs. I ben't noways p'tic'lar.'

'La, Mr Sampson! Who ever heard tell of such a thing?' cried Catherine, giggling in spite of herself.

'That's right!' he chuckled. 'Laugh so much as you've a mind to. Sister laughing too?'

Caroline's nervous titter passed muster.

'Now we'm comfor'ble,' he remarked. 'Reckon I can step inside now, and no scandal.'

In he walked, none hindering, took his usual chair, spread his hands on his knees, and beamed on the sisters.

'Ess,' he continued. 'I'm like the old cat in the bonfire – don't know which course to steer. Never was such a case, s'pose. I've turned it over this way, and I've rolled it over that way, and I can't come to no conclusion. Always seeing you together, you see, I can't part 'e nohow, no more than milk from water. But don't matter, as I said before. If only you'll be so kind as to settle it between yourselfs—'

'We couldn' do that,' said Catherine emphatically.

'Couldn' 'e, now?' He turned inquiringly to Caroline. Caroline shook her head.

'Wouldn' be fitty,' she murmured.

'Well, you do know best,' said Mr Sampson, a little dashed, and pondered, his eyes on the ground, while the sisters shot sidelong glances at him and avoided each other's looks. He lifted his head and caught Caroline's eye.

'Cath'rine's the best to manage things,' said Caroline, in a hurry.

He looked hopefully at Catherine.

'Car'line's the best cook by far,' she hastened to say.

Mr Sampson thumped his knee.

'That's where 'tis!' he exclaimed. 'The pair of 'e rolled up together 'ud make a complete masterpiece. A man couldn' look for a better wife than the two of 'e 'ud make. That's where 'tis, nor I don't see no way out of it – not in a Christian country. Ah!' he added meditatively. 'These heathen Turks – they know a thing or two after all, don't they?'

'Mr Sampson, I wonder at 'e!' cried Catherine, shocked at this libertine sentiment.

' 'Tidn' to be thought of, I know that,' he apologised. 'But I can't think of no other way. Without' – he brightened – 'without we should spin up a ha'penny and bide by the fall of en.'

'Never in this house!' exclaimed Catherine, more shocked than ever.

'Don't see how we shouldn',' he maintained stoutly. ' 'Tis just the same as casting lots, and that's a good Scripture observance. The reg'lar way with these old patriarchs, so I'm given to onderstand; only 'twas shekels with them, I reckon. But shekels or ha'pennies, 'tis all one.'

'If you'm sure 'tis Scriptural,' said Catherine, impressed and half convinced.

'Sound Bible doctrine, my word for'n. An't that so, marm?' he added, appealing to Caroline.

'I mind a text in Proverbs,' said Caroline shyly, 'which say, "The lot causeth contentions to cease".'

'See!' ejaculated Mr Sampson. 'That's of it! "The lot causeth contentions to cease." 'Tis aimed straight at our case. Out o' Proverbs, too! Old Solomon's the chap for we. See how 'a settled that argyment 'bout the baby. And there was two ladies in *that*. Well, then?'

Catherine shook her head doubtfully, but offered no further objection. Mr Sampson produced a handful of coins, chose one with fitting deliberation, and held it up for inspection.

'Now,' he announced. 'If 'a should turn up the old Queen, then 'tis Cath'rine. If 'tis the young person with the prong, then Caroline's the one. And up she goes.'

It was not the spin of an expert, and he failed to catch the flying coin. It fell to the ground in the dark corner by Grandf'er.

Mr Sampson went down on his hands and knees, while the sisters held their breaths.

'Well, I'm darned!'

The ladies jumped. Mr Sampson rose slowly to his feet, holding the halfpenny at arm's length and smiling foolishly upon it.

'If it had been a lime-ash floor, now,' he said.

'What's wrong?' Catherine found breath to ask.

'Fell in a crack of the planching, my dear. Found en sticking there edge up, and no head to en, nor yet no tail. Old Solomon himself couldn' make nothing by en. But how come you to have a timbern floor to your kitchen, when mine's lime-ash?'

' 'Twas father's doing when the house was built,' said Caroline. 'He always liked to take off his boots of a' evening, and lime-ash is that cold-natured, 'tis apt to give 'e chilblains through your stockings.'

'Well, to see how things do turn out!' meditated Mr Sampson.

' 'Twas ordained, I seem,' said Caroline solemnly.

'A token, sure enough,' agreed Catherine. 'And father's eyes upon us this very minute, I shouldn' wonder. Mr Sampson – I doubt 'tis all foolishness, and we'd best say no more about it.'

'Don't see that,' said he. 'If you father didn' choose to wear slippers, that an't no lawful reason why I shouldn' get married if I want to. Must try some other way, that's all.'

Again he pondered, till Caroline broke the silence with a timid suggestion.

'If,' she hesitated, colouring, 'if we should wait a bit, Mr Sampson keeping away from us meanwhile, p'raps his heart 'ud speak.'

'So 'a might,' said the gentleman dubiously; 'and then agin 'a mightn'. A mazy old organ, b'lieve.'

'Absence make the heart grow fonder, so they say,' remarked Catherine.

'That's very well,' he replied. 'Don't doubt but what 'a do. But how if 'a should make en grow fonder of both of 'e? Where'd us be then? But we'll try if you do wish, though I doubt 'tidn' much use.'

75

Taking his leave, he paused at the door.

'All the same,' he said, 'I can't help wishing I'd been born a heathen Turk.'

Left alone, the sisters had plenty of food for thought. They sat without speaking, and the longer they sat the harder it became to break silence. For the first time in their lives a veil of reserve was drawn between them, and every moment it thickened and darkened. At last, with a few constrained words for decency's sake, they lit their candles and went to bed. Next morning two heavy-eyed women confronted each other with mistrustful looks over the breakfast-table. The day dragged through on a minimum of conversation, in which no word of their neighbour found a place. Through the morning of the next they held no communication at all, and the air was heavy with suppressed thunder. In the afternoon Caroline set about her preparations for the usual Saturday baking. The materials were ready on the table, when Catherine came in from the garden. Her searching glance on the table hardened into a fixed glare.

'I thought as much,' she said, in a tense whisper. 'You've been taking those Wyandotte eggs!'

Caroline turned pale.

'S'posing I have!' she made answer at last.

Catherine raised her voice.

'You knowed very well I was going to set Toppy on those eggs today.'

Caroline trembled and clutched the edge of the table.

'S'posing I did!' she whispered.

'Then how come you to take those eggs?'

'I-I shall take what eggs I've a mind to – so there!'

'A mean trick, so 'tis. To take my eggs, what I've been saving up for Toppy, and she as cluck as cluck can be, as you very well know, and in her box this very minute, wearing her heart out over the chaney nest-egg, poor fond little worm! Of all the mean tricks, to take my eggs—'

'Aw, you and your bistly old eggs!'

76

Even for a maiden attempt at scornful sarcasm it was a wretchedly poor one, and its effect was further discounted when the perpetrator instantly burst into a flood of penitential tears. The next moment they were in each other's arms.

'To think of it!' exclaimed Catherine, as their sobs subsided. 'All these years with never a cross word, and now – Aw, drat the man!'

'Sister!'

'Drat the man!' she repeated, revelling in her own profanity. 'Wish we'd never set eyes 'pon him. Sarve him right if we sent him 'bout his business!'

'Sister! When we'm both so good as promised to'n! Beside, 'a wouldn' go. He's terrible obstinate, for all his quiet ways.'

'A week's notice'll settle en,' said Catherine viciously.

'Cath'rine, we couldn'! Good man – to be slighted by two in one day, and turned out of house and home overplush – we couldn'!'

'It do seem hard,' admitted Catherine. 'But we can't go on like this, that's plain.'

'P'raps he've made his ch'ice by now.'

'If 'a have, 'a can't choose but one of us. And then, where'll the other be? Tell me that!'

'Sister,' said Caroline, and paused, and drew a long breath. 'Sister dear; I-I ben't in no p'tic'lar vi'lence to get married.'

'Caroline Stevens, there's the Bible 'pon the shelf. Lay your hand to'n, and say those words agin, if you can.'

Caroline hid her face in her hands. 'I can't,' she faltered.

'Nor I nuther. And here we be, the two of us, geeking round the corner after one man! At our age, too! 'Tis shameful! I'm black-red all over at the thought of it. Two silly old women – that's what we be.'

'Aw, *don't*, sister!' shuddered Caroline.

'Two silly old women,' repeated the merciless self-abaser. 'But it shan't be so. Thanks be, I got some sense left in my brain, though my heart's a caudle of foolishness. It shan't be so. The longer he stay, the worse 'twill be, and go he shall. How couldn' 'a make up his mind 'fore speak? 'Twouldn' have happened so, then.'

' 'Twas fo'ced upon him to speak.'

'So 'a was. I mustn' be hard 'pon him. 'Tis Doom, I reckon; and better-fit Doom should tend to his battles and murders and sudden deaths, 'stead of coming and plaguing quiet, dacent folk. Well, and Doom shan't have it all his own way, nuther. There shan't be no jalous wife nor no sinful-thoughted sister-in-law, not in this locality.'

'Sister, such dreadful talk!'

' 'Tis my duty to speak plain. There's bound to be suffering come out of it, but anyways we can choose to suffer respectable. Go he shall.'

The garden gate clicked.

'Cath'rine! Here 'a do come! And aw! if I do live, he've got his best clo'es up!'

'Then 'a *have* made up his mind after all, and he've come to tell us so. But 'tis too late now, and 'shan't name no names, not if I can help. 'Twill be harder if we do know. Now, Car'line, you'm too soft for this job. You leave en to me, and don't say a word, and, whatever you do, don't start snooling – d'st hear? We got to be hard, or we'll never get rids of him.'

The door was tapped and opened, and Mr Sampson appeared. His hard-pressed holiday suit encased him in its rigid folds, like the stone garments of a statue; his face was one consistent solid smile; a substantial cabbage-rose adorned the lapel of his coat; and his hands – O wonder! – were mailed in enormous black kid gloves. Altogether he made a noble, if stiffish figure, worthy of any woman's affection. Catherine felt her resolution tottering. She advanced one desperate step and shot her bolt.

'Mr Sampson, you'll kindly take your week's notice from today.'

The wide expanse of smile slowly crumbled, and as slowly heaped itself up into a round O of ineffable astonishment. Caroline began to whimper. Catherine stealthily shook her by the arm, while Mr Sampson's eyes roved to the ceiling, the walls, and the floor, in search of symptoms of universal disintegration.

'I'm a dazy old bufflehead, I know,' he began at last, 'and I don't azackly seem to get to the rights o' this.'

'There an't no rights to en!' cried Catherine wildly. '(*Will* 'e stop snooling, sister!) 'Tis all so wrong as can be, and time to put an end to it. Nor you mustn' ask why, for we can never tell 'e. We'm grieved to put 'e out in any way, and we'm grieved to part with 'e; but go you must, and no questions asked.'

Mr Sampson's scattered wits obeyed his summons. 'If I ben't mistook,' he said, not without dignity, 'there was words passed between us consarning matrimony.'

'Foolish words!' interjected Catherine. 'Foolisher words were never spoke. They've got to be took back.'

'If I ben't mistook,' he continued stolidly, 'I was told to go away and make up my mind – or my heart as you may say – if so be I could.'

' 'Tis too late. We'll be thankful if you won't say no more about it.'

'If I ben't mistook,' he went on, with a corroborative glance at his festal attire, 'I come here just now to say I'd come to a conformable conclusion at last. I come here to say – with doo respect to the other lady, who's good enough for anybody – I come to say I'd pitched my ch'ice on the lady I should wish to commit matrimony with. And the name of that lady—'

'Don't say the word!' cried Catherine. ' 'Tis hard enough already; don't 'e go to make it harder. Whichever 'tis, her answer have got to be "No". An't that so, Car'line?'

Caroline speechlessly assented.

'With best thanks all the same,' continued Catherine in softer tones, 'and hoping you won't think too hardly of us, and never shall we think other than kindly o' you, and proud we'd ha' been ayther one of us, if it hadn' been ordained otherwise, as you'll mind I said to once when the ha'penny stood on edge, and – aw, *will* 'e go, and not stand glazing there like a stuck pig!'

Mr Sampson stiffened his back. 'Very well, marm,' he replied, and began peeling off a glove. 'I ben't one to fo'ce myself 'pon nobody.' He attacked the other glove. 'Nor I ben't going to

state no grievance, nor ask no questions, nor mention no names.'
He rolled the gloves into a forlorn and crumpled ball.

'You'll spile 'em,' said Catherine, sniffing audibly. 'Give 'em
here.'

She took them, smoothed them out, laid them together,
turned one neatly inside out over the other, and gave them back.

'Thank 'e,' he said. 'Bought 'em for a funeral I didn' go to;
never put 'em on till today. Queer how things do turn out. Well,
if I got to go, then the sooner the better.' He took the flower
from his buttonhole and laid it on the table. '(Meant for the
lady of my ch'ice, not to mention no names.) So I reckon I'll go
to once.' He fumbled in his pocket. 'I can get a bed over to
Churchtown – very good beds at the inn, so I'm told – and I'll
send along for my things later on.' He counted some silver out
on the table. 'And there's the money owing; two shilling rent
for this week and next.'

'Mr Sampson—' Catherine protested through her tears. He
raised an implacable hand.

'If you plaise, marm. According to the law of the land, and
not wishing to be beholden to nobody. And that's about all,
b'lieve. Good-bye.'

'You'll shake hands 'fore go,' pled Catherine.

'No, I don't think,' said the unforgiving old man. ' 'Tis the
Christian thing to do, I know; but there an't no mistake about
it, I ought to have been born a heathen Turk.'

Without another word he turned and went. His bent figure
passed the window and disappeared.

'He'll scorn us all his life!' wailed Caroline.

'We've done what's right,' said Catherine, 'so don't matter
what he think of us. *I* don't care, for one.'

The rose caught her eye. She took it up and lifted it to her
face.

'Give it me,' said Caroline, dry-eyed of a sudden. 'I'll take
care of it.'

Catherine whipped it behind her back.

'Meant for the lady of his ch'ice,' she said. 'Maybe you
think—'

80

'I've so much right as you to think—'

They held each other's eyes, and gentle Caroline's look was as hard as her sister's. But the crisis passed as quickly as it had come – with Caroline in a fresh flood, with Catherine in a resolute stamp of the foot.

'It shan't be so!' she declared. Going to the fire, she opened the top of the grate and dropped the flower within. It shrivelled and vanished.

'And there's an end to en,' she said. 'Dust and ashes. And now, sister, snooling won't help us, but work will, or so they say else. Time to pitch baking; come, bustle.'

COUNTRY PLACES

Except for the sense of smell, there is nothing which evokes such strong and instant emotions as places – particularly country places. The poet who remembered

> *Four ducks on a pond*
> *A green bank beyond*

for years, and with tears, went to the root of the matter. It is not only memory which responds so piercingly to places. Words, fields, barns and houses – especially houses – have an atmosphere which can be welcoming or the reverse.

I had an example of this once in a Kentish wood. There were a great many yew trees growing from greyish chalky soil and the imponderable sense of doom which hung about the place I attributed to the lack of light and colour. No one could be less psychic than I am, but I was extremely unhappy there and very glad to quit it. Some years later, I heard, the wood was dug up, and with it many ancient bones and weapons. It was thought to be the site of a battle in Saxon times.

But fortunately more pleasure than fear is awakened by country places, and what more dear than one's home? Robert Herrick (1591–1674) sums up this affection with simplicity and elegance.

A THANKSGIVING TO GOD, FOR HIS HOUSE

Lord, Thou has given me a cell
        Wherein to dwell:
A little house, whose humble roof
        Is weather-proof;
Under the spars of which I lie
        Both soft, and dry.
Low is my porch, as is my fate,
        Both void of state;

And yet the threshold of my door
           Is worn by the poor,
Who thither come, and freely get
           Good words, or meat:
Like as my parlour, so my hall
           And kitchen's small:
Some brittle sticks of thorn or briar
           Make me a fire
Close by whose living coal I sit,
           And glow like it.
Lord, I confess too, when I dine,
           The pulse is Thine,
And all those other bits, that be
           There placed by Thee:
The worts, the purslain, and the mess
           Of water-cress.
Thou mak'st my teeming hen to lay
           Her egg each day:
All these, and better Thou dost send
           Me to this end,
That I should render, for my part,
           A thankful heart.

                    Robert Herrick

THE COUNTRY BEDROOM

My room's a square and candle-lighted boat,
In the surrounding depths of night afloat.
My windows are the portholes, and the seas
The sound of rain on the dark apple-trees.

Sea-monster-like beneath, an old horse blows
A snort of darkness from his sleeping nose,
Below, among drowned daisies. Far off, hark!
Far off, one owl amidst the waves of dark.

Frances Cornford

SOME DWELLINGS

The first house on the opposite side of the way is the
blacksmith's; a gloomy dwelling, where the sun never seems to
shine; dark and smoky within and without, like a forge. The
blacksmith is a high officer in our little state, nothing less than
a constable; but, alas! alas! when tumults arise, and the constable is called for, he will commonly be found in the thickest
of the fray. Lucky would it be for his wife and her eight children
if there were no public-house in the land; an inveterate inclina-
tion to enter those bewitching doors is Mr Constable's only
fault.

Next to this official dwelling is a spruce brick tenement, red,
high, and narrow, boasting, one above another, three sash-
windows, the only sash-windows in the village, with a clematis
on one side and a rose on the other, tall and narrow like itself.
That slender mansion has a fine, genteel look. The little parlour
seems made for Hogarth's old maid and her stunted footboy;
for tea and card parties – it would just hold one table; for the
rustle of faded silks, and the splendour of old china; for the
delight of four by honours, and a little snug, quiet scandal between the deals; for affected gentility and real starvation. This
should have been its destiny; but fate has been unpropitious; it
belongs to a plump, merry, bustling dame, with four fat, rosy,
noisy children, the very essence of vulgarity and plenty.

Then comes the village shop, like other village shops, multi-
farious as a bazaar; a repository for bread, shoes, tea, cheese,
tape, ribands, and bacon; for everything, in short, except the
one particular thing which you happen to want at the moment,

and will be sure not to find. The people are civil and thriving, and frugal withal; they have let the upper part of their house to two young women (one of them is a pretty, blue-eyed girl) who teach little children their ABC and make caps and gowns for their mammas – parcel schoolmistress, parcel mantua-maker. I believe they find adorning the body a more profitable vocation than adorning the mind.

Divided from the shop by a narrow yard, and opposite the shoemaker's is a habitation of whose inmates I shall say nothing. A cottage – no – a miniature house, with many additions, little odds and ends of places, pantries, and what not; all angles, and of a charming in-and-outness; a little bricked court before one half, and a little flower-yard before the other; the walls, old and weather-stained, covered with holly-hocks, roses, honeysuckles, and a great apricot-tree; the casement full of geraniums (ah! there is our superb white cat peeping out from among them); the closets (our landlord has the assurance to call them rooms) full of contrivances and corner-cupboards; and the little garden behind full of common flowers, tulips, pinks, larkspurs, peonies, stocks, and carnations, with an arbour of privet, not unlike a sentry-box, where one lives in a delicious green light, and looks out on the gayest of all gay flower-beds. That house was built on purpose to show in what an exceeding small compass comfort may be packed. Well, I will loiter there no longer.

The next tenement is a place of importance, the Rose Inn; a whitewashed building, retired from the road behind its fine swinging sign, with a little bow-window room coming out on one side, and forming, with our stable on the other, a sort of open square, which is the constant resort of carts, wagons, and return chaises. There are two carts there now, and mine host is serving them with beer in his eternal red waistcoat. He is a thriving man and a portly, as his waistcoat attests, which has been twice let out within this twelvemonth. Our landlord has a stirring wife, a hopeful son, and a daughter, the belle of the village; not so pretty as the fair nymph of the shoe-shop, and far less elegant, but ten times as fine; all curl-papers in the morning, like a porcupine, all curls in the afternoon, like a poodle, with more flounces than curl-papers, and more lovers than curls. Miss Phoebe is fitter for town than country; and to do her justice, she has a consciousness of that fitness, and turns her steps townwards as often as she can. She is gone to B——— today with her last and principal lover, a recruiting sergeant – a man as tall as Sergeant Kite, and as impudent. Some day or other he will carry off Miss Phoebe.

Mary Russell Mitford: *Our Village*

This nicely ironic snippet comes from one of Alexander Pope's letters. Pope was born in 1688 of elderly parents, and was deformed and delicate. He became one of our foremost satirists, in prose and poetry of matchless exactitude. He was essentially urban in spirit, as this glimpse of him in the country shows.
He died in 1744.

AN ANCIENT ENGLISH COUNTRY SEAT

Our best room above is very long and low, of the exact proportion of a bandbox; it has hangings of the finest work in the world; those, I mean, which Arachne spins out of her own bowels: indeed, the roof is so decayed, that after a favourable shower of rain, we may, with God's blessing, expect a crop of mushrooms between the chinks of the floors.

All this upper story has for many years had no other inhabitants than certain rats, whose very age renders them worthy of this venerable mansion, for the very rats of this ancient seat are grey. Since these had not quitted it we hope at least this house may stand during the small remainder of days these poor animals have to live, who are now too infirm to remove to another: they have still a small subsistence left them in the few remaining books of the library.

Alexander Pope

BICKERS COTTAGE

Companionable ticking of the clock;
Collapsing of the coal;
The chair-legs warm;
Tobacco in a bowl;
The door sealed up;
The sooted kettle's hiss;
The fire-lit loaf; the cocoa-tin; the cup;
Outside the unplumbed night and pattering storm.

At such an hour as this
A ghost might knock,
Lacking unearthly comfort in its soul.

Frances Cornford

TEA BREAK AT DORCAS LANE'S SMITHY

Tea was not considered a substantial meal. It was for the workmen, as Miss Lane counted time, an innovation. She could remember when bread and cheese and beer were at that hour taken to the forge for the men to consume standing. 'Afternoon bavour,' they had called it. Now a well-covered table awaited them indoors. Each man's plate was stacked with slices of bread and butter and what was called 'a relish' was provided. 'What can we give the men for a relish at tea-time?' was an almost daily question in that household. Sometimes a blue-and-white basin of boiled new-laid eggs would be placed on the table. Three eggs per man was the standard allowance, but two or three extra were usually cooked 'in case,' and at the end of the meal the basin was always empty. On other afternoons there would be brawn, known locally as 'collared head,' or soused herrings, or a pork pie, or cold sausages.

As the clock struck five the scraping of iron-tipped boots would be heard and the men, with leather aprons wound up around their waists, and their faces, still moist from their visit to the pump in the yard, looking preternaturally clean against their work-soiled clothes, would troop into the kitchen. While they ate they would talk of the horses they had been shoeing. 'That new grey o' Squire's wer' as near as dammit to nippin' my ear. A groom ought'r stand by and hold th' young devil,' or 'Poor old Whitefoot! About time he wer' pensioned off. Went to sleep an' nearly fell down top of me today, he did. Let's see, how old is he now, do you reckon?' 'Twenty, if he's a day. Mus' Elliott's father used to ride him to hounds and he's bin dead this ten 'ears. But you leave old Whitefoot alone. He'll drag that station cart for another five 'ears. What's he got to cart? Only young Jim, and he's a seven-stunner, if that, and maybe a bit of fish and a parcel or two. No, you take my word for't, old White-foot ain't going to die while he can see anybody else alive.' Or they would talk about the weather or the crops or some new arrival in the place, extracting the last grain of interest from every trifling event.

Flora Thompson: *Candleford Green*

NIGHT

It is spring, moonless night in the small town, starless and bible-black, the cobblestreets silent and the hunched, courters'-and-rabbits' wood limping invisible down to the sloeblack, slow, black, crowblack, fishingboat-bobbing sea. The houses are blind as moles (though moles see fine tonight in the snouting, velvet dingles) or blind as Captain Cat there in the muffled middle by the pump and the town clock, the shops in mourning, the Welfare Hall in widows' weeds. And all the people of the lulled and dumbfound town are sleeping now.

Hush, the babies are sleeping, the farmers, the fishers, the tradesmen and pensioners, cobbler, schoolteacher, postman and publican, the undertaker and the fancy woman, drunkard, dressmaker, preacher, policeman, the webfoot cocklewomen and the tidy wives. Young girls lie bedded soft or glide in their dreams, with rings and trousseaux, bridesmaided by glow-worms down the aisles of the organ-playing wood. The boys are dreaming wicked or of the bucking ranches of the night and the jolly-rogered sea. And the anthracite statues of the horses sleep in the fields, and the cows in the byres, and the dogs in the wet-nosed yards; and the cats nap in the slant corners or lope sly, streaking and needling, on the one cloud of the roofs.

You can hear the dew falling, and the hushed town breathing. Only *your* eyes are unclosed to see the black and folded town fast, and slow, asleep. And you alone can hear the invisible starfall, the darkest-before-dawn minutely dewgrazed stir of the black, dab-filled sea where the *Arethusa*, the *Curlew* and the *Skylark*, *Zanzibar*, *Rhiannon*, the *Rover*, the *Cormorant*, and the *Star of Wales* tilt and ride.

Dylan Thomas: *Under Milk Wood*

MORNING

The town's half over with its morning. The morning's busy as bees.

There's the clip clop of horses on the sunhoneyed cobbles of the humming streets, hammering of horseshoes, gobble quack and cackle, tomtit twitter from the bird-ounced boughs, braying on Donkey Town. Bread is baking, pigs are grunting, chop goes the butcher, milk-churns bell, tills ring, sheep cough, dogs shout, saws sing. Oh, the Spring whinny and morning moo from the clog dancing farms, the gulls' gab and rabble on the boat-bobbing river and sea and the cockles bubbling in the sand, scamper of sanderlings, curlew cry, crow caw, pigeon coo, clock strike, bull bellow, and the ragged gabble of the beargarden school as the women scratch and babble in Mrs Organ Morgan's general shop where everything is sold: custard, buckets, henna, rat-traps, shrimp-nets, sugar, stamps, confetti, paraffin, hatchets, whistles.

Dylan Thomas: *Under Milk Wood*

THE COAST: NORFOLK

As on the highway's quiet edge
He mows the grass beside the hedge,
The old man has for company
The distant, grey, salt-smelling sea,
A poppied field, a cow and calf,
The finches on the telegraph.

Hung on his faded back a hone,
He slowly, slowly, scythes alone
In silence of the wind-soft air,
With ladies' bedstraw everywhere,
With whitened corn, and tarry poles,
And far-off gulls like risen souls.

Frances Cornford

A NORTH COUNTRY KITCHEN IN WINTER

The perfect setting for tale-telling was firelight, the cave fire for primitive man, the camp fire for explorers, the great fire at the inn for travellers, the kitchen fire with its friendly blaze for farm-house and country folk. There is something in the rise and fall of flames, the deep gold caves in glowing coal, the ever-changing beauty of the tongues of fire that seems to draw forth a story.

The time for tales was night, preferably a winter night, and, ideally, a night of snow or bitter storm when nobody had to go out, for then the contrast between the warm interior and the outer darkness pressing at the shutters, beating on the door, was most marked . . .

. . . Shutters barred and fastened, cottered with the long iron cottering-pins, doors locked and the great keys lying on the end of the oak dresser by the knife-box, outdoor work finished, these were the essential preliminaries. The kitchen was shining and bright and cosy with the blazing fire and the lamplight. The lamp was the parlour lamp, used on special occasions when any-one came. It stood on the table on its square brass base, with raised figures of bronze mermaids and dolphins. Its circular globe was like the full moon, and little transparent stars were cut in the opaque surface through which the light glinted. Every-body stared at the lamp. It drew the eyes of the company to its glories, it seemed to be about to tell stories itself. I always felt proud of it. I felt rich when it was there.

Hands and faces had been washed at the slop-stone, in the bright brass washing-bowl. Hair – unruly black hair, pale gold hair, brown curls, grey whiskers and children's silky heads – had been brushed before the tiny glass with its mahogany frame, that hung above the rose-painted box for brushes and combs. Boots had been removed, the servant-boy taking off my father's, my brother or I taking off the guest's, other men pulling off their own. Slippers were drawn on tired, aching feet, feet that had plodded across ploughfield and pasture all day, or returned from a long cold journey. The meal was over, washing-up done, and milk-cans reared on the wall at the door facing the wild winds, to sweeten them. The hearthstone, sanded each morning, was speckless, and although feet touched the edge of that great yellow stone that stretched in front of the fire, boiler and oven, they did not rest upon it. It was left vacant, and nobody trod there except to lift a heavy pan from the fire. The fire itself was big enough to keep people away.

Its heat streamed into the room and the flames lighted up the faces of young and old gathered round it. Gleaming flashes, dancing shadows, laughter and the sound of a rocking-chair, of kettles hissing and clock ticking, they were the accompaniments of tales. Light glinting on the polished oak cupboard, which stood beyond the slop-stone and reached the ceiling, as it had stood in its beauty for two hundred years and listened to tales; light from the brass face of the grandfather clock, from the copper warming-pan, and brass saucepans – the room sparkled and twinkled with a thousand watching eyes, and I knew very well they were there, sharing our life.

Alison Uttley: *Country Things*

ARRACOMBE WOOD

Some said, because he wud'n spaik
Any words to women but Yes and No,
Nor put out his hand for Parson to shake
He mun be bird-witted. But I do go
By the lie of the barley that he did sow,
And I wish no better thing than to hold a rake
Like Dave, in his time, or to see him mow.

Put up in churchyard a month ago,
'A bitter old soul,' they said, but it wadn't so.
His heart were in Arracombe Wood where he'd used
    to go
To sit and talk wi' his shadder till sun went low,
Though what it was all about us'll never know.
And there baint no mem'ry in the place

Of th' old man's footmark, nor his face;
Arracombe Wood do think more of a crow –
Will be violets there in the Spring: in Summer time
   the spider's lace;
And come the Fall, the whizzle and race
Of the dry, dead leaves when the wind gies chase;
And on the Eve of Christmas, fallin' snow.

Charlotte Mew

THE HALL FARM

Evidently that gate is never opened: for the long grass and the great hemlocks grow close against it; and if it were opened, it is so rusty, that the force necessary to turn it on its hinges would be likely to pull down the square stone-built pillars, to the detriment of the two stone lionesses which grin with a doubtful carnivorous affability above a coat of arms, surmounting each of the pillars. It would be easy enough, by the aid of the nicks in the stone pillars, to climb over the brick wall with its smooth stone coping; but by putting our eyes close to the rusty bars of the gate, we can see the house well enough, and all but the very corners of the grassy enclosure.

D

It is a very fine old place, of red brick, softened by a pale powdery lichen, which has dispersed itself with happy irregularity, so as to bring the red brick into terms of friendly companionship with the limestone ornaments surrounding the three gables, the windows, and the door-place. But the windows are patched with wooden panes, and the door, I think, is like the gate – it is never opened: how it would groan and grate against the stone floor if it were! For it is a solid, heavy, handsome door, and must once have been in the habit of shutting with a sonorous bang behind a liveried lackey, who had just seen his master and mistress off the grounds in a carriage and pair.

But at present one might fancy the house in the early stage of a chancery suit, and that the fruit from that grand double row of walnut-trees on the right hand of the enclosure would fall and rot among the grass, if it were not that we heard the booming bark of dogs echoing from great buildings at the back. And now the half-weaned calves that have been sheltering themselves in a gorse-built hovel against the left-hand wall, come out and set up a silly answer to that terrible bark, doubtless supposing that it has reference to buckets of milk.

Yes, the house must be inhabited, and we will see by whom; for imagination is a licensed trespasser: it has no fear of dogs, but may climb over walls and peep in at windows with impunity. Put your face to one of the glass panes in the right-hand window: what do you see? A large open fireplace, with rusty dogs in it, and a bare boarded-floor; at the far end, fleeces of wool stacked up; in the middle of the floor, some empty corn bags. That is the furniture of the dining-room. And what through the left-hand window? Several clothes-horses, a pillion, a spinning-wheel, and an old box wide open, and stuffed full of coloured rags. At the edge of this box there lies a great wooden doll, which, so far as mutilation is concerned, bears a strong resemblance to the finest Greek sculpture, and especially in the total loss of its nose. Near it there is a little chair, and the butt-end of a boy's leather long-lashed whip.

The history of the house is plain now. It was once the residence of a country squire, whose family, probably dwindling down to mere spinsterhood, got merged in the more territorial name of Donnithorne. It was once the Hall; it is now the Hall Farm. Like the life in some coast-town that was once a watering-place and is now a port, where the genteel streets are silent and grass-grown, and the docks and warehouses busy and resonant, the life at the Hall has changed its focus, and no longer radiates from the parlour, but from the kitchen and the farmyard.

George Eliot: *Adam Bede*

THE FIELD OF WATERLOO

Yea, the coneys are scared by the thud of hoofs,
And their white scuts flash at their vanishing heels,
And swallows abandon the hamlet-roofs.

The mole's tunnelled chambers are crushed by wheels,
The lark's eggs scattered, their owners fled;
And the hedgehog's household the sapper unseals.

The snail draws in at the terrible tread,
But in vain; he is crushed by the felloe-rim;
The worm asks what can be overheard,

And wriggles deep from a scene so grim,
And guesses him safe; for he does not know
What a foul red flood will be soaking him!

Beaten about by the heel and toe
Are butterflies, sick of the day's long rheum,
To die of a worse than the weather-foe.

Trodden and bruised to a miry tomb
Are ears that have greened but will never be gold,
And flowers in the bud that will never bloom.

Thomas Hardy

BIRD, BEAST AND FISH

Animals, both wild and domestic, play an important part in country affairs. Whether they are being tended, or chased, or merely observed, they furnish the countryman with boundless interest and sometimes his livelihood.

James Woodforde's diary provides the opening extract here. If this journal is not already known to you I hope you will procure it without delay. To me, it is the most appealing of all diaries, and I am not forgetting those three giants Pepys, Evelyn and John Wesley.

They lived among great men and knew the world of affairs. James Woodforde did not. He was born in 1740 in Somerset, but in 1774 became rector of Weston Longeville, Norfolk, where he remained until his death on New Year's Day 1803. As John Beresford said in his preface to the diary: 'It is because his life was so tranquil and so obscure that the Diary is uniquely interesting. The ordinary life of ordinary men passes away like a shadow. But by means of Parson Woodforde's Diary we are able, for the second half of the eighteenth century, to meet and to know individually and personally the very men and women who lived in the country . . . Since life in the country, in the immemorial villages of England was – unlike our own urban day – the experience of the vast majority of Woodforde's contemporaries, the record is all the more significant.'

This diary is my bedside book. I met it first at Cambridge when I was eighteen, and read the five sturdy volumes with mounting rapture. I don't mind admitting that I have been in love with James Woodforde ever since.

One of his endearing qualities is his concern for animals in an age which was notoriously callous to them. These entries are typical of his deep interest and humanity.

103

PARSON WOODFORDE'S PIGS

April 15, 1778

My two large Piggs, by drinking some Beer grounds taking out of one of my Barrels today, got so amazingly drunk by it, that they were not able to stand and appeared like dead things almost, and so remained all night from dinner time today. I never saw Piggs so drunk in my life, I slit their ears for them without feeling.

April 16, 1778

We breakfasted, dined and supped and slept again at home. My 2 Piggs are still unable to walk yet, but they are better than they were yesterday. They tumble about the yard and can by no means stand at all steady yet. In the afternoon my 2 Piggs were tolerably sober.

James Woodforde: Diary of a Country Parson

THE POOR MAN'S PIG

Already fallen plum-bloom stars the green,
And apple-boughs as knarred as old toads' backs
Wear their small roses ere a rose is seen;
The building thrush watches old Job who stacks
The fresh-peeled osiers on the sunny fence,

The pent sow grunts to hear him stumping by,
And tries to push the bolt and scamper thence,
But her ringed snout still keeps her to the sty.

Then out he lets her run; away she snorts
In bundling gallop for the cottage door,
With hungry hubbub begging crusts and orts,
Then like the whirlwind bumping round once more;
Nuzzling the dog, making the pullets run,
And sulky as a child when her play's done.

Edmund Blunden

PARSON WOODFORDE'S CAT

October 26, 1768
I had a poor little cat that had one of her ribs broke and that
laid across her belly, and we could not tell what it was, and she
was in great pain. I therefore with a small pen-knife this
morning, opened one side of her and took it out, and performed
the operation very well, and afterwards sewed it up and put
Friars Balsam to it, and she was much better after, the incision
was half an inch. It grieved me much to see the poor creature in
such pain before, and therefore made me undertake the above,
which I hope will preserve the life of the poor creature.

*Betsy Barker's unfortunate cow must be one of the best-known
quadrupeds in English literature. She was certainly well-loved, for
such a feat of dress-making by her owner must have called for a high
degree of patience, ingenuity and motherly solicitude.*
Elizabeth Gaskell (1810–1865) wrote Cranford, *her most
famous novel, in 1853, a simple story of a few Cheshire villagers,*

told with humour and sympathy. It is based on her experiences in Knutsford.

MISS BETSY BARKER'S ALDERNEY

An old lady had an Alderney cow, which she looked upon as a daughter. You could not pay the short quarter-of-an-hour call without being told of the wonderful milk or wonderful intelligence of this animal. The whole town knew and kindly regarded Miss Betsy Barker's Alderney; therefore great was the sympathy and regret when, in an unguarded moment, the poor cow tumbled into a lime pit. She moaned so loudly that she was soon heard and rescued; but meanwhile the poor beast had lost most of her hair, and came out looking naked, cold, and miserable, in a bare skin. Everybody pitied the animal, though a few could not restrain their smiles at her droll appearance. Miss Betsy Barker absolutely cried with sorrow and dismay; and it was said she thought of trying a bath of oil. This remedy, perhaps, was recommended by some one of the number whose advice she asked; but the proposal, if ever it was made, was knocked on the head by Captain Brown's decided 'Get her a flannel waistcoat and flannel drawers, ma'am, if you wish to keep her alive. But my advice is, kill the poor creature at once.'

Miss Betsy Barker dried her eyes, and thanked the Captain heartily; she set to work, and by and by all the town turned out to see the Alderney meekly going to her pasture, clad in dark gray flannel. I have watched her myself many a time. Do you ever see cows dressed in gray flannel in London?

Mrs Gaskell: *Cranford*

AUBADE

Hark! hark! the lark at heaven's gate sings,
And Phoebus 'gins arise,
His steeds to water at those springs

On chaliced flowers that lies;
And winking Mary-buds begin
To ope their golden eyes:
With everything that pretty bin,
My lady sweet, arise!
Arise! arise!

William Shakespeare

Robert Smith Surtees, the creator of Jorrocks, was probably the greatest sporting writer of the nineteenth century. Modern readers may find his comic writings too heavily facetious taken in large doses, but he had a great sense of fun, a racy pen, and boundless infectious energy.

He was particularly fortunate in his illustrators John Leech and Hablot Knight Browne.

A Durham man, Surtees was born in 1803 and died in 1864.

MR JORROCKS AND THE GROUSE

Mr Pippin was a game-seller as well as a fruiterer, and the 12th of August drawing nigh, he had stuck a newly gilt and lettered sign to that effect over his door:

'Pippin, Fruiterer, and Licensed Dealer in Game,' read Mr Jorrocks, in that vacant sort of way that people read anything that comes in their way.

'Pippin, Fruiterer and Game-seller,' said he to himself, shortening the sign. 'Wonders if he's got any cranberries.' Mr J. was very fond of cranberries.'

'Have you got any cranberries?' asked he of Pippin, who, on the look-out for "squalls" now rushed to the door.

'Not any cranberries, sir; particular nice gooseberries, strawberries, cauliflowers, radishes, fish sauces of all kinds, sir; cucumbers, cigars, pickles – expect some peas in tonight, sir – step in, sir; step in.'

Mr Jorrocks complied, but oh! what a sight greeted him on the opposite wall – 'three brace of grouse hanging by the neck!' Mr Jorrocks stood transfixed.

'*How now?*' exclaimed he, as speech returned, and with staring eye-balls he turned to the shopkeeper.

'*How now?*' repeated he, pointing to the birds, 'grouse for sale before the 12th of August.'

'Five shillings a brace,' replied Mr Pippin, quite unconcerned; 'we generally charge six, but the season's coming on, and we shall soon get plenty more.'

'Plenty more,' roared Mr Jorrocks; 'aren't you 'shamed of yourself?'

'Oh dear no, sir, not at all; take the whole for fourteen shillings.'

'*I'll fourteen you!*' repeated Mr Jorrocks, stamping with rage, 'I'll fourteen you, you waggabone. I'm one of Her Majesty's jestices o' the peace – "*nullum tempus occurrit*" somethin' – the Queen stands no nonsense – I'll fine you!'

'What for, sir?' inquired Mr Pippin.

'For havin' game afore the twelfth – I'll summons you directly,' added Mr Jorrocks, hurrying out of the shop.

'Please say *they're stuffed!*' roared Mr Pippin after him.

R. S. Surtees: *Hillingdon Hall*

THE TOWN AND COUNTRY MOUSE

In days of old a country mouse
Welcomed within his humble house
A friend from town (or so they tell);
They long had known each other well.
No sleek or spendthrift mouse was he
Yet given to hospitality.
In short, he gladly went to fetch
His long-eared oats and hoarded vetch,
He gave him half-gnawed bacon scraps
And raisins, hoping that perhaps
The many courses might constrain
His guest to stomach his disdain;
For at the dishes one by one
He took a pick and then had done.
At last the latter, when he saw
His host stretched on the summer's straw
Munching a meal of spelt and tare,
And leaving him the better fare,
Cried out, 'Dear chap, what can you see
In living here so cheerlessly
Mid hills and woods, a country clown?
Why don't you leave, and come to town?
Take my advice and make a start.
We live our lives, but soon depart:
Such is the lot of small and great.
"There is no armour against fate."
So let's be merry while we may,
Knowing we're creatures of a day.'

To this his friend pays ready heed,
Bounds from his house, and both proceed,
Eager to win the walls by dark.
Now night held heaven's midmost arc.
They reach the town, and enter there
The mansion of a millionaire,

Where draperies of crimson dye
Shimmer on seats of ivory,
And baskets bulge with food amassed
From remnants of the night's repast.
The country mouse is now the guest,
Reclining, at his friend's request,
Upon a purple couch, while he
Serves course on course officiously,
Just like a waiter at his worst
(And, true to type, he tastes them first).
The other lies in high content,
Reflecting on his betterment,
And, savouring each new confection,
Plays the smug patron to perfection –
When suddenly with mighty bang
The doors flew open. Up they sprang.
They scurried round and round the room.
Next came the mastiffs' echoing boom.
At that they nearly died of fright.
Then said the country mouse, 'Good night.
This life of yours is far too trying.
I find plain vetch quite satisfying.
Homes in the backwoods have their charms.
At least they're safe from town alarms.'

Horace. Translated by Janet Maclean Todd

Gilbert White, the great naturalist, was born in 1720 at Selborne in Hampshire, and remained there until 1793, when he died, spending most of that time as curate there.

His meticulous regard for detail, his loving patience and his acute powers of observation have been an example to all naturalists.

The Natural History of Selborne was first published in 1789.

FIELD MICE AND HOUSE MICE

As to the small mice, I have farther to remark, that though they hang their nests for breeding up amidst the straws of the standing corn, above the ground; yet I find that, in the winter, they burrow deep in the earth, and make warm beds of grass; but their grand rendezvous seems to be in corn-ricks, into which they are carried at harvest. A neighbour housed an oat-rick lately, under the thatch of which were assembled near an hundred, most of which were taken; and some I saw. I measured them; and found that, from nose to tail, they were just two inches and a quarter, and their tails just two inches long. Two of them, in a scale, weighed down just one copper halfpenny, which is about the third of an ounce avoirdupois; so that I suppose they are the smallest quadrupeds in this island. A full-grown *mus medius domesticus* weighs, I find, one ounce lumping weight, which is more than six times as much as the mouse above; and measures from nose to rump four inches and a quarter, and the same in it's tail.

Gilbert White: *The Natural History of Selborne*

Bertram Smith was born in Cheshire in 1876, but later went to Beattock, Dumfriesshire, where he farmed and wrote. Older readers may remember his light essays in Punch *under the pseudonym 'Bis.' He was a great open-air man, walking, caravanning, shooting and swimming. He died at the early age of 41 in 1918.*

111

My copy of Running Wild *was sent me by his sister, who has since died. She was the first person to write encouragingly to me about my first book* Village School, *and I always wish that I could have met her. She was the only girl in a family of six, and must have led an adventurous childhood, as you will see from this account of one of their many escapades.*

BOYS BY A STREAM

Perhaps the most ingenious of our exploits in this direction was the occasion of the adventure of the ants. (In truth we were never short of ideas.) I do not know what it was that put so happy an inspiration into our heads as to maroon a company of ants upon a rock in mid-stream. We had come upon them in the course of excavations, beneath an upturned stone, and we transferred them forthwith to that perilous position. The stream was very low at the time, and when we dammed it some feet farther down it rose gradually by inches. At first the prisoners paid little attention, though one or two of the more careless were washed away. But as the area narrowed down and the situation became clear to them, there was much running back and forth, consternation and dismay, till at last, when only a point of the rock remained, the whole terrified population was herded together on a space of but a few square inches. Just when a fearful disaster seemed imminent a way of escape was opened up, for we came to the rescue with a bridge, in the form of a twig to a larger rock beyond, from which a second bridge led to the mainland. It was a fine thing to see that distracted throng, hustling and crowding joyously to safety.

Such were the plain facts of this adventure. But it was not thus that we were wont to relate it in later years. It grew into a legend, elaborated by many picturesque embroideries. There was a point in it, I remember, where the leader of the party stood forth at the bridge end, plainly proclaiming 'Women and children first!' And it concluded with a general thanksgiving meeting on the gravel on the bank.

All of which goes to prove that there is much that can be done with a stream.

Bertram Smith: *Running Wild*

THE RUNAWAY

Once when the snow of the year was beginning to fall,
We stopped by a mountain pasture to say, 'Whose colt?'
A little Morgan had one forefoot on the wall,
The other curled at his breast. He dipped his head
And snorted to us. And then he had to bolt.
We heard the miniature thunder where he fled,
And we saw him, or thought we saw him, dim and grey,
Like a shadow against the curtain of falling flakes.
'I think the little fellow's afraid of the snow.
He isn't winter-broken. It isn't play
With the little fellow at all. He's running away.
I doubt if even his mother could tell him, "Sakes,
It's only weather." He'd think she didn't know!
Where is his mother? He can't be out alone.'
And now he comes again with a clatter of stone
And mounts the wall again with whited eyes
And all his tail that isn't hair up straight.
He shudders his coat as if to throw off flies.
'Whoever it is that leaves him out so late,
When other creatures have gone to stall and bin,
Ought to be told to come and take him in.'

Robert Frost

Izaak Walton (1593–1683) needed to write only two books to justify his claim to posterity, his Lives *and* The Compleat Angler. *The latter has delighted generations of country-lovers.*

To a non-fisher, the last part of the following passage sounds ironic. To sew a live frog (albeit 'with only one stitch') seems a strange way of 'using him as though you loved him'! But the felicity of Izaak Walton's prose helps one to overcome these qualms.

INSTRUCTION ON FROGS

And first you are to note, that there are two kinds of frogs, that is to say, if I may so express myself, a flesh and a fish frog. By flesh-frogs, I mean frogs that breed and live on the land; and of these there be several sorts also, and of several colours, some being speckled, some greenish, some blackish, or brown: the green frog, which is a small one, is, by Topsel, taken to be venomous, and so is the padock, or frog-padock, which usually keeps or breeds on the land, and is very large and bony, and big, especially the she-frog of that kind; yet these will sometimes come into the water, but it is not often: and the land-frogs are some of them observed by him, to breed by laying eggs, and others to breed of the slime and dust of the earth, and that in winter they turn to slime again, and that the next summer that very slime returns to be a living creature; this is the opinion of Pliny. And Cardanus undertakes to give a reason for the raining of frogs: but if it were in my power, it should rain none but water-frogs, for those I think are not venomous, especially the right water-frog, which, about February or March, breeds in ditches, by slime, and blackish eggs in that slime, about which time of breeding, the he and she frogs are observed to use divers summersaults, and to croak and make a noise, which the land-frog, or padock-frog, never does.

Now of these water-frogs, if you intend to fish with a frog for a pike, you are to choose the yellowest that you can get, for that the pike ever likes best. And thus use your frog, that he may continue long alive.

Put your hook into his mouth, which you may easily do from the middle of April till August; and then the frog's mouth grows up and he continues so for at least six months without eating, but is sustained, none but He whose name is Wonderful knows how: I say, put your hook, I mean the arming-wire, through his mouth and out at his gills; and then with a fine needle and silk sew the upper part of his leg, with only one stitch, to the arming-wire of your hook; or tie the frog's leg, above the upper joint, to the armed-wire; and, in so doing, use him as though you loved him, that is, harm him as little as you may possibly, that he may live the longer.

Izaak Walton: *The Compleat Angler*

THE BOY FISHING

I am cold and alone,
On my tree-root sitting as still as a stone.
The fish come to my net. I scorned the sun,
The voices on the road, and they have gone.
My eyes are buried in the cold pond, under
The cold, spread leaves; my thoughts are silver-wet.
I have ten stickleback, a half-day's plunder,
Safe in my jar. I shall have ten more yet.

E. J. Scovell

115

WHITE OWLS

White owls seem not (but in this I am not positive) to hoot at all: all that clamorous hooting appears to me to come from the wood kinds. The white owl does indeed snore and hiss in a tremendous manner; and these menaces well answer the intention of intimidating; for I have known a whole village up in arms on such an occasion, imagining the church-yard to be full of goblins and spectres. White owls also often scream horribly as they fly along; from this screaming probably arose the common people's imaginary species of *screech-owl*, which they superstitiously think attends the windows of dying persons. The plumage of the remiges of the wings of every species of owl that I have yet examined is remarkably soft and pliant. Perhaps it may be necessary that the wings of these birds should not make much resistance or rushing, that they may be enabled to steal through the air unheard upon a nimble and watchful quarry.

Gilbert White: *The Natural History of Selborne*

THE TORTOISE

While I was in Sussex last autumn my residence was at the village near Lewes, from whence I had formerly the pleasure of writing to you. On the first of November I remarked that the old tortoise, formerly mentioned, began first to dig the ground in order to the forming it's hybernaculum, which it had fixed on just beside a great turf of hepaticas. It scrapes out the ground with it's fore-feet, and throws it up over it's back with it's hind; but the motion of it's legs is ridiculously slow, little exceeding the hour-hand of a clock; and suitable to the composure of an animal said to be a whole month in performing one feat of copulation. Nothing can be more assiduous than this creature night and day in scooping the earth, and forcing it's great body into the cavity; but, as the noons of that season proved unusually warm and sunny, it was continually interrupted, and called forth by the heat in the middle of the day; and though I continued there till the thirteenth of November, yet the work remained unfinished. Harsher weather, and frosty mornings, would have quickened it's operations. No part of it's behaviour ever struck me more than the extreme timidity it always expresses with regard to rain; for though it has a shell that would secure it against the wheel of a loaded cart, yet does it discover as much solicitude about rain as a lady dressed in all her best attire, shuffling away on the first sprinklings, and running it's head up in a corner. If attended to, it becomes an excellent weather-glass; for as sure as it walks elate, and as it were on tiptoe, feeding with great earnestness in a morning, so sure will it rain before night. It is totally a diurnal animal, and never pretends to stir after it becomes dark. The tortoise, like other reptiles, has an arbitrary stomach as well as lungs; and can refrain from eating as well as breathing for a great part of the year. When first awakened it eats nothing; nor again in the autumn before it retires; through the height of the summer it feeds voraciously, devouring all the food that comes in it's way. I was much taken with it's sagacity in discerning those that do it kind offices: for, as soon as the good old lady comes in sight who has waited on it for more than thirty years, it hobbles towards it's benefactress with aukward alacrity; but remains inattentive to strangers. Thus not only 'the ox knoweth his owner, and the ass his master's crib,' but the most abject reptile and torpid of beings distinguishes the hand that feeds it, and is touched with the feelings of gratitude.

In about three days after I left Sussex the tortoise retired into the ground under the hepatica.

When one reflects on the state of this strange being, it is a matter of wonder to find that Providence should bestow such a profusion of days, such a seeming waste of longevity, on a reptile that appears to relish it so little as to squander more than two thirds of it's existence in a joyless stupor, and be lost to all sensation for months together in the profoundest of slumbers.

While I was writing this letter, a moist and warm afternoon, with the thermometer at 50, brought forth troops of *shell-snails*;

and, at the same juncture, the *tortoise* heaved up the mould and put out it's head; and the next morning came forth, as it were raised from the dead; and walked about till four in the afternoon.

Gilbert White: *The Natural History of Selborne*

THE GRASSHOPPER AND THE CRICKET

The poetry of earth is never dead:
When all the birds are faint with the hot sun,
And hide in cooling trees, a voice will run
From hedge to hedge about the new-mown mead:
That is the grasshopper's – he takes the lead
In summer luxury, – he has never done
With his delights, for when tired out with fun,
He rests at ease beneath some pleasant weed.
The poetry of earth is ceasing never:
On a lone winter evening, when the frost
Has wrought a silence, from the hearth there shrills
The cricket's song, in warmth increasing ever,
And seems to one in drowsiness half lost,
The grasshopper's among some grassy hills.

John Keats

PARSON WOODFORDE'S BEES

We had a Swarm of Bees today about Noon. Will Woodcock hived them for us, for which I gave him some Victuals and Drink and one shilling. They were hived twice as they would not stay in the hive they were first hived in, so that we were obliged to get a new hive for them and in that they continued very well. Tho' the other hive was a new one, yet they did not like it. It had been kept in the Corn Chamber all last year and perhaps Mice or other Animals might have been in it. Bees are particularly Nice and Cleanly.

James Woodforde: *The Diary of a Country Parson*

BIRD WATCHING

June 16th, Wednesday, 1802

I spoke of the little Birds keeping us company, and William told me that that very morning a bird had perched upon his leg. He had been lying very still, and had watched this little creature, it had come under the bench where he was sitting, and then flew up to his leg; he thoughtlessly stirred himself to look further at it, and it flew on to the apple tree above him. It was a little young creature, that had just left its nest, equally unacquainted with man, and unaccustomed to struggle against storms and winds. While it was upon the apple tree the wind blew about the stiff boughs, and the Bird seemed bemazed, and not strong enough to strive with it. The swallows come to the sitting-room window as if wishing to build, but I am afraid they will not have courage for it, but I believe they will build at my room window. They twitter, and make a bustle and a little chearful song, hanging against the panes of glass, with their soft white bellies close to the glass, and their forked fish-like tails. They swim round and round, and again they come. It was a sweet evening.

Dorothy Wordsworth: *Grasmere Journal*

Richard Jefferies (1848–1887) followed closely in the footsteps of Gilbert White in his methods as a naturalist. He wrote several books before Bevis: the story of a boy, *from which the following extract is taken. All show a fine poetic style as well as the keenest eye for detail.*

BEVIS WATCHES SWALLOWS

As he listened and watched the swallows he thought, or rather felt – for he did not think from step to step upwards to a conclusion – he felt that all the power of a bird's wing is in its tip.

It was with the slender-pointed and elastic tip, the flexible and finely divided feather point that the bird flew. An artist has a cumbrous easel, a heavy framework, a solid palette which has a distinct weight, but he paints with a tiny point of camel's hair. With a camel's hair tip the swallow sweeps the sky.

That part of the wing near the body, which is thick, rigid, and contains the bones, is the easel and framework; it is the shaft through which the driving force flows, and in floating it forms a part of the plane or surface, but it does not influence the air. The touch of the wing is in its tip. There, where the feathers fine down to extreme tenuity, so that if held up the light comes through the filaments, they seem to feel the air and to curl over on it as the end of a flag on a mast curls over on itself. So the tail of a fish – his one wing – curls over at the extreme edge of its upper and lower corners, and as it unfolds presses back the water. The swallow, pure artist of flight, feels the air with his wing-tips as with fingers, and lightly fanning, glides.

Richard Jefferies: *Bevis*

The youngest contributor to this collection wrote the following poem. Marjorie Fleming was born in 1803 at Kirkaldy, Fife, and died in 1811 at the age of eight.

THREE TURKEYS

Three turkeys fair their last have breathed
And now this world for ever leaved
Their Father & their Mother too
Will sigh and weep as well as you
Mourning for their offsprings fair
Whom they did nurse with tender care
Indeed the rats their bones have cranched
To eternity they are launched
Their graceful form and pretty eyes
Their fellow fowls did not despise
A direful death indeed they had
That would put any parent mad
But she was more than usual calm
She did not give a single damn
She is as genteel as a lamb
Here ends this melancholy lay
Farewell Poor Turkeys I must say

Marjorie Fleming (aged 7)

Three Men in a Boat *appeared first in 1889, and secured fame
for Jerome K. Jerome (1859–1927), who had struggled against
poverty, and in countless jobs, for many years. He was, he tells us in
his autobiography, 'of a melancholy and brooding disposition,'
although no one would suspect this whilst enjoying the gaiety of his
light-hearted masterpiece.*

SWAN BATTLE

It took us an immense amount of screaming and roaring to
wake Harris up again, and put some sense into him; but we
succeeded at last, and got safely on board.

Harris had a sad expression on him, so we noticed, when we

got into the boat. He gave you the idea of a man who had been through trouble. We asked him if anything had happened, and he said –

'Swans!'

It seemed we had moored close to a swan's nest, and soon after George and I had gone, the female swan came back, and kicked up a row about it. Harris had chivied her off, and she had gone away, and fetched up her old man. Harris said he had had quite a fight with these two swans; but courage and skill had prevailed in the end, and he had defeated them.

Half an hour afterwards they returned with eighteen other swans! It must have been a fearful battle, so far as we could understand Harris's account of it. The swans had tried to drag him and Montmorency out of the boat and drown them; and he had defended himself like a hero for four hours, and had killed the lot, and they had all paddled away to die.

'How many swans did you say there were?' asked George.

'Thirty-two,' replied Harris, sleepily.

'You said eighteen just now,' said George.

'No, I didn't,' grunted Harris; 'I said twelve. Think I can't count?'

What were the real facts about these swans we never found out. We questioned Harris on the subject in the morning, and he said 'What swans?' and seemed to think that George and I had been dreaming.

Jerome K. Jerome: Three Men in a Boat

VINCENZO C. A STORY TOLD IN PRISON

Ever since I was five years old I've looked after animals. You must always be gentle with them, and see to their wants. I understand much more about cows and sheep and goats than I do about Christians. When I look after a cow properly, she pays me back, she gives me milk; I'm good to her, and so she's good to me. But Christians aren't good to me; instead of helping me they do me harm. I know what to do when I'm with animals, but with Christians – no. My animals – they've shown far more love for me than Christians have shown. I had a kid and a lamb that used to follow me wherever I went. My mother and my brothers wish me well, but no one, not even God Himself, has ever cared about me as much as that kid and that lamb did.

Danilo Dolci: *To Feed the Hungry*

Here is a covey of English birds as seen by English poets from Shakespeare's time to our own.

THE CUCKOO

When daisies pied and violets blue,
And lady-smocks all silver-white,
And cuckoo-buds of yellow hue
Do paint the meadows with delight,

The cuckoo then, on every tree,
Mocks married men; for thus sings he,
Cuckoo!
Cuckoo, cuckoo! – O word of fear,
Unpleasing to a married ear!

When shepherds pipe on oaten straws,
And merry larks are ploughmen's clocks,
When turtles tread, and rooks, and daws,
And maidens bleach their summer smocks
The cuckoo then, on every tree,
Mocks married men; for thus sings he,
Cuckoo!
Cuckoo, cuckoo! – O word of fear,
Unpleasing to a married ear!

William Shakespeare

THE RED ROBIN

Cock Robin he got a new tippet in spring,
And he sat in a shed and heard other birds sing,
And he whistled a ballad as loud as he could,
And built him a nest of oak leaves by the wood.

And finished it just as the celandine pressed
Like a bright burning blaze by the edge of its nest,
All glittering with sunshine and beautiful rays,
Like high polished brass, or the fire in a blaze;

Then sung a new song on the bend of the brere;
And so it kept singing the whole of the year.
Till cowslips and wild roses blossomed and died,
The red robin sang by the old spinney side.

John Clare

THE OWL

Downhill I came, hungry, and yet not starved;
Cold, yet had heat within me that was proof
Against the North wind; tired, yet so that rest
Had seemed the sweetest thing under a roof.

Then at the inn I had food, fire, and rest,
Knowing how hungry, cold, and tired was I.
All of the night was quite barred out except
An owl's cry, a most melancholy cry

Shaken out long and clear upon the hill,
No merry note, nor cause of merriment,
But one telling me plain what I escaped
And others could not, that night, as in I went.

And salted was my food, and my repose,
Salted and sobered, too, by the bird's voice
Speaking for all who lay under the stars,
Soldiers and poor, unable to rejoice.

                                    Edward Thomas

THE YELLOWHAMMER

With rural admixture of shrill and sweet,
Forging his fairy letter for the ear
Of passing folks, from pollards close the wheat,
The yellowhammer gives the sun a cheer.
   Delighted with his leafy maze
   Like dancing elves he nods and sways,
   And now trills out a chime that's fair,
   And now grates out what he might spare,
While from the totter-grass gazes the humble hare.

                                    Edmund Blunden

THE DARKLING THRUSH

I leant upon a coppice gate
When Frost was spectre-gray,
And Winter's dregs made desolate
The weakening eye of day.
The tangled bine-stems scored the sky
Like strings from broken lyres,
And all mankind that haunted nigh
Had sought their household fires.

The land's sharp features seemed to be
The Century's corpse outleant,
His crypt the cloudy canopy,
The wind his death-lament.
The ancient pulse of germ and birth
Was shrunken hard and dry,
And every spirit upon earth
Seemed fervourless as I.

At once a voice burst forth among
The bleak twigs overhead
In a full-hearted evensong
Of joy illimited;
An aged thrush, frail, gaunt, and small,
In blast-beruffled plume,
Had chosen thus to fling his soul
Upon the growing gloom.

So little cause for carollings
Of such ecstatic sound
Was written on terrestrial things
Afar or nigh around,
That I could think there trembled through
His happy good-night air
Some blessed Hope, whereof he knew
And I was unaware.

Thomas Hardy

MAGPIES

One for sorrow, Two for mirth,
Three for a wedding, Four for a birth;
Five for the rich, Six for the poor,
Seven for a witch, Eight for one more;
Nine for a burying, Ten for a dance,
Eleven for England, Twelve for France.

Old Rhyme

SOLUTIONS

The swallow flew like lightning over the green
And through the gate-bars (a hand's breadth between);
He hurled his blackness at that chink and won;
The problem scarcely rose and it was done.

The spider, chance-confronted with starvation,
Took up another airy situation;
His working legs, as it appeared to me,
Had mastered practical geometry.

The old dog dreaming in his frowsy cask
Enjoyed his rest and did not drop his task;
He knew the person of 'no fixed abode,'
And challenged as he shuffled down the road.

These creatures which (Buffon and I agree)
Lag far behind the human faculty
Worked out the question set with satisfaction
And promptly took the necessary action.

By this successful sang-froid I, employed
On 'Who wrote Shakespeare?' justly felt annoyed,
And seeing an evening primrose by the fence
Beheaded it for blooming insolence.

Edmund Blunden

THE GALLOWS

There was a weasel lived in the sun
With all his family,
Till a keeper shot him with his gun
And hung him up on a tree,
Where he swings in the wind and rain,
In the sun and in the snow,
Without pleasure, without pain,
On the dead oak tree bough.

There was a crow who was no sleeper,
But a thief and a murderer
Till a very late hour; and this keeper
Made him one of the things that were,
To hang and flap in rain and wind,
In the sun and in the snow.
There are no more sins to be sinned
On the dead oak tree bough.

There was a magpie, too,
Had a long tongue and a long tail;
He could both talk and do –
But what did that avail?
He, too, flaps in the wind and rain
Alongside weasel and crow,
Without pleasure, without pain,
On the dead oak tree bough.

And many other beasts
And birds, skin, bone and feather,
Have been taken from their feasts

128

And hung up there together,
To swing and have endless leisure
In the sun and in the snow,
Without pain, without pleasure,
On the dead oak tree bough.

Edward Thomas

Stacey Aumonier is recognised as one of the most distinguished modern short-story writers. As his name suggests, he was of French extraction, and brought to his work a certain Gallic elegance and irony. He was adept at keeping the story moving, and leading his reader steadily to his climax. His characters live, his countryside is real. Never for a moment does he forget his duty to his reader and become boring.

I have admired The Octave of Jealousy *for many years. This eight-sided tale ends where it began. Its form is perfect, each little story leading to the next with mounting tension, until the octagonal circle (if there is such a geometrical figure) is complete.*

It comes from a book of short stories called Ups and Downs, *published by Heinemann in 1929.*

Stacey Aumonier was born in 1887 and died in 1928.

THE OCTAVE OF JEALOUSY

I

A tramp came through a cutting by old Jerry Shindle's nursery, and crossing the stile, stepped into the glare of the white road. He was a tall swarthy man with stubby red whiskers which appeared to conceal the whole of his face, except a small portion under each eye about the size of a two shilling piece. His skin showed through the rents in a filthy old black green garment, and was the same colour as his face, a livid bronze. His toes protruded from his boots, which seemed to be home-made contraptions of canvas and string. He carried an ash stick, and the rest of his worldly belongings in a spotted red and white handkerchief. His worldly belongings consisted of some rags, a doorknob, a portion of a foot-rule, a tin mug stolen from a workhouse, half a dozen date stones, a small piece of very old bread, a raw onion, the shutter of a camera and two empty matchboxes.

He looked up and down the road as though uncertain of his direction. To the north it curved under the wooded opulence of Crawshay Park. To the south it stretched like a white ribbon across a bold vista of shadeless downs. He was hungry and he eyed, critically, the potential possibilities of a cottage, standing back from the road. It was a shabby little three-roomed affair with fowls running in and out of the front door, some washing on a line, and the sound of a child crying within. While he was hesitating, a farm labourer came through a gate to an adjoining field, and walked towards the cottage. He, too, carried property tied up in a red handkerchief. His other hand balanced a steel fork across his left shoulder. He was a thick-set, rather dour-looking man. As he came up the tramp said:

'Where does this road lead to, mate?'

The labourer replied brusquely:

'Pondhurst.'

'How far?'

'Three and a half miles.'

Without embroidering this information any further he walked stolidly across the road and entered the garden of the cottage. The tramp watched him put the fork down by the lintel door. He saw him enter the cottage, and he heard a woman's voice. He sighed and muttered into his stubbly red beard: 'Lucky devil!' Then, hunching his shoulders, he set out with long flat-footed strides down the white road which led across the downs.

II

Having kicked some mud off his boots, the labourer, Martin Crosby, said to his wife:

'Dinner ready?'

Emma Crosby was wringing out some clothes. Her face was shiny with the steam and the heat of the day. She answered petulantly:

'No, it isn't. You'll have to wait another ten minutes, the 'taters aren't cooked. I've enough to do this morning I can tell you, what with the washing, and Lizzie screaming with her teeth, and the biler going wrong.'

'Ugh! There's allus somethin'.'

Martin knew there was no appeal against delay. He had been married four years; he knew his wife's temper and mode of life sufficiently well. He went out into the garden and lighted his pipe. The fowls clucked round his feet and he kicked them away. He, too, was hungry. However, there would be food of a sort – in time. Some greasy pudding and potatoes boiled to a liquid mash, a piece of cheese perhaps. Well, there it was. When you work in the open air all day you can eat anything. The sun was pleasant on his face, the shag pungent and comforting. If only old Emma weren't such a muddler! A good enough piece of goods when at her best, but always in a muddle, always behind time, no management, and then resentful because things went wrong. Lizzie: seven months old and two teeth through already and another coming. A lovely child, the spit and image of – what her mother must have been. Next time it would be a boy. Life wasn't so bad – really.

The gate clicked, and the tall figure of Ambrose Baines appeared. He was dressed in a corduroy coat and knickers, stout brown gaiters and square thick boots. Tucked under his arm was a gun with its two barrels pointing at the ground. He was the gamekeeper to Sir Septimus Letter. He stood just inside the gate and called out:

'Mornin', Martin.'

Martin replied: 'Mornin'.'

'I was just passin'. The missus says you can have a cookin' or so of runner beans if you wants 'em. We've got more than enough, and I hear as yours is blighty.'

'Oh! . . . ay, thank 'ee.'

'Middlin' hot today.'

'Ay . . . terrible hot.'

'When'll you be comin'?'

'I'll stroll over now. There's nowt to do. I'm waitin' dinner. I 'specks it'll be a half-hour or so. You know what Emma is.'

He went inside and fetched a basket. He said nothing to his wife, but rejoined Baines in the road. They strolled through the cutting and got into the back of the gamekeeper's garden just inside the wood. Martin went along the row and filled his basket. Baines left him and went into his cottage. He could hear Mrs Baines singing and washing up.

Of course *they* had had their dinner. It would be like that. Mrs Baines was a marvel. On one or two occasions Martin had entered their cottage. Everything was spick and span, and done on time. The two children always seemed to be clean and quiet. There were pretty pink curtains and framed oleographs. Mrs Baines could cook, and she led the hymns at church – so they said. Even the garden was neat, and trim, and fruitful. Of course *their* runner beans would be prolific while his failed. Mrs Baines appeared at the door and called out:

'Mornin', Mr Crosby.'

He replied gruffly: 'Mornin', Mrs Baines.'

'Middlin' hot.'

'Ay . . . terrible hot.'

She was not what you would call a pretty, attractive woman; but she was natty, competent, irrepressibly cheerful. She would make a shilling go as far as Emma would a pound. The cottage had five rooms, all in a good state of repair. The roof had been newly thatched. All this was done for him, of course, by his employer. He paid no rent; Martin had to pay five shillings a week, and then the roof leaked, and the boiler never worked properly – but perhaps that was Emma's fault. He picked up his basket and strolled towards the outer gate. As he did so, he heard the two children laughing, and Baines's voice joining in.

'Some people do have luck,' Martin murmured, and went back to his wife.

III

> Jack and Jill went up the hill
> To fetch a pail of water;
> Jack fell down and broke his crown
> And Jill came tumbling after!

It was very pretty – the way Winny Baines sang that, balancing the smaller boy on her knee, and jerking him skyward on the last word. Not what the world would call a pretty woman, but pretty enough to Ambrose, with her clear skin, kind motherly eyes, and thin brown hair. Her voice had a quality which somehow always expressed her gentle and unconquerable nature.

'She's too good for me,' Ambrose would think at odd moments. 'She didn't ought to be a gamekeeper's wife. She ought to be a lady – with carriages, and comforts, and well-dressed friends.'

The reflection would stir in him a feeling of sullen resentment, tempered with pride. She was a wonderful woman. She managed so well; she never complained. Of course, so far as the material necessities were concerned, there was enough and to spare. The cottage was comfortable, and reasonably well furnished – so far as he could determine. Of food there was abundance; game, rabbits, vegetables, eggs, fruit. The only thing he had to buy in the way of food was milk from the farm, and a few groceries from Mr Mead's shop. He paid nothing for the cottage and yet – he would have liked to have made things better for Winny. His wages were small, and there were clothes to buy, all kinds of little incidental expenses. There never seemed a chance to save and soon there would be the boy's schooling.

In spite of the small income, Winny always managed to keep herself and the children neat and smart, and even to help others like the more unfortunate Crosbys. She did all the work of the cottage, the care of the children, the mending and washing, and still found time to make jam, to preserve fruit, to grow flowers, and to sing in the church choir. She was the daughter of a piano-tuner at Bladestone, and the glamour of this early connection always hung between Ambrose and herself. To him a piano-tuner appeared a remote and romantic figure. It suggested a world of concerts, theatres, and Bohemian life. He was never quite clear about the precise functions of a piano-tuner, but he regarded his wife as the daughter of a public man, coming from a world far removed from the narrow limits of the life she was forced to lead with him.

In spite of her repeated professions of happiness, Ambrose

always felt a shade suspicious, not of her, but of his own ability to satisfy her every demand. Sometimes he would observe her looking round the little rooms, as though she were visualising what they might contain. Perhaps she wanted a grand piano, or some inlaid chairs, or embroidered coverings. He had not the money to buy these things, and he knew that she would never ask for them; but still it was there – that queer gnawing sense of insecurity. At dawn he would wander through the coppices drenched with dew, the gun under his arm, and the dog close to heel. The sunlight would come rippling over the jewelled leaves, and little clumps of primroses and violets would reveal themselves. Life would be good then, and yet somehow – it was not Winny's life. Only through their children did they seem to know each other.

> Jack and Jill went up the hill
> To fetch a pail of water;
> Jack fell down and broke his crown
> And Jill came tumbling after!

'Oo – Ambrose,' the other boy was tugging at his beard, when Winny spoke. He pretended to scream with pain before he turned to his wife.

'Yes, my dear?'

'Will you be passing Mr Mead's shop? We have run out of candles.'

'Oh? Roight be, my love. I'll be nigh there afore sundown. I have to order seed from Crumblings.'

He was later than he expected at Mr Mead's shop. He had to wait whilst several women were being served. The portly owner's new cash register went 'tap-tapping!' five times before he got a chance to say:

'Evenin', Mr Meads, give us a pound of candles, will ye?'

Mrs Meads came in through a parlour at the back, in a rustling black dress. She was going to a welfare meeting at the vicar's. She said:

'Good evening, Mr Baines, hope you are all nicely.'

A slightly disturbing sight met the eye of Ambrose. The parlour door was open, and he could see a maid in a cap and apron clearing away tea things in the gaily furnished room. The Meads had got a servant! He knew that Meads was extending his business. He had a cheap clothing department now, and he was building a shed out at the back with the intention of supplying petrol to casual motorists, but – a servant!

He picked up his packet of candles and muttered gruffly: 'Good evenin'.'

Before he had reached the door he heard 'tap-tapping! *His* one and twopence had gone into the box. As he swung down the street, he muttered to himself:

'God! I wish I had his money!'

IV

When Mrs Meads returned from the welfare meeting at half-past eight, she found Mr Meads waiting for her in the parlour, and the supper laid. There was cold veal and beetroot, apple pie, cheese and stout.

'I'm sorry I'm late, dear,' she said.

'That's all right, my love,' replied Mr Meads, not looking up from his newspaper.

'We had a lovely meeting – Mrs Wonnicott was there, and Mrs Beal, and Mrs Edwin Pillcreak, and Mrs James, and Ada, and both the Jamiesons, and the Vicar was perfectly sweet. He made two lovely speeches.'

'Oh, that was nice,' said Mr Meads, trying to listen and read a piquant paragraph about a divorce case at the same time.

'I should think you want your supper.'

'I'm ready when you are, my love.'

Mr Meads put down his newspaper, and drawing his chair up to the table, began to set about the veal. He was distinctly a man for his victuals. He carved rapidly for her, and less rapidly for himself. From this you must not imagine that he treated his wife meanly. On the contrary, he gave her a large helping, but a close observer could not help detecting that when carving for himself he seemed to take more interest in his job. Then he rang a little tinkly hand-bell and the new maid appeared.

'Go into the shop, my dear,' he said, 'and get me a pot of pickled walnuts from the second shelf on the left before you come to them bales of calico.'

The maid went, and Mrs Meads clucked:

'Um – being a bit extravagant tonight, John.'

'The labourer is worthy of his hire,' quoted Mr Meads sententiously. He put up a barrage of veal in the forefront of his mouth – he had no back teeth, but managed to penetrate it with an opaque rumble of sound. 'Besides we had a good day today – done a lot of business. Pass the stout—'

'I'm glad to hear it,' replied Mrs Meads. 'It's about time things began to improve, considerin' what we've been through. Mrs Wonnicott was wearin' her biscuit-coloured taffeta with a new lace yoke. She looked smart, but a bit stiff for the Welfare to my way of thinkin'.'

'Ah!' came rumbling through the veal.

'Oh, and did I tell you Mrs Mounthead was there, too? She was wearing her starched ninon – no end of a swell she looked.'

Mr Mead's eyes lighted with definite interest at last. Mrs Mounthead was the wife of James Mounthead, the proprietor of that handsome hostelry, 'The Die is Cast.' When his long day's work was over, Mr Meads would not infrequently pop into 'The Die is Cast' for an hour or so before closing time and have a long chat with Mr James Mounthead. He swallowed half a glass of stout at a gulp, and helped himself liberally to the pickled walnuts which the maid had just brought in. Eyeing the walnuts thoughtfully, he said:

'Oh, so she's got into it, too, has she?'

'Yes, she's really quite a pleasant body. She told me coming down the street that her husband has just bought Bolder's farm over at Pondhurst. He's setting up his son there who's marrying Kate Steyning. Her people have got a bit of money, too, so they'll be all right. By the way, we haven't heard from Charlie for nearly three weeks.'

Mr Meads sighed. Why were women always like that? There was Edie. He was trying to tell her that things were improving, going well in fact. The shed for petrol and motor accessories was nearly finished; the cheap clothing department was in full swing; he had indulged in pickled walnuts for supper (her supper, too); and there she must needs talk about – Charlie! Everybody in the neighbourhood knew that their son Charlie was up in London, and not doing himself or anybody else any good. And almost in the same breath she must needs talk about old Mounthead's son. Everyone knew that young Mounthead was a promising industrious fellow. Oh! and so James had bought him Bolder's farm, had he? That cost a pretty penny, he knew. Just bought a farm, had he? Not put the money into his business; just bought it in the way that he, Sam Meads, might buy a gramophone, or an umbrella. Psaugh!

'I don't want no tart,' he said, on observing Edie begin to carve it.

'No tart!' she exclaimed. 'Why, what's wrong?'

'Oh, I don't know,' he replied. 'Don't feel like it – working too hard – bit flatulent. I'll go out for a stroll after supper.'

An hour later he was leaning against the bar of 'The Die is Cast,' drinking gin and water, and listening to Mr Mounthead discourse on dogs. The bar of 'The Die is Cast' was a self-constituted village club. Other cronies drifted in. They were all friends of both Mr Meads and Mr Mounthead. Mrs Mounthead seldom appeared in the bar, but there was a potman and a barmaid named Florrie; and somewhere in the rear a cook, two housemaids, a scullerymaid, a boy for knives and boots, and an ostler. Mr Mounthead had a victoria and a governess car, as well as a van for business purposes, a brown mare and a pony. He also had his own farm well stocked with pigs, cattle, and poultry. While taking his guests' money in a sleepy leisurely way, he regaled them with the rich fruits of his opinions and experiences. Later on he dropped casually that he was engaging an overseer at four hundred a year to take his son's place. And Mr Meads glanced round the bar and noted the shining glass and pewter, the polished mahogany, the little pink and green glasses winking at him insolently.

'He doesn't know what work is either,' suddenly occurred to him. Mr Mounthead's work consisted mostly in a little book-keeping, and in ordering people about. He only served in the shop as a kind of social relaxation. If he, Sam Meads, didn't serve in his shop himself all day from early morning till late evening, goodness knows what would happen to the business. Besides – the pettiness of it all! Little bits of cheese, penny tins of mustard, string, weighing out sugar and biscuits, cutting bacon, measuring off ribbons and calico, and flannelette. People gossiping all day, and running up little accounts it was always hard to collect. But here – oh, the snappy quick profit. Every-body paying on the nail, served in a second, and what a profit! Enough to buy a farm for a son as though it was – an umbrella. Walking home, a little dejectedly, later on, he struck the road with his stick, and muttered:

'Damn that man!'

V

Mrs James Mounthead was rather pleased with her starched ninon. She leant back luxuriously in the easy chair, yawned, and pressed her hands along the sides of her well-fitting skirt. Gilt bangles round her wrists rattled pleasantly during this per-formance. A paste star glittered on her ample bosom. She heard James moving ponderously on the landing below; the bar had closed. He came puffily up the stairs and opened the door.

'A nightcap, Queenie?' he wheezed through the creaking machinery of his respiratory organs.

Mrs Mounthead smiled brightly. 'I think I will tonight, Jim.'

He went to a cabinet and poured out two mixed drinks. He handed his wife one, and raising the other to his lips said:

'Well, here's to the boy!'

'Here's to James the Second!' she replied, and drank deeply. Her eyes sparkled. Mrs Mounthead was excited. The bangles clattered against the glass as she set it down.

'Come and give me a kiss, old dear,' she said leaning back.

Without making any great show of enthusiasm, James did as he was bidden. He, too, was a little excited, but his excitement was less amorous than commercial. He had paid nearly twelve hundred pounds less for Bolder's farm than he had expected. The news of his purchase was all over the neighbourhood. It had impressed everyone. People looked at him differently. He was becoming a big man, *the* big man in those parts. He could buy another farm tomorrow, and it wouldn't break him. And the boy – the boy was a good boy; he would do well, too.

A little drink easily affected Mrs Mounthead. She became garrulous.

'I had a good time at the Welfare, though some of the old cats didn't like me, I know. Ha, ha, ha, what do I care? We could buy the whole lot up if we wanted to, except perhaps the Wonnicotts. Mine was the only frock worth a tinker's cuss. Lord! You should have seen old Mrs Meads! Looked like a washerwoman on a Sunday. The vicar was ever so nice. He called me madam, and said he 'oped I often come. I gave a fiver to the fund. Ha, ha, ha, I didn't tell 'em that I made it backing 'Ringcross' for the Nunhead Stakes yesterday! They'd have died.'

During this verbal explosion, James Mounthead thoughtfully regarded his glass. And he thought to himself:

'Um. It's a pity Queenie gives herself away sometimes.'

He didn't particularly want to hear about the Welfare. He wanted to talk about 'James the Second' and the plans for the future. He wanted to indulge in the luxury of talking about their success, but he didn't want to boast about wealth in quite that way. He had queer ambitions not unconnected with the land he lived on. He had not always been in the licensing trade. His father had been a small landed proprietor and a stock breeder; a man of stern, unrelenting principles. From his father, he, James Mounthead, had inherited a kind of reverence for the ordered development of land and cattle, an innate respect for the sanctity of tradition, caste, property and fair dealing. His wife had always been in the licensing trade. She was the daughter of a publican at Pondhurst. As a girl she had served in the bar.

All her relations were licensing people. When she had a little to drink – she was apt to display her worst side, to give herself away. James sighed.

'Did Mrs Wonnicott say anything about her husband?' he asked, to change the subject.

'You bet she did. Tried to put it across us – when I told her about us buying Bolder's farm – said her old man had thought of bidding for it, but he knew it was poor in root crops and the soil was no good for corn, and that Sturge had neglected the place too long. The old cat! I said: "Yes, and p'raps it wouldn't be convenient to pay for it just now, after 'aving bought a lawn mower!" Ha, ha, ha. He, he, he. O my!!'

'I shouldn't have said that,' mumbled Mr Mounthead, who knew, however, that anything was better than one of Queenie's violent reactions to quarrelsomeness. 'Come on, let's go and turn in, old girl.'

An hour later, James Mounthead was tossing restlessly between the sheets. Queenie's reference to the Wonnicotts had upset him. He could read between what she had said sufficiently to envisage a scene, which he himself deplored. Queenie, of course, had given herself away again to Mrs Wonnicott. He knew that both the Wonnicotts despised her, and through her, him. He had probably as much money as Lewis Wonnicott, if not more. He certainly had a more fluid and accumulative way of making it, but there the matter stopped. Wonnicott was a gentleman; his wife a lady. He, James, might have been as much a gentleman as Wonnicott if – circumstances had been different. Queenie could never be a lady in the sense that Mrs Wonnicott was a lady. Wonnicott led the kind of life *he* would like to live – a gentleman farmer, with hunters, a little house property, and some sound vested interests; a man with a great knowledge of land, horses, finance, and politics.

He loved Queenie in a queer enduring kind of way. She had been loyal to him, and she satisfied most of his needs. She loved him, but he knew that he could never attain the goal of his vague ambitions with her clinging to his heels. He thought of Lewis Wonnicott sleeping in his white panelled bedroom with chintz curtains and old furniture, and his wife in the adjoining room, where the bay window looked out on to the downs; and the heart of James became bitter with envy.

VI

'I don't think I shall attend those Welfare meetings any more,' remarked Mrs Lewis Wonnicott with a slight drawl. She gathered up her letters from the breakfast table and walked to the window.

In the garden below, Leach, the gardener, was experimenting with a new mower on the well-clipped lawns. The ramblers on the pergola were at their best. Her husband in a broad check suit and a white stock, looked up from *The Times* and said:

'Oh, how is that, my dear?'

'They are getting such awful people in. That dreadful woman, the wife of Mounthead, the publican, has joined.'

'Old Mounthead's all right – not a bad sort. He knows a gelding from a blood mare.'

'That may be, but his wife is the limit. I happened to say something about the new mower, and she was simply rude. An awful vulgar person, wears spangles, and boasts about the money her husband makes out of selling whisky.'

'By gad! I bet he does, too. I wouldn't mind having a bit in his pub. Do you see Canadian Pacifics are still stagnant?'

'Lewis, I sometimes wish you wouldn't be so material. You think about nothing but money.'

'Oh, come, my dear, I'm interested in a crowd of other things – things which I don't make any money out of, too.'

'For instance?'

'The land, the people who work on it, horses, cattle, game, the best way to do things for everybody. Besides, ain't I interested in the children? The two girls' careers at Bedales? Young Ralph at Rugby and going up to Cambridge next year?'

'You know they're there, but how much interest you take, I couldn't say.'

'What is it you want me to do, my dear?'

'I think you might bestir yourself to get amongst better people. The girls will be leaving school soon and coming home. We know no one, no one at all in the neighbourhood.'

'No one at all! Jiminy! Why, we know everyone!'

'You spend all your time among horse-breeders and cattle-dealers, and people like Mounthead, and occasionally call on the Vicar, but who is there of any importance that we know?'

'Lord! What do you want? Do you want me to go and call at Crawshay Park, and ask Sir Septimus and Lady Letter to come and make up a four at bridge?'

'Don't be absurd! You know quite well that the Letters are entirely inaccessible. He's not only an M.P. and owner of half the newspapers in the country, but a millionaire. They entertain house parties of ministers and dukes, and even royalty. They can afford to ignore even the county people themselves. But there are others. We don't even know the county.'

'Who, for instance?'

'Well, the Burnabys. You met St John Burnaby at the Constitutional Club two or three times and yet you have never attempted to follow it up. They're very nice people and neighbours. And they have three boys all in the twenties, and the girl Sheila – she's just a year younger than Ralph.'

'My word! Who's being material now?'

'It isn't material, it's just – thinking of the children.'

'Women are wonderful,' muttered Lewis Wonnicott into his white stock, without raising his head. Mrs Wonnicott swept to the door. Her thin lips were drawn in a firm straight line. Her refined hard little face appeared pinched and petulant. With her hand on the door-handle she said acidly:

'If you can spare half an hour from your grooms and pigs, I think you might at least do this to please me – call on Mrs Burnaby today.'

And she went out of the room, shutting the door crisply.

'Oh, Jiminy-Piminy!' muttered Mr Wonnicott. 'Jiminy-Piminy!'

He stood up and shook himself. Then with feline intentness he walked quickly to the French window, and opening it walked down the steps into the garden. All the way to the sunk rose-garden he kept repeating, 'Jiminy-Piminy!'

Once among the rose-bushes he lighted his pipe. (His wife objected to smoking in the house.) He blew clouds of tobacco smoke amongst imaginary green-fly. Occasionally he would glance furtively out at the view across the downs. Half buried amongst the elms near Basted Old Church he could just see the five red gables of the Burnaby's capacious mansion.

'I can't do it,' he thought, 'I can't do it, and I shall have to do it.'

It was perfectly true he had been introduced to St John Burnaby and had spoken to him once or twice. It was also true that Burnaby had never given any evidence of wishing to follow up the acquaintanceship. Bit of a swell, Burnaby, connected with all sorts of people, member of half a dozen clubs, didn't race but went in for golf, and had a shooting box in Scotland. Some said he had political ambitions, and meant to try for Parliament at the next election. He didn't racket round in a check suit and a white stock and mix with grooms and farm hands; he kept up the flair of the gentleman, the big man, acres of conservatory, and peacocks, and a son in the diplomatic service, a daughter married to a bishop. His wife, too, came of a poor but aristo-cratic family. Over at the 'Five Gables' they kept nine gar-deners and twenty odd servants. Everything was done tip-top.

Lewis Wonnicott turned and regarded his one old man gardener, trying the new mower, which Mrs Mounthead had been so rude about to Dorothy. Poor Dorothy! She was touchy, that's what it was. Of course she *did* think of the children – no getting away from it. She was ambitious more for them than for herself or himself. She had given up being ambitious for him. He knew that she looked upon him as a slacker, a kind of cabbage. Well, perhaps he had been. He hadn't accomplished all he ought to. He had loved the land, the feel of horse-flesh, the smell of wet earth when the morning dews were on it. He had been a failure . . . a failure. He was not up to county people. He was unworthy of his dear wife's ambitions. Jiminy-Piminy!

145

it would be a squeeze to send Ralph up to Cambridge next year!

He looked across the valley at the five red gables among the red elms, and sighed.

'Lucky devil!' he murmured. 'Damn it all! I suppose I must go.'

VII

'You don't seem to realise the importance of it,' said Gwendolen St John Burnaby as her husband leant forward on his seat on the terrace and tickled the ear of Jinks, the Airedale. 'A career in the diplomatic service without influence is about as likely to be a success as a – as a performance on a violin behind a sound-proof curtain. There's Lal, wasting his – his talents and genius at that wretched little embassy at Oporto, and all you've got to do is to drive three miles to Crawshay Park and put the matter before Sir Septimus.'

'These things always seem so simple to women,' answered Sir John, a little peevishly.

'Well, isn't it true? Do you deny that he has the power?'

'Of course he has power, my dear, but you may not realise the kind of life a man like that lives. Every minute of the day is filled up, all kinds of important things crowding each other out. He's always been friendly enough to me, and yet every time I meet him I have an idea he has forgotten who I am. He deals in movements in which men are only pawns. If I told him about Lal he would say yes, he would do what he could – make a note of it, and forget about it directly I turned my back.'

Mrs St John Burnaby stamped her elegant Louis heels.

'Is nothing ever worth trying?'

'Don't be foolish, Gwen, haven't I tried? Haven't I ambition?'

'For yourself, yes. I am thinking of Lal.'

'Women always think of their sons before their husbands. He knows I've backed his party for all I'm worth. He knows I'm standing for the constituency next time. When I get elected will be the moment. I shall then have a tiny atom of power. For a man without even a vote in Parliament do you think Letter is going to waste his time?'

'Obstinate!' muttered Mrs Burnaby with metallic clearness. The little lines round the eyes and mouth of a face that had once been beautiful became accentuated in the clear sunlight. The constant stress of ambitious desires had quickened her vitality, but in the process had aged her body before its time. She knew that her husband was ambitious, too, but there was always just that little something he lacked in the great moments, just that little special effort that might have landed him among the gods – or in the House of Lords. He had been successful enough in a way. He had made money – a hundred thousand or so – in brokerage and dealing indirectly in various manufactured commodities; but he had not even attained a knighthood or a seat in Parliament. His heavy dark face betokened power and courage, but not vision. He was indeed as she had said – obstinate. In minnow circles he might appear a triton, but living within the same county as Sir Septimus Letter – Bah!

About to leave him, her movement was arrested by the approach of a butler followed by a gentleman in a check suit and a white stock, looking self-conscious.

Mrs St John Burnaby raised her lorgnette. 'One of these local people,' she reflected.

On being announced the gentleman in the check suit exclaimed rapidly:

'Excuse the liberty I take – neighbours, don't you know. Remember me at the Constitutional Club, Mr Burnaby? Thought I would drop in and pay my respects.'

St John Burnaby nodded.

'Oh, yes, yes, quite. I remember, Mr-er-Mr—'

'Wonnicott.'

'Oh yes, of course. How do you do? My wife – Mr Wonnicott.'

The wife and the Wonnicott bowed to each other, and there was an uncomfortable pause. At last Mr Wonnicott managed to say:

'We live over at Wimpstone, just across the valley – my wife, the girls are at school, boy's up at Rugby.'

'Oh, yes – really?' This was Mrs Burnaby, who was thinking to herself:

'The man looks like a dog fancier.'

'Very good school' said St John Burnaby. 'Hot today, isn't it!'

'Yes, it's exceedingly warm.'

'Do you golf?'

'No, I don't golf. I ride a bit.'

'You must excuse me,' said Mrs St John Burnaby. 'I have got to get a trunk call to London.'

She fluttered away across the terrace, and into the house. Mr Wonnicott chatted away for several minutes, but St John Burnaby was preoccupied and monosyllabic. The visitor was relieved to rescue his hat at last and make his escape. Walking down the drive he thought:

'It's no good. He dislikes me.'

As a matter of fact St John Burnaby was not thinking about him at all. He was thinking of Sir Septimus Letter, the big man, the power he would have liked to have been. He ground his teeth and clenched his fists:

'Damn it!' he muttered. 'I will not appeal for young Lal. Let him fight his own battles.'

VIII

On a certain day that summer when the sun was at its highest in the heavens, Sir Septimus Letter stood by the bureau in his cool library and conversed with his private secretary.

Sir Septimus was wearing what appeared to be a ready-made navy serge suit and a low collar. His hands were thrust into his trouser pockets. The sallow face was heavily marked, the strange restless eyes peered searchingly beneath dark brows which almost met in one continuous line. The chin was finely modelled, but not too strong. It was not indeed what is usually known as a strong face. It had power, but of the kind which has been mellowed by the friction of every human experience. It had alert intelligence, a penetrating absorption, above all things it indicated vision. The speech and the movements were incisive; the short wiry body a compact tissue of nervous energy. He listened with the watchful intensity of a dog at a rabbit-hole.

Through the door at the end of the room could be heard the distant click of many typewriters.

The secretary was saying:

'The third reading of the Nationalisation of Paper Industries Bill comes on at five-thirty, sir. Boneham will be up, and I do not think you will be called till seven. You will, of course, however, wish to hear what he has to say.'

'I know what he'll say. You can cut that out, Roberts. Get Libby to give me a précis at six forty-five.'

'Very good, sir. Then there will be time after the Associated News Service Board at four to see the minister with regard to this question of packing meetings in East Riding. Lord Lampreys said he would be pleased if I could fix an appointment. He has some information.'

'Right. What line are Jennins and Castwell taking over this?'

'They're trying to side-track the issue. They have every unassociated newspaper in the North against you.'

'H'm, h'm. Well, we've fought them before.'

'Yes, sir. The pressure is going to be greater this time, but everyone has confidence you will get them down.'

The little man's eyes sparkled. 'Roberts, get through on the private wire to – Lambe; no, get through to all of them, and make it quite clear. This is not to be a party question. They're to work the unctious rectitude stuff, you know – liberty of the subject and so on.'

'Very good, sir. The car comes at one-fifteen. You are lunching with Cranmer at Shorn Towers, the Canadian paper interests will be strongly represented there. I will be at Whitehall Court at three with the despatches. It would be advisable, if possible, to get Loeb of the finance committee. Oh, by the way, sir, I had to advise you from Loeb. They have received a cabled report of the expert's opinion from Labrador. There are two distinct seams of coal on that land you bought in '07. A syndicate from Buffalo have made an offer. They offer a million and a quarter dollars down.'

'What did we pay?'

'One hundred and twenty thousand.'

149

'Don't sell.'

'Very good, sir.'

'Have you seen my wife lately?'

'I have not seen Lady Letter for some days, sir. I believe she is at Harrogate.'

The little man sighed, and drew out a cigarette case, opened it and offered one to Roberts, who accepted it with an elegant gesture. Then he snapped it to, and replaced it in his pocket.

'Damn it, Roberts, Reeves says I mustn't smoke.'

'Oh, dear! – only a temporary disability, I trust, sir.'

'Everything is temporary, Roberts.'

With his hands still in his pockets, he walked abstractedly out of the room. A little ormolu clock in the outer corridor indicated twenty minutes to one. The car was due at one-fifteen. Thirty-five minutes; oh, to escape for only that brief period! Through the glass doors he could see his sister, talking to two men in golfing clothes, some of the house party. The house party was a perpetual condition at Crawshay. He turned sharply to the right, and went through a corridor leading out to the rear of the garage. He hurried along and escaped to a path between two tomato houses. In a few moments he was lost to sight. He passed through a shrubbery, and came to a clearing. Without slackening his pace, he walked across it, and got amongst some trees. The trees of Crawshay Park – his trees! . . . He looked up at the towering oaks and elms. Were they his trees – because he had bought them? They were there years before he was born. They would be there years after his death. He was only passing through them – a fugitive. 'Everything is temporary, Roberts—' Yes, even life itself. Jennins and Castwell! Of course they wanted to get him down! Were they the only ones? Does one struggle to the top without hurting others to get there? Does one get to the top without making enemies? Does one get to the top without suffering, and bitterness, and remorse? The park sloped down to a low stone wall, with an opening where one could obtain a glorious view across the weald of Sussex. The white ribbon of a road stretched away into infinity.

As he stood there, he saw a dark swarthy figure clamber

down a bank, and stand hesitating in the middle of the road. He was a tramp with a stubbly red beard nearly concealing his face, and a filthy black green suit. In his hand he carried a red hand-kerchief containing his worldly belongings – a door-knob, a portion of a foot-rule, a tin mug stolen from a workhouse, some date stones, an onion, the shutter of a camera, and two empty match boxes.

Sir Septimus did not know this fact; he merely regarded the tramp as an abstraction. He observed him hesitate, exchange a word with a field labourer, look up at the sky, hunch his shoulders, and suddenly set out with long swinging strides down the white road. Whither? There stirred within the breast of the millionaire a curious wistful longing. Oh, to be free! To be free! To walk across those hills without a care, without a re-sponsibility. The figure, with its easy gait, fascinated him. The dark form became smaller and smaller, swallowed up in the immensity of nature. With a groan, Sir Septimus Letter buried his face in his hands and murmured:

'Lucky devil! . . . lucky devil! O God! If I could die . . .'

Stacey Aumonier: *Ups and Downs*

THE CHANGING SEASONS

In a climate as capricious as ours it is small wonder that the weather takes first place in our conversation, and that the seasons are anticipated with some joy or foreboding.

Here you will find some literary reactions to the English climate, and I have given pride of place to Spring, when we are at our most hopeful, beginning with a fresh Elizabethan sonnet, gay as Spring itself but for the dying fall of the last five poignant words.

DESCRIPTION OF SPRING

Wherein each thing renews, save only the Lover

The soote season, that bud and bloom forth brings,
With green hath clad the hill and eke the vale:
The nightingale with feathers new she sings;
The turtle to her mate hath told her tale.
Summer is come, for every spray now springs:
The hart hath hung his old head on the pale;
The buck in brake his winter coat he flings;
The fishes float with new repaired scale.
The adder all her slough away she slings;
The swift swallow pursueth the flies smale;
The busy bee her honey now she mings;
Winter is worn that was the flowers' bale.

And thus I see among these pleasant things
Each care decays, and yet my sorrow springs.

Henry Howard, Earl of Surrey

APRIL MORNING

April 29th, Thursday, 1802

A beautiful morning – the sun shone and all was pleasant. We went to John's Grove, sate a while at first. Afterwards William lay, and I lay, in the trench under the fence – he with his eyes shut, and listening to the waterfalls and the birds. There was no one waterfall above another – it was a sound of waters in the air – the voice of the air. William heard me breathing and rustling now and then, but we both lay still, and unseen by one another; he thought that it would be as sweet thus to lie so in the grave, to hear the *peaceful* sounds of the earth, and just to know that our dear friends were near. The lake was still; there was a boat out. Silver How reflected with delicate purple and yellowish hues, as I have seen Spar; Lambs on the island, and running races together by the half-dozen, in the round field near us. The copses green*ish*, hawthorn green. Came home to dinner, then went to Mr Simpson – we rested a long time under a wall, sheep and lambs were in the field – cottages smoking. As I lay down on the grass, I observed the glittering silver line on the ridge of the backs of the sheep, owing to their situation respecting the sun, which made them look beautiful, but with something of strangeness, like animals of another kind, as if belonging to a more splendid world.

Dorothy Wordsworth: *Grasmere Journal*

A MAY MORNING

The bisy larke, messager of day,
Salueth in hir song the morwe gray,
And firy Phebus riseth up so bright
That al the orient laugheth of the light,
And with his stremes dryeth in the greves
The silver dropes hangynge on the leves.
And Arcita, that is in the court roial
With Theseus his squier principal,
Is risen and looketh on the myrie day.
And for to doon his observaunce to May,
Remembrynge on the poynt of his desir,
He on a courser, starlynge as the fir,
Is riden into the feeldes hym to pleye,
Out of the court, were it a myle or tweye.
And to the grove of which that I yow tolde
By aventure his wey he gan to holde,
To maken hym a gerland of the greves
Were it of wodebynde or hawethorn leves,
And loude he song ayeyn the sonne shene:
'May, with alle thy floures and thy grene,
Welcome be thou, faire, fresshe May,
In hope that I som grene gete may.'

Geoffrey Chaucer: *The Knight's Tale*

SPRING GOETH ALL IN WHITE

Spring goeth all in white,
Crowned with milk-white may:
In fleecy flocks of light
O'er heaven the white clouds stray:

White butterflies in the air;
White daisies prank the ground:
The cherry and hoary pear
Scatter their snow around.

Robert Bridges

PERDITA'S SPEECH

I would I had some flowers o' the spring that might
Become your time of day; and yours, and yours,
That wear upon your virgin branches yet
Your maidenheads growing: O Proserpina!
For the flowers now that frighted thou let'st fall
From Dis's waggon! daffodils,
That come before the swallow dares, and take
The winds of March with beauty; violets dim,
But sweeter than the lids of Juno's eyes
Or Cytherea's breath; pale prim-roses,
That die unmarried, ere they can behold
Bright Phoebus in his strength, a malady
Most incident to maids; bold oxlips and
The crown imperial; lilies of all kinds,
The flower-de-luce being one.

William Shakespeare: The Winter's Tale

This extract from a letter to James Rice was written by John Keats at his home in Wentworth Place. A year later, in Rome, on February 23rd, 1821, Keats died.

LEAVING THE WORLD

How astonishingly does the chance of leaving the world impress a sense of its natural beauties on us. Like poor Falstaff, though I do not 'babble,' I think of green fields. I muse with the greatest affection of every flower I have known from my infancy – their shapes and colours are as new to me as if I had just created them with a superhuman fancy. It is because they are connected with the most thoughtless and happiest moments of our Lives. I have seen foreign flowers in hothouses of the most beautiful nature, but I do not care a straw for them. The simple flowers of our spring are what I want to see again.

John Keats: *A letter to James Rice*, 14 February, 1820

DOROTHY'S DAFFODILS...

April 15th, Thursday, 1802

When we were in the woods beyond Gowbarrow park we saw a few daffodils close to the water-side. We fancied that the lake had floated the seeds ashore, and that the little colony had so sprung up. But as we went along there were more and yet more; and at last, under the boughs of the trees, we saw that there was a long belt of them along the shore, about the breadth of a country turnpike road. I never saw daffodils so beautiful. They grew among the mossy stones about and about them; some rested their heads upon these stones as on a pillow for weariness; and the rest tossed and reeled and danced, and seemed as if they verily laughed with the wind, that blew upon them over the lake; they looked so gay, ever glancing, ever changing. This wind blew directly over the lake to them. There was here and there a little knot, and a few stragglers a few yards higher up; but they were so few as not to disturb the simplicity, unity, and life of that one busy highway.

Dorothy Wordsworth: *Grasmere Journal*

... AND HER BROTHER'S

I wandered lonely as a Cloud
That floats on high o'er Vales and Hills,
When all at once I saw a crowd
A host of golden Daffodils;
Along the Lake, beneath the trees,
Fluttering and dancing in the breeze.

The waves beside them danced, but they
Outdid the sparkling waves in glee: –
A Poet could not but be gay
In such a laughing company:
I gaz'd – and gaz'd – but little thought
What wealth the shew to me had brought:

For oft, when on my couch I lie
In vacant or in pensive mood,
They flash upon that inward eye
Which is the bliss of solitude;
And then my heart with pleasure fills,
And dances with the Daffodils.

William Wordsworth

*And here is another Elizabethan sonnet from the greatest
countryman of all time.*

From you have I been absent in the spring,
When proud-pied April, dress'd in all his trim,
Hath put a spirit of youth in everything,
That heavy Saturn laugh'd and leap'd with him.
Yet nor the lays of birds, nor the sweet smell
Of different flowers in odour and in hue,
Could make me any summer's story tell,

160

Or from their proud lap pluck them where they grew;
Nor did I wonder at the Lily's white,
Nor praise the deep vermilion in the Rose;
They were but sweet, but figures of delight,
Drawn after you, you pattern of all those.
    Yet seem'd it Winter still, and you away,
    As with your shadow I with these did play.

William Shakespeare

AN OCTOBER DAY

October 20th, Monday, 1800

William worked in the morning at the sheepfold. After dinner we walked to Rydale, crossed the stepping-stones, and while we were walking under the tall oak trees the Lloyds called out to us. They went with us on the western side of Rydale. The lights were very grand upon the woody Rydale Hills. Those behind dark and topp'd with clouds. The two lakes were divinely beautiful. Grasmere excessively solemn and the whole lake was calm, and dappled with soft grey ripples. The Lloyds staid with us till 8 o'clock. We then walked to the top of the hill at Rydale. Very mild and warm. About six glow-worms shining faintly. We went up as far as the grove. When we came home the fire was out. We ate our supper in the dark, and went to bed immediately. William was disturbed in the night by the rain coming into his room, for it was a very rainy night. The Ash leaves lay across the Road.

Dorothy Wordsworth: Grasmere Journal

*'There's a change in the weather,' says one. 'The wind has turned,'
says another. 'The glass is falling,' says a third. What does it
presage? Rain, usually. Here are five poems inspired by an element
which most people find depressing.*

GLASS FALLING

The glass is going down. The sun
Is going down. The forecasts say
It will be warm, with frequent showers.
We ramble down the showery hours
And amble up and down the day.
Mary will wear her black goloshes
And splash the puddles on the town;
And soon on fleets of macintoshes
The rain is coming down, the frown
Is coming down of heaven showing
A wet night coming, the glass is going
Down, the sun is going down.

Louis Macneice

*This is a poem which I always associate with young children, for I
taught it to many between the ages of six and eight. It was always a
favourite, and by some felicitous arrangement of consonant and
vowel best known to a Welsh poet, it was beautifully said. The
children savoured it – it is the only word – and let each syllable have
its full weight, 'drop after drop.'*

THE RAIN

I hear leaves drinking Rain;
I hear rich leaves on top
Giving the poor beneath

Drop after drop;
'Tis a sweet noise to hear
These green leaves drinking near.

And when the Sun comes out,
After this Rain shall stop,
A wondrous Light will fill
Each dark, round drop;
I hope the Sun shines bright:
'Twill be a lovely sight.

W. H. Davies

AFTER THE STORM

There was a roaring in the wind all night;
The rain came heavily and fell in floods;
But now the sun is rising calm and bright;
The birds are singing in the distant woods;
Over his own sweet voice the Stock-dove broods;
The Jay makes answer as the Magpie chatters;
And all the air is filled with pleasant noise of waters.

All things that love the sun are out of doors;
The sky rejoices in the morning's birth;
The grass is bright with rain drops; – on the moors
The hare is running races in her mirth;
And with her feet she from the plashy earth
Raises a mist; that, glittering in the sun,
Runs with her all the way, wherever she doth run.

William Wordsworth

RAIN

I woke in the swimming dark
And heard, now sweet, now shrill,
The voice of the rain-water,
Cold and still,

Endlessly sing; now faint,
In the distance borne away;
Now in the air float near,
But nowhere stay;

Singing I know not what,
Echoing on and on;
Following me in sleep,
Till night was gone.

Walter de la Mare

PLUVIOSE

At the black wood's corner, not one green bud
On the oak, but the boughs weeping
In steady rain, bright drops.
Low clouds, through all
The wet day fall.
Gurgling ditch, by the copse;
Down the rushy furrow seeping,
Comes the water, running through hoof-poached mud.
Stream and pond cream-brown with the loam:
The outlet swirling with heaped foam.
Noisily through
Hatchets and culverts, leaping, goes
The stream that to the water meadows
Runs, and floods blue.

                                          Julian Bell

*If rain is depressing, snow surely is exhilarating – I hasten to
add*, when it begins to fall. *The first hour is quite enough. One can
soon have too much of a good thing, as you will see when you read
the account of Elizabeth Woodcock's adventure in 1799.*

*Cold weather has its devotees (although I am not among them),
and here for those who enjoy snow, ice, hoar frost – not to mention
chilblains, coughs, and colds – are a few gelid offerings.*

THE TRUE TALE OF ELIZABETH WOODCOCK

However extraordinary the following account may appear, our
readers may depend on the truth of it, as the principal circumstances were taken from the information of the poor sufferer.

On Sunday last, about half past one o'clock, as *Mr Muncey* of
Impington was coming to Cambridge, he observed a handkerchief upon a snowdrift, and on approaching the spot, heard the
sound of a human voice, upon which he called *a shepherd* who was

then in the field, and they found that the person under the snow was Elizabeth Woodcock, who had been missing since Saturday evening the 2nd inst. as mentioned in our last paper.

The shepherd, whose name is Stittle, on coming to the spot called out, 'Mrs Woodcock!' and was immediately answered, 'John Stittle! I know your voice: for God's sake help me out.' Muncey then ran for her husband, who came with assistance, and after considerable labour, extricated the poor woman from her miserable situation, and conveyed her in a cart to her husband's house at Impington, where she was immediately put to bed and proper care taken of her by the directions of *Mr Okes*, surgeon, of this place, who fortunately passed her as she was conveying home in the cart, and who, we hope, will favour the public with an account of all the peculiarities attending this interesting case.

On enquiring into the circumstances of her being lost, she said, that as she was returning from market, between 7 and 8 o'clock on Saturday evening, about half a mile on this side of Impington her horse started, and threw her off, together with her basket in which were some meat, candles and other articles which she had bought at Cambridge; that the horse ran from her and that she wandered with her basket a considerable distance from the road till she was exhausted, having lost one of her shoes in the snow, when she sat down under a bush in the expectation of the snow abating. Being very much fatigued, it is conjectured that she fell asleep, and the wind being high, the snow drifted over her to the height of several feet, and there she remained for eight nights, without any sustenance except what she received from eating the snow. She says that she heard the bells ring for church at Impington, Histon and Chesterton on Sunday 3rd, that she frequently heard people passing near her.

She had beat down the snow as far as her hands could reach, which formed a space for her more easily breathing, and she says it was so light as to enable her to read an Almanac which she had with her. Her basket with the meat etc., was not more than two yards from her, but her legs being buried in the snow, were so benumbed, that she was unable to get it, or even to extricate

166

herself till she perceived the snow waste on Saturday last, when she slipt off a branch from the bush under which she sheltered, and finding she could thrust it thro' the snow above her, she thought of tying her handkerchief to the top of the branch, by which means she was providentially discovered.

It is reasonable to suppose that she must have slept a considerable part of the time (tho' she appears to have kept a regular account of the days and nights), otherwise it seems impossible for her to have existed in so dreadful a situation for nearly eight days and nights.

Mrs Woodcock is the wife of a small farmer at Impington, four miles from Cambridge, in such circumstances as to render the contributions of the benevolent acceptable. She is about 45 years of age, and has five children, to one of whom, upwards of two years old, she gave suck at the time the accident happened. When first taken out of the snow, her voice and pulse were strong as in full health: her legs appeared like those of a drowned person, and a mortification has taken place in consequence of their being buried in the snow for such a length of time.

The Cambridge Chronicle, 15 February, 1799

ON A NIGHT OF SNOW

Cat, if you go outdoors you must walk in the snow,
You will come back with little white shoes on your feet,
Little white slippers of snow that have heels of sleet.
Stay by the fire, my Cat. Lie still, do not go.
See how the flames are leaping and hissing low,
I will bring you a saucer of milk like a marguerite,
So white and so smooth, so spherical and so sweet –
Stay with me, Cat. Out-doors the wild winds blow.

Out-doors the wild winds blow, Mistress, and dark is the
    night.
Strange voices cry in the trees, intoning strange lore,

167

And more than cats move, lit by our eyes' green light,
On silent feet where the meadow grasses hang hoar –
Mistress, there are portents abroad of magic and might,
And things that are yet to be done. Open the door!

Elizabeth J. Coatsworth

When icicles hang by the wall,
And Dick the shepherd blows his nail,
And Tom bears logs into the hall,
And milk comes frozen home in pail,
When blood is nipp'd, and ways be foul,
Then nightly sings the staring owl,
                    To-whit!
To-who! – a merry note,
While greasy Joan doth keel the pot.

When all aloud the wind doth blow,
And coughing drowns the parson's saw,
And birds sit brooding in the snow,
And Marian's nose looks red and raw,
When roasted crabs hiss in the bowl,
Then nightly sings the staring owl,
                    To-whit!
To-who! – a merry note,
While greasy Joan doth keel the pot.

William Shakespeare

THE VIRTUOSO

As he stands at the brim
Of the virgin rink
He holds within him
Like an endless thread
The track he is to spin.

On armoured feet
That prowl and push
His sharp blades
With flash and flourish
Etch the ice.

Sometimes he leaps,
And the line snaps
But is not lost,
For his metal heels
Pick up the clew.

– Now in the dead
Centre of the rink
Beneath the spots he burns
And turns on himself
Till he becomes

Transparent, but still
He turns, still faster,
Brighter, and spins
So fast, in the end,
Look! he's vanished!

James Kirkup

SNOW TOWARD EVENING

Suddenly the sky turned grey,
The day,
Which had been bitter and chill,
Grew soft and still.
Quietly
From some invisible blossoming tree
Millions of petals cool and white
Drifted and blew,
Lifted and flew,
Fell with the falling night.

Melville Cane

That time of year thou may'st in me behold
When yellow leaves, or none, or few, do hang
Upon those boughs which shake against the cold –
Bare ruin'd choirs where late the sweet birds sang.
In me thou see'st the twilight of such day
As after Sunset fadeth in the West
Which by and by black night doth take away,
Death's second self, that seals up all in rest.
In me thou see'st the glowing of such fire
That on the ashes of his youth doth lie,
As the death-bed whereon it must expire,
Consumed with that which it was nourish'd by.
   This thou perceiv'st, which makes thy love more
      strong
   To love that well which thou must leave ere long.

William Shakespeare

STOPPING BY WOODS ON A SNOWY EVENING

Whose woods these are I think I know.
His house is in the village though;
He will not see me stopping here
To watch his woods fill up with snow.

My little horse must think it queer
To stop without a farmhouse near
Between the woods and frozen lake
The darkest evening of the year.

He gives his harness bells a shake
To ask if there is some mistake.
The only other sound's the sweep
Of easy wind and downy flake.

The woods are lovely, dark and deep,
But I have promises to keep,
And miles to go before I sleep,
And miles to go before I sleep.

                                    Robert Frost

BRIGHT MORNING

Now it is more noble to sit like Jove than to fly like Mercury
– let us not therefore go hurrying about and collecting honey,
bee-like buzzing here and there impatiently from a knowledge
of what is to be aimed at; but let us open our leaves like a flower
and be passive and receptive – budding patiently under the eye
of Apollo and taking hints from every noble insect that favours
us with a visit – sap will be given us for meat and dew for drink.

I was led into these thoughts, my dear Reynolds, by the beauty
of the morning operating on a sense of Idleness – I have not
read any Books – the Morning said I was right – I had no idea
but of the morning, and the thrush said I was right – seeming
to say,

> O thou whose face hath felt the Winter wind,
> Whose eye has seen the snow-clouds hung in mist,
> And the black elm-tops 'mong the freezing stars,
> To thee the Spring will be a harvest-time.
> O thou, whose only book has been the light
> Of supreme darkness which thou feddest on
> Night after night when Phoebus was away,
> To thee the Spring shall be a triple morn.
> O fret not after knowledge – I have none,
> And yet my song comes native with the warmth.
> O fret not after knowledge – I have none,
> And yet the Evening listens. He who saddens
> At thought of idleness cannot be idle,
> And he's awake who thinks himself asleep.

Now I am sensible all this is a mere sophistication (however
it may neighbour to any truths), to excuse my own indolence –
so I will not deceive myself that Man should be equal with
Jove – but think himself very well off as a sort of scullion-
Mercury, or even a humble Bee. It is no matter whether I am
right or wrong, either one way or another, if there is sufficient
to lift a little time from your shoulders.

Your affectionate friend
John Keats

A letter to John Hamilton Reynolds, 19 February, 1818

REMEDIES AND RECIPES

Some of these old remedies make gruesome reading. An Anglo-Saxon unfortunate enough to suffer from eruptive rash, for instance, had the choice of applying squashed anglers' worms, warm calf's dung, or a swallow's nest mixed with vinegar to ease his pain. It is easy enough to dismiss this early medical advice as something belonging entirely to the Dark Ages, but within living memory equally revolting cures have been suggested for man's sufferings.

A friend of mine told me recently that her mother was at school with a girl who was 'in a decline' as they put it then. This must have been in the 1870s. The child was obliged to call at the headmistress's study every morning to drink a glassful of warm milk in which two live fat slugs disported themselves.

Another person who was present at the relation of this tale pointed out that the large Roman snails of Provence are still collected there, taken to the local pharmacy, put into a large jar with plenty of salt, and the resulting viscous liquid is taken for chest complaints.

Not far from the village where I live an old lady was heard to recommend most earnestly a fried mouse, to be served up whole, as an infallible cure for whooping cough.

Many of the less horrifying remedies may remind readers of their own household cures. I can remember having a stye rubbed with my mother's wedding ring, just as Alison Uttley describes, and enjoying too a delicious mixture of butter and sugar when in bed with a cold. But ours was moistened with lemon juice, I remember, and was served in an egg-cup with an apostle spoon standing upright in the comforting golden pile.

OLD REMEDIES

The yardman, he with coins on his watch-chain, stood
Joking the housewife where she tied to the rafter
A monstrous puffball found in the dust of the wood.

'You'll come when you cut yourself next.' He replied in
    laughter,
'Them old remedies won't do a morsel of good.'

This I heard;
This like many a chance-arriving word
About my brain with the iron refrain of a mill-wheel's
    round recurred.
Yet, being in the day's machine fresh-hacked,
This night I pray the dewy stars to act,
The stars, and moon, once of sweet influence known,
Has even the moon a dusty puffball grown?
Are those old remedies of sovran grace
Unable now to touch the case?

Edmund Blunden

DOROTHY OSBORNE'S MEDICINE

Saturday, 5 March, 1652/3

I drink your health every morning in a drench that would
Poyson a horse I beleeve, and 'tis the only way I have to perswade my self to take it, 'tis the infusion of steell, and makes
mee soe horridly sick that every day at ten a clock I am makeing
my will, and takeing leave of all my freind's, you will beleeve
you are not forgot then: They tell mee I must take this ugly
drink a fortnight, and then begin another as Bad, but unlesse
you say soe too I doe not thinke I shall, 'tis worse then dyeing,
by the halfe.

Saturday, 12 March, 1652/3

I am soe farre from thinking you ill natured for wisheing I
might not outlive you, that I should not have thought you at all
kinde, if you had done otherwise; Noe, in Earnest I was never
soe in love with my life, but that I could have parted with it

upon a much lesse occasion then your Death, and 'twill bee noe
complement to you, to say it would bee very uneasy to mee then,
since 'tis not very pleasant to mee now. Yet you will say I take
great paines to preserve it, as ill as I like it; but noe, i'le sweare
'tis not that I intende in what I doe, all that I ayme at, is but to
keep myself from groweing a Beast. They doe soe fright mee
with strange Story's of what the Spleen will bring mee to in
time, that I am kept in awe with them like a Childe. They tell
mee 'twill not leave mee common sence, that I shall hardly bee
fitt company for my owne dog's, and that it will ende, either in
a Stupidnesse that will make mee uncapable of any thing, or fill
my head with such whim's as will make mee, rediculous; to
prevent this, whoe would not take steel or any thing? though I
am partly of your opinion, that 'tis an ill kinde of Phisick. Yet
I am confident that I take it the safest way, for I doe not take
the powder, as many doe, but onely lay a peece of steel in white
wine over night, and drink the infusion next morning, which one
would think were nothing, and yet 'tis not to bee imagin'd how
sick it makes mee for an hower or two and, which is the missery,
all that time one must be useing some kinde of Exercise. Your
fellow servant has a blessed time on't, I make her play at
shutlecock with mee, and she is the veryest bungler at it that
ever you saw, then am I ready to beate her with the batledore,
and grow soe peevish as I grow sick, that i'le undertake she
wishes there were noe steel in Englande; but then to recom-
pence the morning I am in good humor all the day after, for Joy
that I am well againe. I am tolde 'twill doe mee goode, and am
content to beleeve; if it do's not, I am but where I was.

Letters of Dorothy Osborne to William Temple

MISS LANE'S WINE JELLY

Once, when one of Miss Lane's own friends fell ill, she herself
brought out from somewhere a cooking apron of fine white linen
and, with her own hands, made him a wine jelly. The history of

that jelly was far removed from that of those we now buy in bottles from the grocer. To begin upon, calf's feet were procured and simmered for the better part of a day to extract the nourishment.

Then the contents of the stewpan were strained and the stock had another long boiling in order to render it down to the desired strength and quantity. Then more straining and sweetening and lacing with port, sufficient to colour it a deep ruby, and clearing with eggshells, and straining and straining. Then it was poured into a flannel jellybag, the shape of a fool's cap, which had to hang from a hook in the larder ceiling all night to let its contents ooze through into the vessel placed beneath, without squeezing, and when, at last, all the complicated processes were completed, it was poured into a small mould and allowed yet one more night in which to set. No gelatine was used.

What Miss Lane called 'a taster' was reserved for herself in a teacup, and of this she gave Laura and Zillah a teaspoonful each that they might also taste. To Laura's untutored palate, it tasted no better than the red jujube sweets of which she was fond, but Zillah, out of her greater experience, declared that a jelly so strong and delicious would 'a'most raise the dead.'

Flora Thompson: *Candleford Green*

SALAMANDERING

Another cooking process Laura was never to see elsewhere and which perhaps may have been peculiar to smithy families was known as 'salamandering.' For this thin slices of bacon or ham were spread out on a large plate and taken to the smithy, where the plate was placed on the anvil. The smith then heated red-hot one end of a large, flat iron utensil known as the 'salamander' and held it above the plate until the rashers were crisp and curled. Shelled boiled, or poached, eggs were eaten with this dish.

Flora Thompson: *Candleford Green*

PARSON WOODFORDE HAS EARACHE

April 14, 1781

I got up very ill this morning about 8 o'clock, having had none or very little sleep all the night, owing to the pain in my Ear which was much worse in the night and broke, and a good deal of blood only came away. The pain continued still very bad all the morning tho' not quite so bad as before. It made me very uneasy abt. it. A throbbing pain in my Ear continued till I went to bed. I put a rosted onion into my Ear going to bed tonight.

179

TOOTHACHE

June 4, 1776

I breakfasted, dined, supped and slept again at Weston. My tooth pained me all night, got up a little after 5 this morning, & sent for one Reeves a man who draws teeth in this parish, and about 7 he came and drew my tooth, but shockingly bad indeed, he broke away a great piece of my gum and broke one of the fangs of the tooth, it gave me exquisite pain all the day after, and my Face was swelled prodigiously in the evening and much pain. Very bad and in much pain the whole day long. Gave the old man that drew it however 0.2.6. He is too old, I think, to draw teeth, can't see very well.

James Woodforde: *Diary of a Country Parson*

Note that 'one Reeves the Farrier' is still drawing teeth nine years later, despite the earlier comment that 'he is too old to draw teeth – can't see very well.'

Perhaps (to be hopeful!) this Reeves is a son of the former dentist.

TOOTHACHE AGAIN

October 24, 1785

The Tooth-Ach so very bad all night and the same this Morn' that I sent for John Reeves the Farrier who lives at the Hart and often draws Teeth for People, to draw one for me. He returned with my Man about 11 o'clock this Morning and he pulled it out for me the first Pull, but it was a monstrous Crash and more so, it being one of the Eye Teeth, it had but one Fang but that was very long. I gave Johnny Reeves for drawing it 0.2.6. A great pain in the Jaw Bone continued all Day and Night but nothing so bad as the Tooth Ach. To Mr Cary for things from Norwich &c. pd. 0.8.8.

James Woodforde: *Diary of a Country Parson*

CURE FOR AGUE

May 22, 1779

My boy Jack had another touch of the Ague about noon. I gave him a dram of gin at the beginning of the fit and pushed him headlong into one of my Ponds and ordered him to bed immediately and he was better after it and had nothing of the cold fit after, but was very hot.

James Woodforde: *Diary of a Country Parson*

PARSON WOODFORDE'S COW POLLY

Feb. 5, 1790

My poor Cow Polly not able to get up yet as she has a Disorder which I never heard of before or any of our Somersett Friends. It is called Tail-Shot, that is, a separation of some of the Joints of the Tail about a foot from the tip of the Tail, or rather a slipping of one Joint from another. It also makes all her Teeth quite loose in her head. The Cure is to open that part of the Tail so slipt lengthways and put in an Onion boiled and some salt, and bind it up with some coarse Tape.

James Woodforde: *Diary of a Country Parson*

PARSON WOODFORDE'S STYE

March 11, Friday, 1791

Mem. The Stiony on my right Eye-lid still swelled and inflamed very much. As it is commonly said that the Eye-lid being rubbed by the tail of a black Cat would do it much good if not entirely cure it, and having a black Cat, a little before dinner I made a trial of it, and very soon after dinner I found my Eye-lid much abated of the swelling and almost free from Pain. I cannot therefore but conclude it to be of the greatest service to a Stiony on the Eye-lid. Any other Cats Tail may have the above effect in all probability – but I did my Eye-lid with my own black Tom Cat's Tail.

March 15, Tuesday, 1791

My right Eye again, that is, its Eye-lid much inflamed again and rather painful. I put on a plaistor to it this morning, but in the Aft. took it off again, as I perceived no good from it.

James Woodforde: *Diary of a Country Parson*

TO CURE A STYE

To cure a stye, or a bloodshot eye, the eylid was rubbed very gently with pure gold. A wedding-ring was used for this, without of course removing it from the finger – which would have been unlucky. It had to be drawn three times across the afflicted eye. My mother often touched somebody's stye with her ring, and the most obstinate sore certainly disappeared in a few hours. Whether this was an act of faith or some strange charm, I do not know. It is an ancient cure, and people in country places still use it.

Alison Uttley: *Country Things*

BAD COLDS

There were delicious remedies for bad colds. We had linseed tea, a thick liquor made from linseed, flavoured with sticks of black liquorice. We loved to sip this smooth, sweet drink, which was not dissimilar from a cure we gave the cows for colds. No wonder the cattle supped it eagerly! We had thin gruel, sweetened with honey, and hot caudles and treacle possets. We had bowls of bread and boiling milk, with cream poured on the top, to cool it, and a sprinkle of nutmeg and brown sugar over it. In the night we drank blackcurrant tea.

There were other delectable things for bad colds – camphor on sugar which we loved, Doncaster butterscotch with its silver-paper wrapping, horehound goodies, and treacle toffee. One of the simplest and best remedies was a mixture of sugar and fresh butter, blended together and flavoured with a few drops of vinegar. It was piled on a little plate, a golden morsel, and we took a spoonful now and then, always wanting more.

Alison Uttley: *Country Things*

HOMELY CURES

Many of our cures came from the little medicinal herb patch at the end of the kitchen garden. Here, in a corner of warm ground sheltered by walls and hedges from the winds, bathed in sunshine, was a little half-wild secret garden where I often sat.

There was an old seat, a bench of mossy oak with ferns growing under it and in it, and in the dark massive wall behind. A sage bush grew on one side like a tree in miniature, and on the herb-garden side were bushes of rue, and wormwood, with tarragon, fennel, pennyroyal, and some unknown, forgotten herbs. The rest of the ground was green with mint. Overhead a nut tree spread a little shade in that hot corner. The bushes of rue and wormwood were strongly aromatic. The smell of the grey-green wormwood was repulsive to me because I knew the taste of that bitter herb, but it is really a clean and good smell. We made a wholesome medicine called wormwood tea from it. It was like strong tea, and we drank half a cupful with groans and grumbles.

Alison Uttley: *Country Things*

THE POWER OF PLANTS

O! mickle is the powerful grace that lies
In herbs, plants, stones, and their true qualities;
For nought so vile that on the earth doth live
But to the earth some special good doth give,
Nor aught so good but strain'd from that fair use
Revolts from true birth, stumbling on abuse:
Virtue itself turns vice, being misapplied,
And vice sometime's by action dignified.
Within the infant rind of this weak flower
Poison hath residence and medicine power:
For this, being smelt, with that part cheers each part;
Being tasted, slays all senses with the heart.
Two such opposed foes encamp them still
In man as well as herbs, grace and rude will;
And where the worser is predominant,
Full soon the canker death eats up that plant.

William Shakespeare: *Romeo and Juliet* (Friar Laurence)

ANGLO-SAXON MEDICINE

For eruptive rash:
Anglers' worms. Rub up thoroughly. Add vinegar and bind on and smear therewith.

Calf's dung warm, or that of an old ox, and apply.

Take a swallow's nest, and break all up together, and burn up with dung and all, and rub to dust and mix with vinegar, and smear therewith.

For the ears a noble drink: Take radish, the lower part, and helenium, broad bishopwort and hassock, rue and rose, savine, feverfew. Beat up all together; drench with a sester full of ale before thou take food.

Make a good drink for stitch in the side: Boil betony and pulegium in old wine. Add twenty-seven ground peppercorns. Give him after the night's fast a good cupful of it warm, and let him rest a good while on his sore side after the drink.

For foot trouble: Take betony. Boil in water, boil away a third part. Give then to drink. And pound the plant; lay it on. Wonderfully soon will the pain be lightened, so learned leeches say.

For heaviness of the belly: Give to eat radish with salt, and vinegar to sip; soon his mood will lighten.

If there be a pock in the eye: Take marrow soap and hind's milk; mix and beat together; let stand until it be clear. Then take the clear fluid; put into the eyes. With God's help the pock shall away. Take clote roots. Pound thoroughly and boil in beer. Give to drink when thou see that they are breaking out. With God's help no harm will come to him.

In case a man or beast swallow a worm: If it be of male kind sing this lay, which is written hereafter, into the right ear; if it be of a female kind sing into the left ear. 'Gonomil orgomil marbumil marbsai ramun tofeo tengo docuillo biran cuidaer caefmiil scuiht cuillo scuiht cuib duill marbsiramum.' Sing this charm nine times into the ear, and a single Paternoster.

J. H. G. Grattan and Charles Singer:
Anglo-Saxon Magic and Medicine

Quinces fascinate me. I like the queer ancient smell of them, their golden pear shape, and the wonderful earthy fruitiness of the jam they make. In late September or early October I begin my search for a few quinces, and every year the search becomes more difficult, as the trees become rarer. Sometimes a kind friend finds me some. Sometimes I send a message to the Women's Institute market stall, begging to be remembered if quinces are brought in. Usually I am lucky, and am able to set about making a few pounds of this delectable preserve. I know it will be the last of the year's jam making, for the leaves are already turning and falling as I stir my brew.

This is the recipe I use:

Peel, core and slice 8 or 10 quinces. Just cover with water to which the juice of a lemon has been added. Simmer until the fruit is soft. Add 2–3 lbs. of preserving sugar, boil rapidly, stirring frequently, until jam sets on a saucer.

This makes about 5 or 6 lbs. of ruby-red preserve to delight your eye and tongue.

Culpeper, it seems, is as enamoured of the quince as I am, and far more enterprising with its products.

Nicholas Culpeper, the famous herbalist, was born in 1616, the year in which Shakespeare died. He was interested in astrology as well as medicine, and set up as an apothecary in Spitalfields in 1640. During the Civil War he fought for the Parliamentarians and was wounded in the chest.

He was the father of seven children, and perforce lived humbly. During his short life (he died in 1654), he collected a vast number of herbal remedies, many of which are in use today.

Culpeper's Complete Herbal *is still in print*, and makes *fascinating reading.*

QUINCE TREE (*PYRUS CYDONIA*)

Descrip – This tree grows to the height of a good-sized apple-tree, crooked, with a rough bark, spreading branches far abroad. The leaves resemble those of the apple-tree, but thicker, broader, and fuller of veins, and whiter on the under-side, not dented about the edges. The flowers are large and white, somewhat dashed over with a blush. The fruit is yellow, being near ripe, and covered with a white frieze; thick set on the younger, growing less, as they get nearer ripe, bunches out oftentimes in some places: some being like an apple, some like a pear, of a strong heady scent, and not durable to keep; it is sour, harsh, and of an unpleasant taste to eat fresh; but being scalded, roasted, baked, or preserved, becomes more pleasant.
Place – It grows plentifully near ponds and water sides.
Time – It flowers not until the leaves come forth. The fruit is ripe in September or October.

Government and Virtues – Saturn owns this tree. The fruit has a strong, very pleasant smell, and acid taste. Its expressed juice, taken in small quantities, is a mild, astringent stomachic medicine, and is of efficacy, in sickness, vomiting, eructations, and purgings. A grateful cordial, and lightly restringent syrup, is made by digesting three pints of the clarified juice, with a dram of cinnamon, half a dram of ginger, the same of cloves, in warm ashes, for six hours, then adding a pint of red port, and dissolving nine pounds of sugar in liquor, and straining it. And a useful jelly is made by boiling the juice with a sufficient quantity of sugar, till it attains a due consistence. The seeds abound with a soft mucilaginous substance, which they readily impart to boiling water, making it like the white of an egg. This is excellent for sore mouths, and useful to soften and moisten the mouth and throat in fevers, and other diseases. The green fruit helps all sorts of fluxes in man or woman, and in choleric laxes. The crude juice is preservative against the force of poison. The oil is useful to bind outwardly hot fluxes; it strengthens the stomach and belly by anointing, and the sinews that are loosened by sharp humours falling on them, and restrains immoderate sweatings. The mucilage taken from the seeds, and boiled in water, is good to cool the heat, and heal the sore breasts of women. The same, with a little sugar is good to lenify the harshness and soreness of the throat, and the roughness of the tongue. The cotton or down boiled, and applied to plague sore, heals them up; and laid as a plaster, made up with wax, it brings hair to those who are bald, and keeps it from falling off, if it be ready to shed.

Culpeper's Complete Herbal

Whenever I pick parsley I remember a young mother whom I knew years ago. She had one small boy of three who had no interest in food at all. The child, rather naturally, was frail, and a source of intense anxiety to his poor mother.

One day she read an account of the miraculous properties of parsley. I forget how many calories and vitamins she told me there were to a parsley leaf, but the knowledge was enough to send us into the garden to pick a large bunch of it for her to take home. It was no use, she knew, attempting to offer any directly to the child. His lip would curl, his face would be turned away, with the same disgust he showed for all the tempting morsels his mother prepared.

But, just occasionally, he had been known to pick up a sliver of apple left on one side, or a crumb of biscuit, and eat it absent-mindedly. Surely, if parsley were put at strategic points in the house, there was a faint chance that some small shred of this wonderful herb might find its way into the right quarter?

The hopeful mother put sprigs in little jugs and egg-cups in various accessible spots. More sprigs were scattered among his toys, on the coverlet of his cot, and even up the stairs. For the rest of the day the mother watched her son intently, hoping to see him rosy and bright-eyed, munching raw parsley and begging for more.

You can guess the end of the story. When the child was in bed (after throwing the parsley leaves through the bars of his cot with considerable distaste), his mother swept up the wilting sprigs and dropped them, with her hopes, in the dustbin.

PARSLEY (COMMON)
(PETROSELINUM SATIVUM)

Descrip – The roots are long, thick, and white, having a wrinkled bark; from which spring many shining, green, winged leaves, growing on long footstalks; which are divided into three sections, and each of those subdivided into three more, which are triangular, and cut in at the ends. The stalks grow to be two feet high, much branched and divided: they are smooth and striated, beset with smaller and finer leaves; and on their tops have small umbels of little, five-leaved, white flowers, which are succeeded by small, round, striated, brown seed.

Place – It is sown in gardens.

Time – It flowers in summer. The roots, leaves, and seeds are used.

Government and Virtues – It is under the dominion of Mercury; is very comforting to the stomach: helps to provoke urine and the courses, to break wind, both in the stomach and bowels, and opens the body, but the root much more. It opens obstructions both of liver and spleen, it is good against falling-sickness, and to provoke urine, especially if the roots be boiled and eaten like parsnips. The seed provokes urine, and women's courses, expels wind, breaks the stone, and eases the pains thereof; it is effectual in the lethargy, and good against coughs. The distilled water is a familiar medicine with nurses to give children when troubled with wind in the stomach or belly, and it is also of service to upgrown persons. The leaves laid to the eyes inflamed with heat, or swollen, helps them, if used with bread or meal, or fried with butter, and applied to women's breasts that are hard through the curding of their milk, it abates the hardness, and takes away black and blue marks coming of bruises or falls. The juice dropped into the ears with a little wine, eases the pains. It helps the jaundice, falling-sickness, the dropsy, and stone in the kidneys in this manner: Take of Parsley seed, fennel, annise, and carraways of each one ounce, of the roots of Parsley, burnet, saxifrage, and carraways, of each an ounce and a half; let the seeds be bruised, and the roots washed and cut small, let them lie all night and steep in a bottle of white wine; and in the morning be boiled in a close earthen vessel to a third of the quantity; of which being strained and cleared, take four ounces night and morning fasting. This opens obstructions of the liver and spleen, and expels the dropsy and jaundice by urine.

Culpeper's Complete Herbal

GARDEN MINT or GARDEN SPEAR (*MENTHA VIRIDIS*)

Descrip – This Mint has many square stalks, which, in good ground, will grow to two or three feet high, having two long sharp-pointed leaves, set opposite at a joint, without footstalks, high-veined underneath, thinly serrated at the edges. The flowers grow in long spikes on the tops of the stalks, set on verticillatim, being small and purplish, having a galea and labella so small, that they are hardly perceivable, a white, long pontel standing out of their mouths. The root creeps and spreads much in the earth, being long and slender. The leaves, stalks, and flowers, have a pleasant and agreeable smell.

Place – It is planted in gardens.

Time – It flowers in July.

Government and Virtues – It is an herb of Venus, and has a binding, drying quality; the juice taken in vinegar, stays bleeding, stirs up venery, or bodily lust; two or three branches taken in the juice of four pomegranates, stays the hiccough, vomiting, and allays the choler. It dissolves imposthumes being laid to with barley-meal. It is good to repress the milk in women's breasts. Applied with salt, it helps the bites of mad dogs: with mead or honeyed water, it eases the pains of the ears, and takes away the roughness of the tongue, being rubbed thereupon. It suffers not milk to curdle in the stomach, if the leaves be steeped or boiled in it before being drunk; it is very profitable to the stomach. Often using it will stay women's courses and the whites. Applied to the forehead and temples, it eases the pains in the head, and is good to wash the heads of young children with, against all manner of breakings out, sores or scabs, and heals the chops in the fundament. It is also profitable against the poison of venomous creatures. The distilled water of mint is available for all the purposes aforesaid, yet more weakly. But if a spirit thereof be chemically drawn, it is more powerful than the herb. It helps a cold liver, strengthens the belly, causes digestion, stays vomiting and the hiccough; it is good against the gnawing of the heart, provokes appetite, takes away obstructions of the liver, but too much must not be taken, because it makes the blood thin, and turns it into choler, therefore choleric persons must abstain from it. The dried powder taken after meat, helps digestion, and those that are splenetic. Taken in wine, it helps women in their sore travail in child-bearing. It is good against the gravel and stone in the kidneys, and the strangury. Being smelled unto, it is comforting to the head. The decoction gargled in the mouth, cures the mouth and gums that are sore, and amends an ill-favoured breath. Mint is an herb that is useful in all disorders of the stomach, as weakness, squeamishness, loss of appetite, pain, and vomiting; it is likewise very good to stop gonorrhoea, the fluor albus, and the immoderate flow of the menses; a cataplasm of the green leaves applied to the stomach, stays vomiting, and to women's breasts, prevents the hardness and curding of the milk. A decoction is good to wash the hands of children when broken out with scabs and blotches.

Official preparations of Mint are, a simple water and spirit, a compound spirit, and a distilled oil.

Culpeper's Complete Herbal

BURDOCK *(ARCTIUM LAPPA)*

It is also called Personata, and Happy-Major, Great Burdoak, and Clot-bur: it is so well known even by the little boys, who pull off the burs to throw at one another, that I shall spare to write any description of it.

Place – They grow plentifully by ditches and watersides, and by the high-ways almost everywhere through this land.

Government and Virtues – Venus challengeth this herb for her own: and by its leaf or seed you may draw the womb which way you please, either upward by applying it to the crown of the head in case it falls out; or downwards in fits of the mother, by applying it to the soles of the feet: or if you would stay it in its place, apply it to the navel, and that is one good way to stay the child in it. See more of it in my Guide for Women.

The Burdock leaves are cooling, moderately drying, and discussing withal, whereby it is good for old ulcers and sores. A dram of the roots taken with pine kernels, helpeth them that spit foul, mattery, and bloody phlegm. The leaves applied to the places troubled with the shrinking in of the sinews or arteries, give much ease: the juice of the leaves, or rather the roots themselves, given to drink with old wine, doth wonderfully help the biting of any serpents; the root beaten with a little salt, and laid on the place, suddenly easeth the pain thereof, and helpeth those that are bit by a mad dog: the juice of the leaves being drunk with honey, provoketh urine and remedieth the pain of the bladder: the seed being drunk in wine forty days together, doth wonderfully help the sciatica: the leaves bruised with the white of an egg and applied to any place burnt with fire, taketh out the fire, gives sudden ease and heals it up afterwards; the decoction of them fomented on any fretting sore or canker, stayeth the corroding quality, which must be afterwards anointed with an ointment made of the same liquor, hog's grease, nitre, and vinegar boiled together. The root may be preserved with sugar, and taken fasting or at other times for the same purposes, and for consumptions, the stone, and the lax. The seed is much commended to break the stone, and cause it to be expelled by urine, and is often used with other seeds and things for that purpose.

Culpeper's Complete Herbal

HOW TO MAKE EEL A MOST EXCELLENT
DISH OF MEAT...

First, wash him in water and salt; then pull off his skin: having done that, take out his guts as clean as you can, but wash him not: then give him three or four scotches with a knife; and then put into his belly and those scotches, sweet herbs, an anchovy, and a little nutmeg grated or cut very small; and your herbs and anchovies must also be cut very small; and mixed with good butter and salt: having done this, then pull his skin over him, all but his head, which you are to cut off, to the end you may tie his skin about that part where his head grew; and it must be so tied as to keep all his moisture within his skin. And having done this, tie him with tape or packthread to a spit, and roast him leisurely; and baste him with water and salt till his skin breaks, and then with butter; and having roasted him enough, let what was put into his belly, and what he drips, be his sauce.

When I go to dress an eel thus, I wish he were as long and as big as that which was caught in Peterborough River, in the year 1667; which was a yard and three-quarters long. If you will not believe me, then go and see at one of the coffee-houses in King Street in Westminster.

Izaac Walton: *The Compleat Angler*

An earlier herbalist was John Gerard (1545–1612). As you will see, he not only gave careful descriptions of plants and their qualities of healing, but also poured scorn on a number of contemporary super-stitions or 'vaine and trifling toies' as he calls them. His famous Herball was first published in 1597.

I have included his account of the African Marigold because it is a flower much in vogue just now as a showy annual. Evidently its smell has not improved since Gerard's time.

It is interesting to see that in Elizabeth I's reign Lilies of the Valley were to be found on 'Hampstead Heath, foure miles from London.'

I could not resist including the English Jacinth (Bluebell) 'full of slimic glewish juice,' as every bluebell picker knows to his cost.

OF CLOWNES WOUND-WORT, OR ALL-HEALE

The Description

Clownes All-heale, or the Husbandmans Wound-wort, hath long slender square stalkes of the height of two cubits: at the top of the stalkes grow the floures spike fashion, of a purple colour mixed with some few spots of white, in forme like to little hoods.

The Place

It groweth in moist medowes by the sides of ditches, and likewise in fertile fields that are somewhat moist, almost every where; especially in Kent about South-fleet, neer to Gravesend, and likewise in the medowes by Lambeth neere London.

The Time

It floureth in August, and bringeth his seed to perfection in the end of September.

The Names

That which hath been said in the description shall suffice touching the names, as well in Latine as English.

The Vertues

The leaves hereof stamped with *Axungia* or hogs grease, and applied unto greene wounds in manner of a pultesse, heale them in short time, and in such absolute manner, that it is hard for any that have not had the experience thereof to beleeve: for being in Kent about a Patient, it chanced that a poore man in mowing of Peason did cut his leg with a sithe, wherein hee made a wound to the bones, and withall very large and wide, and also with great effusion of bloud; the poore man crept unto this herbe, which he bruised with his hands, and tied a great quantitie of it unto the wound with a piece of his shirt, which presently stanched the bleeding, and ceased the paine, insomuch that the poore man presently went to his daies worke againe, and so did from day to day, without resting one day untill he was perfectly whole; which was accomplished in a few daies, by this herbe stamped with a little hogs grease, and so laid upon it in manner of a pultesse, which did as it were glew or sodder the lips of the wound together, and heale it according to the first intention, as wee terme it, that is, without drawing or bringing the wound to suppuration or matter; which was fully performed in seven daies, that would have required forty daies with balsam it selfe. I saw the wound and offered to heale the same for charity; which he refused, saying that I could not heale it so well as himselfe: a clownish answer I confesse, without any thankes for my good will: whereupon I have named it Clownes Wound-wort, as aforesaid. Since which time my selfe have cured many grievous wounds, and some mortall, with the same herbe; one for example done upon a Gentleman of Grayes Inne in Holborne, Mr *Edmund Cartwright*, who was thrust into the lungs, the wound entring in at the lower part of the *Thorax*, or the brest-blade, even through that cartilaginous substance called *Mucronata Cartilago*, insomuch that from day to day the frothing and puffing of the lungs did spew forth of the wound such excrements as it was possessed of, besides the Gentleman was most dangerously vexed with a double quotidian fever; whom by Gods permission I perfectly cured in very short time, and with this Clownes experiments, and some of my foreknowne helpes, which were as followeth.

First I framed a slight unguent hereof thus: I tooke foure handfulls of the herbe stamped, and put them into a pan, whereunto I added foure ounces of Barrowes grease, halfe a pinte of oyle Olive, wax three ounces, which I boyled unto the consumption of the juyce (which is knowne when the stuffe doth not bubble at all) then did I straine it, putting it to the fire againe, adding thereto two ounces of Turpentine, the which I suffered to boile a little, reserving the same for my use.

The which I warmed in a sawcer, dipping therein small soft tents, which I put into the wound, defending the parts adjoyning with a plaister of *Calcitheos*, relented with oyle of roses: which manner of dressing and preserving I used even untill the wound was perfectly whole: notwithstanding once in a day I gave him two spoonfulls of this decoction following.

I tooke a quart of good Claret wine, wherein I boyled an handfull of the leaves of *Solidago Saracenica*, or Saracens consound, and foure ounces of honey, whereof I gave him in the morning two Spoonfulls to drinke in a small draught of wine tempered with a little sugar.

In like manner I cured a Shoo-makers servant in Holborne, who intended to destroy himselfe for causes knowne unto many now living: but I deemed it better to cover the fault, than to put

the same in print, which might move such a gracelesse fellow
to attempt the like: his attempt was thus; First, he gave himselfe a most mortall wound in the throat, in such sort, that when
I gave him drinke it came forth at the wound, which likewise
did blow out the candle: another deepe and grievous wound in
the brest with the said dagger, and also two others in *Abdomine*:
the which mortall wounds, by Gods permission, and the vertues
of this herbe, I perfectly cured within twenty daies: for the
which the name of God be praised.

Gerard's Herball

OF TEASELS

The Description

Garden Teasell is also of the number of the Thistles; it
bringeth forth a stalke that is straight, very long, jointed, and
ful of prickles: the leaves grow forth of the joynts by couples,
not onely opposite or set one right against another, but also
compassing the stalke about, and fastened together; and so
fastened, that they hold dew and raine water in manner of a
little bason: these be long, of a light greene colour, and like to
those of Lettice, but full of prickles in the edges, and have on the
outside all alongst the ridge stiffer prickles: on the tops of the
stalkes stand heads with sharpe prickles like those of the Hedgehog, and crooking backward at the point like hookes: out of
which heads grow little floures: The seed is like Fennell-seed,
and in taste bitter: the heads wax white when they grow old,
and there are found in the midst of them when they are cut,
certaine little magots: the root is white, and of a meane length.

The Place

The first called the tame Teasell is sowne in this country in
gardens, to serve the use of Fullers and Clothworkers.

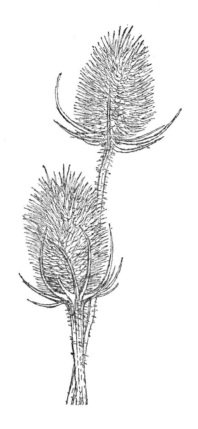

The Time

These floure for the most part in June and July.

The Names

Teasell is called in Latine, *Dipsacus*, and *Laver Lavacrum*, of the forme of the leaves made up in fashion of a bason, which is never without water: in English, Teasell, Carde Teasell, and Venus bason.

The Vertues

There is small use of Teasell in medicines: the heads (as we have said) are used to dresse woollen cloth with.

It is needlesse here to alledge those things that are added touching the little wormes or magots found in the heads of the

198

Teasell, and which are to be hanged about the necke, or to mention the like thing that *Pliny* reporteth of Galedragon: for they
are nothing else but most vaine and trifling toies, as my selfe
have proved a little before the impression hereof, having a most
grievous ague, and of long continuance: notwithstanding
Physicke charmes, these worms hanged about my neck, spiders
put into a walnut shell, and divers such foolish toies that I was
constrained to take by fantasticke peoples procurement; notwithstanding, I say, my helpe came from God himselfe, for
these medicines and all other such things did me no good at all.

Gerard's Herball

OF AFRICAN MARIGOLD

The Description

The common Africane, or as they vulgarly terme it French
Marigold, hath small weake and tender branches trailing upon
the ground, reeling and leaning this way and that way, beset with
leaves consisting of many particular leaves, indented about the
edges, which being held up against the sunne, or to the light,
are seene to be full of holes like a sieve, even as those of Saint
Johns woort: the floures stand at the top of the springy branches
forth of long cups or husks, consisting of eight or ten small
leaves, yellow underneath, on the upper side of a deeper yellow
tending to the colour of a darke crimson velvet, as also soft in
handling: but to describe the colour in words, it is not possible,
but this way; lay upon paper with a pensill a yellow colour called
Masticot, which being dry, lay the same over with a little
saffron steeped in water or wine, which setteth forth most lively
the colour. The whole plant is of a most ranke and unwholesome
smell, and perisheth at the first frost.

The Nature and Vertues

The unpleasant smel, especially of that common sort with
single floures doth shew that it is of a poisonsome and cooling

qualitie; and also the same is manifested by divers experiments:
for I remember, saith *Dodonaeus*, that I did see a boy whose
lippes and mouth when hee began to chew the floures did swell
extreamely; as it hath often happened unto them, that playing or
piping with quils or kexes of Hemlockes, do hold them a while
betweene their lippes: likewise he saith, we gave to a cat the
floures with their cups, tempered with fresh cheese, shee forthwith mightily swelled, and a little while after died: also mice
that have eaten of the seed thereof have been found dead. All
which things doe declare that this herbe is of a venomous and
poysonsome facultie; and that they are not to be hearkened
unto, that suppose this herb to be a harmlesse plant: so to conclude, these plants are most venomous and full of poison, and
therefore not to be touched or smelled unto, much lesse used
in meat or medicine.

Gerard's Herball

OF LILLY IN THE VALLEY, OR MAY LILLY

The Description

The Convall Lilly, or Lilly of the Vally, hath many leaves
like the smallest leaves of Water Plantaine; among which riseth
up a naked stalke halfe a foot high, garnished with many white
floures like little bels, with blunt and turned edges, of a strong
savour, yet pleasant enough; which being past, there come small
red berries, much like the berries of *Asparagus*, wherein the seed
is contained. The root is small and slender, creeping far abroad
in the ground.

The second kinde of May Lillies is like the former in every
respect; and herein varieth or diffreth, in that this kinde hath
reddish floures, and is thought to have the sweeter smell.

The Place

The first groweth on Hampsted heath, foure miles from
London, in great abundance: neere to Lee in Essex, and upon

Bushie heath, thirteene miles from London, and many other places.

The other kinde with the red floure is a stranger in England: howbeit I have the same growing in my garden.

The Time

They floure in May, and their fruit is ripe in September.

The Names

The Latines have named it *Lilium Convallium*: in French, *Muguet*: yet there is likewise another herbe which they call *Muguet*, commonly named in English, Woodroof. It is called in English, Lilly of the Valley, or the Convall Lillie, and May Lillies, and in some places Liriconfancie.

The Vertues

The floures of the Valley Lillie distilled with wine, and drunke the quantitie of a spoonefull, restore speech unto those that have the dumb palsie and that are falne into the Apoplexie, and are good against the gout, and comfort the heart.

The water aforesaid doth strengthen the memory that is weakened and diminished; it helpeth also the inflammations of the eies, being dropped thereinto.

The floures of May Lillies put into a glasse, and set in a hill of ants, close stopped for the space of a moneth, and then taken out, therein you shall finde a liquor that appeaseth the paine and griefe of the gout, being outwardly applied; which is commended to be most excellent.

Gerard's Herball

OF DAFFODILS

The Description

The first of the Daffodils is that with the purple crowne or circle, having small narrow leaves, thicke, fat, and full of slimie juice; among the which riseth up a naked stalke smooth and hollow, of a foot high, bearing at the top a faire milke white floure growing forth of a hood or thin filme such as the flours of onions are wrapped in: in the midst of which floure is a round circle or small coronet of a yellowish colour, purfled or bordered about the edge of the said ring or circle with a pleasant purple colour; which being past, there followeth a thicke knob or button, wherein is contained blacke round seed. The root is white, bulbous or Onion-fashion.

The second kinde of Daffodil is that sort of *Narcissus* or Primrose peerelesse that is most common in our country gardens, generally knowne everie where. It hath long fat and thick leaves, full of a slimie juice; among which riseth up a bare thicke stalke, hollow within and full of juice. The floure groweth at the top, of a yellowish white colour, with a yellow crowne or circle in the middle, and floureth in the moneth of Aprill, and sometimes sooner. The root is bulbous fashion.

Gerard's Herball

OF THE ENGLISH JACINTH, OR HARE-BELLS

The Description

The blew Hare-bells or English Jacinth is very common throughout all England. It hath long narrow leaves leaning towards the ground, among the which spring up naked or bare stalks loden with many hollow blew floures, of a strong sweet smell somewhat stuffing the head: after which come the cods or round knobs, containing a great quantitie of small blacke shining seed. The root is bulbous, full of a slimie glewish juice, which will serve to set feathers upon arrowes instead of glew, or to paste bookes with: hereof is made the best starch next unto that of Wake-robin roots.

Gerard's Herball

PARSON WOODFORDE'S ANTIDOTE

January 28, 1780
We had for dinner a Calf's Head, boiled Fowl and Tongue, a Saddle of Mutton Rosted on the Side Table, and a fine Swan rosted with Currant Jelly Sauce for the first Course. The second Course a couple of Wild Fowl called Dun Fowls, Larks, Blamange, Tarts, etc. and a good Desert of Fruit after amongst which was a Damson Cheese. I never eat a bit of a Swan before, and I think it good eating with sweet sauce.

(*A few days later the diarist says:* 'Sister Clarke, Nancy, Sam and myself, all took it in our heads to take a good dose of Rhubarb going to bed.')

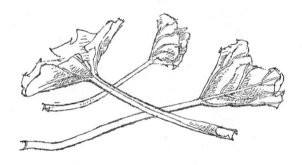

COUNTRY OCCASIONS
AND JUNKETINGS

DIEU · ET · MON · DROIT

CAMBRIDGE
CORONATION
FESTIVAL.

Rustic Sports,

In Celebration of the CORONATION of her Most Gracious
Majesty QUEEN VICTORIA.
On THURSDAY the 28th day of JUNE, 1838.

The Committee appointed for conducting the RUSTIC SPORTS on the approaching
Festival announce to the Public, that the following Amusements will commence
precisely at Four o'clock in the afternoon,

ON MIDSUMMER GREEN.

NEWMARKET BAULK
OR HOW TO RISE IN LIFE!

Well-shaped Scaffold Poles, stout, no middling-rate cut of the proper-looking—will be offered for, by prohibit and unexploit-cated Gamuts, for Breeches, Leaps of Mutton, &c. &c. If any competitor obtains an elevation two yards higher than the top of the pole—all is no go!

Jumping in Sacks.

A distance of 20 yards for Six Men. Each man to jump in a three-feet Sack (to be procured by himself for the occasion.)
The winner to receive a NEW PAIR of Boots.—Second best, a NEW Hat, warranted to Do.—The Third, a Pair of Shoes.

BISCUIT BOLTING.

Twelve Boys to eat a Pennyworth of Biscuits each. The first shall have a Victoria Waistcoat. Second a New White Beaver Tile. Third, a regular out-and-out Wide-awake.

A JINGLING MATCH,
Or, Blind Buff and the Bellman.

This Match will take place in a 25 yard ring, between 12 young Men, (not less than 16 years of age) for a Best pair of Cord Trousers. The time allowed for this Match is 20 Minutes; and the Bellman will not be allowed to allow this Bell longer than 20 Seconds at any time.

WHEELBARROW RACE,

for Ten Men, Blindfolded. The winner in this Match to receive a pair of High Shoes. Second best a pair of Low Shoes. Third best, a Melton Mowbray Cravat, or Coronation Stock!

Bobbing for Oranges in Wash Troughs

by Twelve Youngsters with hands tied behind them, to be approved of by the Committee at the time. No one need apply whose mouth is more than twelve inches wide—or who can drink a bucket of water at one draught!

ROYAL PIG RACES.

for 10 Men. The tail to be soaped. The First Man who fairly catches it by the tail, and fairly suspends it over his shoulder, to receive the Pig as a Prize.

An Elegant Pie-bald Short-legged Well-fed Curley-tailed PIG,
To be run for and caught in some manner or feel Pig, for the more prime.—Also, 3 other Royal Pig Races—on some terms

GRINNING MATCH.
OR, WHICH IS THE UGLIEST PRIZE!

This Match will be contested by Men of all ages, and all complexions—of the opinion of physiognomy—and every degree of ugliness and beauty—whether short or tall, little or big, born or fat, young or old, green or grey—and must be patronised according to the social excellence of those occasions, exhibiting, in Odonatidae excellence and deaf colour, the various Contortions of the "Human Face Divine," by peeping through a Pigtailous Cravat:—or, as the vulgar would profanely proclaim it, the Horse's Collar!—The party who shall be declared the winner will be rewarded with a brave new pair of Velveteen Trousers, and a New Wipe. The other competitors will be rewarded with a gallon of Sam Moore's Popular Vel-vet, Head-dainty, Delandfeet, Stomp-boiled, Bare-pan, Groos-a-strong, Lift-er-up, Knock-em-down, Nice Pye-Eh-ot, Strandy- Sidesumer-Green Stings! and a New Hat ect!

A RAM RACE.

To be Run for—A Elegant RAM, of science and speed remarkable—Positively described from the Close Derby Shoe

ROOTING EXTRAORDINARY,

By Boys to a Tub of Meal, for Sixpences,
PENNY LOAVES AND TREACLE.
by Six Boys, with their hands tied behind them, for a New Hat.

RACES

Twelve Men, (not less than 14 stone weight) to run 100 yards. All sixteen-stones eligible—top (send) boys! First, New Boots. Second, Pair Cord Trousers. Third, Pair of Velveteens Inexpressibles.

YOUNG LAD'S MATCH.

Six Lads, whose ages will not exceed 13 next grass, to run 100 yards. The winner to receive a pound of the best Gunpowder Tea & Pair Coronation Braces. Second Best, A new Bell!—Third best, A Wharfedale waistcoat. Twelve Boys, whose ages (if grass,) do not 100 yards, (Three boats.) Winner a New Hat. 2d pair Trou-sers. 3d pair shoes.

DIPPING FOR EELS,

for Six Boys. First Prize a New Hat. Second Prize of High town.

ROLLING MATCH.

Winner first, New Skin, for a New Shirt. Second Best, a Coronation Neckcloth. Rolling in Reverse No Prize!

A WHISTLING MATCH,

By Six and over, for a new Copper Tea Kettle. The Second best to have a Tea Kettle and Tobacco Box—GOD SAVE THE QUEEN.

DONKEY RACE.

For a handsome New Bridle and a Splendid Whip.

SECOND RACE.

The several Donkeys entered for this Prize will not be ridden by the Owners, but will be contended for after the manner of that adopted by the ancients—each Donkey mount for exchanging an opposite party and being the Rider of the actual Donkey at the last race, and the first Donkey to be the winner of the prize. The winner to receive a New Birdtile. WITH A VARIETY OF OTHER SPORTS.

The commencement of each Sport will be announced by the ringing of a bell.
No carriages, horses, or donkeys, will be allowed on the ground, except such by the Stewards, and no booth or Booths erected, but such as are licensed, and on the conditions, let the Stewards, who have attended all the arrangements of the Committee, and no manufactures, for the amusement of the public, in the Sundry Stewards then appointed of the Committee of Sports, will be thankfully received.

JEREMIAH WHIPPEM.

A Grand Display of FIREWORKS
Will take Place on Parker's Piece, at 10 o'clock.

You will find a good mixed bag here, ranging from a grinning match to a Norfolk hanging, but on the whole they show the lively boisterous side of rural junketing. Because most of our country frolics take place in the open air there is a zest and freshness about them which is lacking in the indoor entertainments of town-dwellers.

For sheer exuberance of spirit I think this poster announcing the Coronation Festivities in Cambridge, in June 1838, takes a lot of beating.

CAMBRIDGE CORONATION FESTIVAL

On Thursday the 28th of June, 1838

The Committee appointed for conducting the RUSTIC SPORTS on the approaching Festival announce to the Public, that the following Amusements will commence precisely at Four o'clock in the afternoon,

ON MIDSUMMER GREEN

THE NEWMARKET BAULK
or How to Rise in Life

Well soaped scaffold poles, stuck up indifferently out of the perpendicular . . . will be climbed for by youthful and unsophisticated Cantabs, for BREECHES, LEGS OF MUTTON, etc. If any competitor obtains an elevation two yards higher than the top of the pole . . . it is no go!

BISCUIT BOLTING

Twelve boys to eat a pennyworth of biscuits each. The first shall have a VICTORIA WAISTCOAT. Second a new WHITE BEAVER TILE. Third, a regular out-and-out WIDE-AWAKE.

JUMPING IN SACKS

A distance of 50 yards by Six men. Each man to jump in a 4-bushel sack (to be provided by himself for the occasion). The winner to receive a NEW PAIR OF BOOTS. Second best A NEW HAT, warranted to fit. The third A PAIR OF SHOES.

A JINGLING MATCH
or BLIND BUFF AND THE BELLMAN

This match will take place in a 24-ft. roped ring, between 12 young men (not less than 18 years of age) for a NEW PAIR OF CORD TROWSERS. The time allowed for this match is 16 minutes, and the Bellman will not be allowed to silence his bell longer than 30 seconds at one time.

WHEELBARROW RACE

By ten men blindfolded. The winner in this Match to receive a pair of HIGH SHOES, Second best a PAIR OF LOW SHOES, Third best a MELTON MOWBRAY CRAVAT, or CORONATION STOCK.

BOBBING FOR ORANGES IN WASH TROUGHS

By twelve youngsters with hands tied behind them. No one need apply whose mouth is more than twelve inches wide . . . or who can drink a bucket of water at one draught!

ROYAL PIG RACES

By ten men. The tail to be soaped. The first man who twice catches it by the tail and fairly suspends it over his shoulder, to receive the pig as a prize.

AN ELEGANT PIEBALD SHORT-LEGGED WELL-FED CURLEY-TAILED PIG

To be run for and caught in the same manner as the first pig, for the same prize. Also two other Royal Pig Races, on same terms.

GRINNING MATCH
or WHICH IS THE UGLIEST PHIZ!!

This match will be contested by men of all ages, and all complexions, all descriptions of physiognomy and every degree of ugliness and beauty, whether short or tall, little or big, lean or fat, young or old, grey or green, and must be performed according to the usual custom on these occasions, exhibiting, in Grimaldian excellence and BOLD RELIEF the various Contortions of the Human Face Divine, by peeping through a Pegasus Cravat . . . or, as the vulgar would profanely designate it . . . a Horse's Collar! The party who shall be declared the winner will be rewarded with a bran new pair of VELVETEEN TROUSERS, and a NEW WIPE. The other competitors will be rewarded with a gallon of Sam Moore's regular right-sort, Headstrong, Out-and-out, Strong-bodied, Ram-jam, Come-it-strong, Lift-me-up, Knock-me-down, How d'ye like it, Genuine Midsummer Green Stingo, and a new HAT each.

A RAM RACE

To be run for . . . A GIGANTIC RAM of stature and speed remarkable . . . positively descended from the Great Derby Ram.

ROOTING EXTRAORDINARY

By boys in a tub of meal for SIXPENCES.

PENNY LOAVES AND TREACLE

By six boys with hands tied behind them for a NEW HAT.

RACES

All complexions eligible . . . no bandy legs. Twelve men (not less than 14 stoneweight) to run 100 yards. The winner to receive a NEW PAIR OF BOOTS. Second PAIR OF CORD TROUSERS. Third pair of VELVETEEN INEXPRESSIBLES.

YOUNG LADS' MATCH

Six lads whose ages will not exceed 15 next grass, to run 100 yards. The winner to receive a pound of the best Souchonga-catamaranchoochoo origindumfefafumrumpecoannuscoronation-mirablis-flavoured GUNPOWDER TEA and PAIR OF SHOES. Second best A NEW HAT. Third best a PAIR OF SHOES.

DIPPING FOR EELS

By six boys. First Prize A NEW HAT. Second, A PAIR OF HIGH LOWS.

ROLLING MATCH

By not less than 4 men, for a NEW HAT. Second, A CORONATION NECKCLOTH. Rolling in river no prize!

A WHISTLING MATCH

By six old men for a new COPPER TEA KETTLE. The second best to have A TIN KETTLE AND TOBACCO. TUNE 'God Save The Queen.'

DONKEY RACE

For a handsome new BRIDLE AND SPLENDID WHIP.

A VARIETY OF OTHER SPORTS

The commencement of each sport will be announced by the ringing of a bell. No carriages, horses or donkeys will be suffered on the ground, except rode by Stewards, and no stalls or booths erected, but under the direction of the Committee. Contributions for the Sports to Mr Bridge's Auction Mart will be thankfully received.

STEWARDS . . . HEZEKIAH MUGGINS AND JEM CROW . . . Clerk of the Sports . . . JEREMIAH WHIPWELL.

A GRAND DISPLAY OF FIREWORKS WILL TAKE PLACE
ON PARKER'S PIECE
at 10 o'clock

COUNTRY FROLIC

December 3, 1776

My Frolic for my People to pay Tithe to me was this day. I gave them a good dinner, surloin of Beef rosted, a Leg of Mutton boiled and plumb Puddings in plenty. Recd. today only for

Tithe and Glebe of them . . . 236.2.0. Mr Browne called on me this morning and he and myself agreed and he paid me for Tithe only 55.0.0 included in the above, he could not stay to dinner. They all broke up about 10 at night. Dinner at 2. Every Person well pleased, and were very happy indeed. They had to drink Wine, Punch and Ale as much as they pleased; they drank of wine 6 Bottles, of Rum 1 gallon and half, and I know not what ale. Old Harry Andrews, my clerk, Harry Dunnell and Harry Andrews at the Heart all dined etc. in Kitchen. Some dined in the Parlour and some in the Kitchen. 17 dined etc. that paid my Tithe, that is to say, Stepn. Andrews, Baker, Burton, Cary, Man, Pegg, Norton, Bowles, Dade, Case, Pratt, Legate Senr. and son of Ringland, Bidewell, Michael Andrews, Borrows and Legate Junr. at the Horse. Mr Peachment came just at dinner time, but he had dined; he spent the afternoon and evening however. There was no supper at all provided for them. We had many droll songs from some of them. I made use of about 13 lemons and about 2 Pds of sugar. Bill and myself both well tired when we went to bed.

James Woodforde : *Diary of a Country Parson*

PILGRIMAGE IN SPRING

Whan that Aprille with his shoures soote
The droghte of March hath perced to the roote,
And bathed every veyne in swich licour
Of which vertu engendred is the flour;
Whan Zephirus eek with his sweete breeth
Inspired hath in every holt and heeth
The tendre croppes, and the yonge sonne
Hath in the Ram his halfe cours yronne,
And smale foweles maken melodye,
That slepen al the nyght with open ye

211

(So priketh hem nature in hir corages);
Thanne longen folk to goon on pilgrimages,
And palmeres for to seken straunge strondes,
To ferne halwes, kowthe in sondry londes;
And specially from every shires ende
Of Engelond to Caunterbury they wende,
The hooly blisful martir for to seke,
That hem hath holpen whan that they were seeke.

Geoffrey Chaucer: *Prologue to the Canterbury Tales*

William Temple and Dorothy Osborne were married in 1654, and their first child Jack was born on 18 December, 1655. This letter to her husband was written from Reading in Berkshire, when the child was about nine months old.

A GREAT FAIR AT READING

I might perhaps beethought som thing mire dull then ordinary when I writt last for as I remember I was sleepy too and not soe much with sitting up late as with riseing Early wch I haue done ever since you went Either because I am weary of my bed or that tis good to make mee leane again; but know soe little what to be with myselfe when I am up that I am fain to send for Jack into my chamber, see him rest there, and when I am weary of playing with him goe to worke for him, but alasse, he has a great defeate his Coate was made and I had gott him linnen redy to weare with it but Mrs Carter has sent him noe shoo's and stockings I beleeue twas Tom's fault that did not carry her Janes letter soone enough. You tell mee nothing of my Aunt nor of my Cousin Thorolde. I suppose tis that you have not seen any of them yett.

I shall observe your orders to morrow and write to you againe on Monday tis like to bee a great faire they say, something more then ordinary sure it will bee or else Mr Mayor and his Brethren would nere have put themselves to the trouble of comeing all to my Aunte two dayes agon to tell her that they would pull down our freind Mr Harrisons hedge to make roome for it. they threatend her Garden too and question her right to the ffishing and the hundred Egg's; Mighty hott words past and many more then the buisnesse was worth I thought, but that the gravity of Mr Mayor's Ruffe bare it out well. would I could borrow it to send with this letter for tis as little to the purpose mee thinks as all that hee sayed. see what you get by putting mee upon long letters, if you would confesse it you are glad with all your heart to finde yourselfe soe neer the End on't. Good night to you my dearest.

I am

Your

D. Temple

Dorothy Osborne's letters to William Temple

And here is another reference to Reading, as a Thames-side town, written well over two hundred years later.

WASHING CLOTHES

We stayed two days at Streatley, and got our clothes washed. We had tried washing them ourselves, in the river, under George's superintendence, and it had been a failure. Indeed, it had been more than a failure, because we were worse off after we had washed our clothes than we were before. Before we had washed them, they had been very, very dirty, it is true; but they were just wearable. *After* we had washed them – well, the river between Reading and Henley was much cleaner, after we had washed our clothes in it, than it was before. All the dirt contained in the river between Reading and Henley we collected, during that wash, and worked it into our clothes.

The washerwoman at Streatley said she felt she owed it to herself to charge us just three times the usual prices for that wash. She said it had not been like washing, it had been more in the nature of excavating.

We paid the bill without a murmur.

Jerome K. Jerome: *Three Men in a Boat*

HARVEST TIME IN THE '80s

In the fields where the harvest had begun all was bustle and activity. At that time the mechanical reaper with long, red, revolving arms like windmill sails had already appeared in the locality, but it was looked upon by the men as an auxiliary, a farmer's toy; the scythe still did most of the work and they did not dream it would ever be superseded. So while the red sails revolved in one field and the youth on the driver's seat of the machine called cheerily to his horses and women followed behind to bind the corn into sheaves, in the next field a band of men would be whetting their scythes and mowing by hand as their fathers had done before them.

With no idea that they were at the end of a long tradition, they still kept up the old country custom of choosing as their leader the tallest and most highly skilled man amongst them, who was then called 'King of the Mowers.' For several harvests in the 'eighties they were led by the man known as Boamer. He had served in the Army and was still a fine well-set-up young fellow with flashing white teeth and a skin darkened by fiercer than English suns.

With a wreath of poppies and green bindweed trails around his wide, rush-plaited hat, he led the band down the swathes as they mowed and decreed when and for how long they should halt for 'a breather' and what drinks should be had from the yellow stone jar they kept under the hedge in a shady corner of the field. They did not rest often or long; for every morning they set themselves to accomplish an amount of work in the day that they knew would tax all their powers till long after sunset. 'Set yourself more than you can do and you'll do it' was one of their maxims, and some of their feats in the harvest field astonished themselves as well as the onlooker.

Old Monday, the bailiff, went riding from field to field on his long-tailed, grey pony. Not at that season to criticise, but rather to encourage, and to carry strung to his saddle the hooped and handled miniature barrel of beer provided by the farmer.

One of the smaller fields was always reserved for any of the women who cared to go reaping. Formerly all the able-bodied women not otherwise occupied had gone as a matter of course; but, by the 'eighties, there were only three or four, beside the regular field women, who could handle the sickle. Often the Irish harvesters had to be called in to finish the field.

Patrick, Dominick, James (never called Jim), Big Mike and Little Mike, and Mr O'Hara seemed to the children as much a part of the harvest scene as the corn itself. They came over from Ireland every year to help with the harvest and slept in the farmer's barn, doing their own cooking and washing at a little fire in the open. They were a wild-looking lot, dressed in odd clothes and speaking a brogue so thick that the natives could only catch a word here and there. When not at work, they went about in a band, talking loudly and usually all together, with the purchases they had made at the inn bundled in blue-and-white check handkerchiefs which they carried over their shoulders at the end of a stick. 'Here comes they jabberin' old Irish,' the country people would say, and some of the women pretended to be afraid of them. They could not have been serious, for the

Irishmen showed no disposition to harm anyone. All they desired was to earn as much money as possible to send home to their wives, to have enough left for themselves to get drunk on a Saturday night, and to be in time for Mass on a Sunday morning. All these aims were fulfilled; for, as the other men confessed, they were 'gluttons for work' and more work meant more money at that season; there was an excellent inn handy, and a Catholic church within three miles.

After the mowing and reaping and binding came the carrying, the busiest time of all. Every man and boy put his best foot forward then, for when the corn was cut and dried it was imperative to get it stacked and thatched before the weather broke. All day and far into the twilight the yellow-and-blue painted farm wagons passed and repassed along the roads between the field and the stackyard. Big carthorses returning with an empty wagon were made to gallop like two-year-olds. Straws hung on the roadside hedges and many a gatepost was knocked down through hasty driving. In the fields men pitchforked the sheaves to the one who was building the load on the wagon, and the air resounded with *Hold tights* and *Wert ups* and *Who-o-oas*. The *Hold tight!* was no empty cry; sometimes, in the past, the man on top of the load had not held tight or not tight enough. There were tales of fathers and grandfathers whose necks or backs had been broken by a fall from a load, and of other fatal accidents afield, bad cuts from scythes, pitchforks passing through feet, to be followed by lockjaw, and of sunstroke; but, happily, nothing of this kind happened on that particular farm in the 'eighties.

At last, in the cool dusk of an August evening, the last load was brought in, with a nest of merry boys' faces among the sheaves on the top, and the men walking alongside with pitchforks on shoulders. As they passed along the roads they shouted:

Harvest home! Harvest home!
Merry, merry, merry harvest home!

and women came to their cottage gates and waved, and the few passers-by looked up and smiled their congratulations. The joy

217

and pleasure of the labourers in their task well done was pathetic, considering their very small share in the gain. But it was genuine enough; for they still loved the soil and rejoiced in their own work and skill in bringing forth the fruits of the soil, and harvest home put the crown on their year's work.

As they approached the farmhouse their song changed to:

Harvest home! Harvest home!
Merry, merry, merry harvest home!
Our bottles are empty, our barrels won't run,
And we think it's a very dry harvest home,

and the farmer came out, followed by his daughters and maids with jugs and bottles and mugs, and drinks were handed round amidst general congratulations. Then the farmer invited the men to his harvest home dinner, to be held in a few days' time, and the adult workers dispersed to add up their harvest money and to rest their weary bones. The boys and youths, who could never have too much of a good thing, spent the rest of the evening circling the hamlet and shouting 'Merry, merry, merry harvest home!' until the stars came out and at last silence fell upon the fat rickyard and the stripped fields.

Flora Thompson: *Lark Rise*

COUNTRY FUNERAL

September 3rd, Wednesday, 1800

A fine coolish morning. I ironed till $\frac{1}{2}$ past 3 – now very hot – I then went to a funeral at John Dawson's. About 10 men and 4 women. Bread, cheese and ale. They talked sensibly and chearfully about common things. The dead person, 56 years of age, buried by the parish. The coffin was neatly lettered and painted black, and covered with a decent cloth. They set the corpse down at the door; and, while we stood within the threshold, the men with their hats off sang with decent and solemn countenances a verse of a funeral psalm. The corpse was then borne down the hill, and they sang till they had got past the Town-End. I was affected to tears while we stood in the house, the coffin lying before me. There were no near kindred, no children. When we got out of the dark house the sun was shining, and the prospect looked so divinely beautiful as I never saw it. It seemed more sacred than I had ever seen it, and yet more allied to human life. The green fields, neighbours of the churchyard, were as green as possible; and, with the brightness of the sunshine, looked quite gay. I thought she was going to a quiet spot, and I could not help weeping very much. When we came to the bridge, they began to sing again, and stopped during four lines before they entered the churchyard.

Dorothy Wordsworth: *Grasmere Journal*

COUNTRY DANCING IN CUMBERLAND

July 1st – We are this morning at Carlisle. After Skiddaw, we walked to Ireby, the oldest Market town in Cumberland – where we were greatly amused by a Country Dancing School holden at the Inn, it was indeed 'no new cotillon fresh from France.' No, they kickit and jumpit with mettle extraordinary, and whiskit, and friskit, and toed it, and go'd it, and twirld it, and whirl'd it, and stamp't it, and sweated it, tattooing the floor like mad. The difference between our Country Dances and these Scottish figures is about the same as leisurely stirring a cup o' Tea and beating up a batter pudding . I was extremely gratified to think, that if I had pleasures they knew nothing of, they had also some into which I could not possibly enter. I hope I shall not return without having got the Highland fling, there was as fine a row of boys and girls as you ever saw, some beautiful faces, and one exquisite mouth. I never felt so near the glory of Patriotism, the glory of making by any means a Country happier. This is what I like better than scenery.

John Keats: *A letter to Thomas Keats, 1818*

AFTER HONEY-TAKING

Geoffrey Day's storehouse at the back of his dwelling was hung with bunches of dried horehound, mint, and sage; brown-paper bags of thyme and lavender; and long ropes of clean onions. On shelves were spread large red and yellow apples, and choice selections of early potatoes for seed next year; –vulgar crowds of commoner kind lying beneath in heaps. A few empty beehives were clustered around a nail in one corner, under which stood two or three barrels of new cider of the first crop, each bubbling and squirting forth from the yet open bunghole.

Fancy was now kneeling beside the two inverted hives, one of which rested against her lap, for convenience in operating upon the contents. She thrust her sleeves above her elbows, and inserted her small pink hand edgewise between each white lobe of honeycomb, performing the act so adroitly and gently as not to unseal a single cell. Then cracking the piece off at the crown of the hive by a slight backward and forward movement, she lifted each portion as it was loosened into a large blue platter, placed on a bench at her side.

'Bother these little mortals!' said Geoffrey, who was holding the light to her, and giving his back an uneasy twist. 'I really think I may as well go indoors and take 'em out, poor things! for they won't let me alone. There's two a stinging wi' all their might now. I'm sure I wonder their strength can last so long.'

'All right, friend; I'll hold the candle whilst you are gone,' said Mr Shiner, leisurely taking the light, and allowing Geoffrey to depart, which he did with his usual long paces.

He could hardly have gone round to the house-door when other footsteps were heard approaching the outbuilding; the tip of a finger appeared in the hole through which the wood latch was lifted, and Dick Dewy came in, having been all this time walking up and down the wood, vainly waiting for Shiner's departure.

Fancy looked up and welcomed him rather confusedly. Shiner grasped the candlestick more firmly, and, lest doing this in silence should not imply to Dick with sufficient force that he was quite at home and cool, he sang invincibly –

' "King Arthur he had three sons." '

'Father here?' said Dick.

'Indoors, I think,' said Fancy, looking pleasantly at him.

Dick surveyed the scene, and did not seem inclined to hurry
off just at that moment. Shiner went on singing –

> ' "The miller was drown'd in his pond,
> The weaver was hung in his yarn,
> And the d—— ran away with the little tail—or
> With the broadcloth under his arm." '

'That's a terrible crippled rhyme, if that's your rhyme!' said
Dick, with a grain of superciliousness in his tone.

'It's no use your complaining to me about the rhyme!' said
Mr Shiner. 'You must go to the man that made it.'

Fancy by this time had acquired confidence.

'Taste a bit, Mr Dewy,' she said, holding up to him a small
circular piece of honeycomb that had been the last in the row of
layers, remaining still on her knees and flinging back her head
to look in his face; 'and then I'll taste a bit too.'

'And I, if you please,' said Mr Shiner. Nevertheless the
farmer looked superior, as if he could even now hardly join the
trifling from very importance of station; and after receiving the
honeycomb from Fancy, he turned it over in his hand till the
cells began to be crushed, and the liquid honey ran down from
his fingers in a thin string.

Suddenly a faint cry from Fancy caused them to gaze at her.

'What's the matter, dear?' said Dick.

'It is nothing, but O-o! a bee has stung the inside of my lip!
He was in one of the cells I was eating!'

'We must keep down the swelling, or it may be serious!' said
Shiner, stepping up and kneeling beside her. 'Let me see it.'

'No, no!'

'Just let *me* see it,' said Dick, kneeling on the other side; and
after some hesitation she pressed down her lip with one finger
to show the place. 'O, I hope 'twill soon be better! I don't mind
a sting in ordinary places, but it is so bad upon your lip,' she
added with tears in her eyes, and writhing a little from the pain.

Shiner held the light above his head and pushed his face close to Fancy's, as if the lip had been shown exclusively to himself, upon which Dick pushed closer, as if Shiner were not there at all.

'It is swelling,' said Dick to her right aspect.

'It isn't swelling,' said Shiner to her left aspect.

'Is it dangerous on the lip?' cried Fancy. 'I know it is dangerous on the tongue.'

'O no, not dangerous!' answered Dick.

'Rather dangerous,' had answered Shiner simultaneously.

'I must try to bear it!' said Fancy, turning again to the hives.

'Hartshorn-and-oil is a good thing to put to it, Miss Day,' said Shiner, with great concern.

'Sweet-oil-and-hartshorn I've found to be a good thing to cure stings, Miss Day,' said Dick with greater concern.

'We have some mixed indoors; would you kindly run and get it for me?' she said.

Now, whether by inadvertence, or whether by mischievous intention, the individuality of the *you* was so carelessly denoted that both Dick and Shiner sprang to their feet like twin acrobats, and marched abreast to the door; both seized the latch and lifted it, and continued marching on, shoulder to shoulder, in the same manner to the dwelling-house. Not only so, but entering the room, they marched as before straight up to Mrs Day's chair, letting the door in the oak partition slam so forcibly, that the rows of pewter on the dresser rang like a bell.

'Mrs Day, Fancy has stung her lip, and wants you to give me the hartshorn, please,' said Mr Shiner, very close to Mrs Day's face.

'O, Mrs Day, Fancy has asked me to bring out the hartshorn, please, because she has stung her lip!' said Dick, a little closer to Mrs Day's face.

'Well, men alive! that's no reason why you should eat me, I suppose!' said Mrs Day, drawing back.

She searched in the corner-cupboard, produced the bottle, and began to dust the cork, the rim, and every other part very carefully, Dick's hand and Shiner's hand waiting side by side.

'Which is head man?' said Mrs Day. 'Now, don't come mumbudgeting so close again. Which is head man?'
Neither spoke; and the bottle was inclined towards Shiner.

Thomas Hardy: *Under the Greenwood Tree*

Why Gooseberry Pye with a 'y' should appear so much more indigestible than our present-day 'pie,' I don't quite know, but it does. And certainly Parson Woodforde's spelling of 'Plumb Pudding' which occurs elsewhere in the Diary, gives one a weighty feeling immediately.

A CHEERFUL PARTY

May 18, 1779

Mr Howes and Wife and Mrs Davy, Mr Bodham and his Brother, and Mr du Quesne all dined and spent the afternoon and part of the evening with us today. I gave them for dinner a dish of Maccarel, 3 young Chicken boiled and some Bacon, a neck of Pork rosted and a Gooseberry Pye hot. We laughed immoderately after dinner on Mrs Howes's being sent to Coventry by us for an Hour. What with laughing and eating hot Gooseberry Pye brought on me the Hickupps with a violent pain in my stomach which lasted till I went to bed. At Cards Quadrille this evening – lost 0.2.6.

James Woodforde: *Diary of a Country Parson*

There are scores of accounts of cricket matches in our literature, but I have chosen Miss Mitford's because it is probably the best given by a woman.

THE CRICKET MATCH

We had now ten of our eleven, but the choice of the last occasioned some demur. Three young Martins, rich farmers of the neighbourhood, successively presented themselves, and were all rejected by our independent and impartial general for want of merit – *cricketal* merit. 'Not good enough,' was his pithy answer. Then our worthy neighbour, the half-pay lieutenant, offered his services, – he, too, though with some hesitation and modesty, was refused – 'Not quite young enough,' was his sentence. John Strong, the exceeding long son of our dwarfish mason, was the next candidate; a nice youth, – everybody likes John Strong, – and a willing, but so tall and so limp, bent in the middle, – a thread-paper, six feet high! We were all afraid that, in spite of his name, his strength would never hold out. 'Wait till next year, John,' quoth William Grey, with all the dignified seniority of twenty speaking to eighteen. 'Coper's a year younger,' said John. 'Coper's a foot shorter,' replied William: so John retired: and the eleventh man remained unchosen, almost to the eleventh hour. The eve of the match arrived, and post was still vacant, when a little boy of fifteen, David Willis, brother to Harry, admitted by accident to the last practice, saw eight of them out, and was voted in by acclamation.

That Sunday evening's practice (for Monday was the important day) was a period of great anxiety, and, to say the truth, of great pleasure. There is something strangely delightful in the innocent spirit of party. To be one of a numerous body, to be authorised to say *we*, to have a rightful interest in triumph or defeat, is gratifying at once to social feeling and to personal pride. There was not a ten-year-old urchin, or a septuagenary woman in the parish who did not feel an additional importance, a reflected consequence, in speaking of 'our side.' An election interests in the same way, but that feeling is less pure. Money is there, and hatred, and politics, and lies. Oh, to be a voter, or a voter's wife, comes nothing near the genuine and hearty sympathy of belonging to a parish, breathing the same air, looking on the same trees, listening to the same nightingales! Talk of a patriotic elector! Give me a parochial patriot, a man who loves his parish! Even we, the female partisans, may partake the common ardour. I am sure I did. I never, though tolerably eager and enthusiastic at all times, remember being in a more delicious state of excitement than on the eve of that battle. Our hopes waxed stronger and stronger. Those of our players who were present were excellent. William Grey got forty notches off his own bat; and that brilliant hitter, Tom Coper, gained eight from two successive balls. As the evening advanced, too, we had encouragement of another sort. A spy, who had been despatched to reconnoitre the enemy's quarters, returned from their practising ground with a most consolatory report. 'Really,' said Charles Grover, our intelligence, – fine old steady judge, one who had played well in his day – 'they are no better than so many old women. Any five of ours would beat their eleven.' This sent us to bed in high spirits . . .

. . . *They* began the warfare, – thos boastful men of B. And what think you, gentle reader, was the amount of their innings! These challengers, – the famous eleven, – how many did they get? Think! imagine! guess! – You cannot? – Well! – they got twenty-two, or, rather, they got twenty; for two of theirs were short notches, and would never have been allowed, only that, seeing what they were made of, we and our umpires were not particular. – They should have had twenty more if they had chosen to claim them. Oh how well we fielded! and how well we bowled! our good play had quite as much to do with their miserable failure as their bad. Samuel Long is a slow bowler, George Simmons a fast one, and the change from Long's lobbing to Simmons's fast balls posed them completely. Poor simpletons! they were always wrong, expecting the slow for the quick, and the quick for the slow. Well, we went in. And what were our innings? Guess again! guess! A hundred and sixty-nine! in spite of soaking showers, and wretched ground, where the ball would not run a yard, we headed them by a hundred and forty-seven; and then they gave in, as well they might. William Grey pressed them much to try another innings. 'There was so much chance,' as he courteously observed, 'in cricket, that advantageous as our position seemed, we might, very possibly, be overtaken. The B. men had better try.' But they were beaten sulky, and would not move – to my great disappointment; I wanted to prolong the pleasure of success. What a glorious sensation it is to be for five hours together – winning – winning! always feeling what a whist-player feels when he takes up four honours, seven trumps! Who would think that a little bit of leather, and two pieces of wood, had such a delightful and delighting power!

The only drawback on my enjoyment was the failure of the pretty boy, David Willis, who, unjudiciously put in first, and playing for the first time in a match amongst men and strangers, who talked to him, and stared at him, was seized with such a fit of shamefaced shyness, that he could scarcely hold his bat, and was bowled out without a stroke, from actual nervousness.

'He will come off that,' Tom Coper says; – I am afraid he will. I wonder whether Tom had ever any modesty to lose. Our modest lad, John Strong, did very well; his length told in fielding, and he got good fame. Joel Brent, the rescued mower, got into a scrape, and out of it again; his fortune for the day. He ran out his mate, Samuel Long; who, I do believe, but for the excess of Joel's eagerness, would have stayed in till his time, by which exploit he got into sad disgrace; and then he himself got thirty-seven runs, which redeemed his reputation. Will Grey made a hit which actually lost the cricket-ball. We think she lodged in a hedge, a quarter of a mile off, but nobody could find her. And George Simmons had nearly lost his shoe, which he tossed away in a passion, for having been caught out, owing to the ball glancing against it. These, together with a very complete somerset of Ben Appleton, our long-stop, who floundered about in the mud, making faces and attitudes as laughable as Grimaldi, none could tell whether by accident or design, were the chief incidents of the scene of action. Amongst the spectators nothing remarkable occurred, beyond the general calamity of two or three drenchings, except that a form, placed by the side of a hedge, under a very insufficient shelter, was knocked into the ditch, in a sudden rush of the cricketers to escape a pelting shower, by which means all parties shared the fate of Ben Appleton, some on land and some by water; and that, amidst the scramble, a saucy gipsy of a girl contrived to steal from the

knee of the demure and well-apparelled Samuel Long, a smart
handkerchief which his careful dame had tied round it to preserve his new (what is the mincing feminine word?) – his new
– inexpressibles, thus reversing the story of Desdemona and
causing the new Othello to call aloud for his handkerchief, to
the great diversion of the company. And so we parted; the
players retired to their supper, and we to our homes; all wet
through, all good-humoured and happy – except the losers.

Today we are happy too. Hats, with ribands in them, go
glancing up and down; and William Grey says, with a proud
humility, 'We do not challenge any parish; but if we be
challenged, we are ready.'

Mary Russell Mitford: Our Village

COUNTRY SALE

Under the thin green sky, the twilight day,
The old home lies in public sad array,
Its time being come, the lots ranged out in rows,
And to each lot a ghost. The gathering grows
With every minute, neckcloths and gold pins;
Poverty's purples; red necks, horny skins,
Odd peeping eyes, thin lips and hooking chins.

Then for the skirmish, and the thrusting groups
Bidding for tubs and wire and chicken coops,
While yet the women hang apart and eye
Their friends and foes and reckon who will buy.
The noisy field scarce knows itself, not one
Takes notice of the old man's wavering moan
Who hobbles with his hand still brushing tears
And cries how this belonged here sixty years,
And picks his brother's picture from the mass
Of frames; and still from heap to heap folks pass.

The strife of tongues even tries the auctioneer,
Who, next the dealer smirking to his leer,
A jumped-up jerky cockerel in his box,
Runs all his rigs, cracks all his jokes and mocks;
'Madam, now never weary of well-doing,'
The heavy faces gleam to hear him crowing.
And swift the old home's fading. Here he bawls
The white four-poster, with its proud recalls,
But we on such old-fashioned lumber frown;
'Passing away at a florin,' grins the clown.
Here Baskett's Prayer Book with his black and red
Finds no more smile of welcome than the bed,
Though policeman turn the page with wisdom's looks:
The hen-wives see no sense in such old books.
Here painted trees and well-feigned towers arise
And ships before the wind, that sixpence buys.

All's sold; then hasty vanmen pile and rope,
Their loads, and ponies stumble up the slope.
And all are gone, the trampled paddock's bare;
The children round the buildings run and blare,
Thinking what times these are! not knowing how
The heavy-handed fate has brought them low,
Till quartern loaf be gone too soon today,
And none is due tomorrow. Long, then, play,
And make the lofts re-echo through the eve,
And sweeten so the bitter taking-leave.

So runs the world away. Years hence shall find
The mother weeping to her lonely mind,
In some new place, thin set with makeshift gear,
For the home she had before the fatal year;
And still to this same anguish she'll recur,
Reckoning up her fine old furniture,
The tall clock with his church-bell time of day,

The mirror where so deep the image lay,
The china with its rivets numbered all,
Seeming to have them in her hands – poor soul,
Trembling and crying how these, loved so long,
So beautiful, all went for an old song.

Edmund Blunden

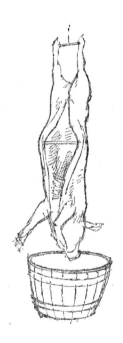

LAURA AND THE PIG-KILLING

A little later in her life came the evening after a pig-killing when she stood alone in the pantry where the dead animal hung suspended from a hook in the ceiling. Her mother was only a few feet away. She could hear her talking cheerfully to Mary Ann, the girl who fetched their milk from the farm and took the children for walks when their mother was busy. Through the thin wooden partition she could hear her distinctive giggle as she poured water from a jug into the long, slippery lengths of chitterlings her mother was manipulating. Out there in the wash-house they were busy and cheerful, but in the pantry where Laura stood was a dead, cold silence.

She had known that pig all its life. Her father had often held her over the door of its sty to scratch its back and she had pushed lettuce and cabbage-stalks through the bars for it to enjoy. Only that morning it had routed and grunted and squealed because it had had no breakfast. Her mother said its noise got on her nerves and her father had looked uncomfortable, although he had passed it off by saying: 'No. No breakfast today, piggy. You're going to have a big operation by and by and there's no breakfast before operations.'

Now it had had its operation and there it hung, cold and stiff and so very, very dead. Not funny at all any more, but in some queer way dignified. The butcher had draped a long, lacy piece of fat from its own interior over one of its forelegs, in the manner in which ladies of that day sometimes carried a white lacy shawl, and that last touch seemed to Laura utterly heartless. She stayed there a long time, patting its hard, cold side and wondering that a thing so recently full of life and noise could be so still. Then, hearing her mother call her, she ran out of the door farthest from where she was working, lest she should be scolded for crying over a dead pig.

There was fried liver and fat for supper and when Laura said, 'No, thank you,' her mother looked at her rather suspiciously, then said: 'Well, perhaps better not, just going to bed and all; but here's a nice bit of sweetbread. I was saving it for Daddy, but you have it. You'll like that.' And Laura ate the sweetbread and dipped her bread in the thick, rich gravy and refused to think about the poor pig in the pantry, for, although only five years old, she was learning to live in this world of compromises.

Flora Thompson: *Over to Candleford*

THETFORD ASSIZES 1785

March 26, 1785

At the Assizes at Thetford in this County 8 Prisoners were condemned, three of the above were reprieved. – The other five left for execution – One Js. Cliffen a most daring Fellow was hanged on Thursday. Js. Cliffen as mentioned on the last mentioned was hanged on Thursday last at Norwich on Castle-Hill and behaved most daringly audacious – His crime was robbing 2 old Men, Brothers, by names Seaman on the Yaxham Road, knocked them both down first, of which Blows one of them died soon after – the other recovered. Cliffen's Body was this Day carried to Badley Moor and there hung in Chains at one Corner of the said Moor.

James Woodforde: Diary of a Country Parson

I have lived near Newbury for many years, so that this contemporary account of a record achievement is of particular interest to me, and, I hope, to you.

The coat is called both 'The Newbury Coat' and 'The Throckmorton Coat,' for obvious reasons. It can still be seen at Coughton Court, Warwickshire, the home of the Throckmorton family.

THE FABULOUS COAT

The attention of the town and neighbourhood of Newbury was uncommonly excited, on Tuesday last, in an experiment attempted and effected by Mr John Coxeter, of Greenham Mill, near that town – At about five o'clock that morning, Sir John Throckmorton, Bart., presented 2 Southdown wether sheep to Mr Coxeter, he having engaged to make from their wool a complete Coat, for Sir John Throckmorton, by 9 in the evening; accordingly the sheep were shorn, the wool spun, the yarn

ILLUSTRATIVE
OF
MANUFACTURING CELERITY
TO PROVE THE POSSIBILITY OF
WOOL

BEING MANUFACTURED INTO
CLOTH
AND MADE INTO A
COAT
BETWEEN
SUNRISE AND SUNSET
AND WHICH WAS SUCCESSFULLY ACCOMPLISHED on
TUESDAY, the 25th of JUNE, 1811.
AT FIVE O'CLOCK THAT MORNING
TWO SHEEP
BELONGING TO
Sir John Throckmorton, Bart.
WERE SHEARED BY HIS OWN SHEPHERD
FRANCIS DRUETT
AND THE WOOL GIVEN TO
Mr. JOHN COXETER
AT GREENHAM MILLS, NEAR
NEWBURY, BERKSHIRE:
WHO HAD

The WOOL Spun, The YARN Spooled,
Warped, Loomed, and Wove. The
CLOTH Burred, Milled, Rowed, Dyed,
Dryed, Sheared, and Pressed
BY FOUR O'CLOCK - ALL the
processes of MANUFACTURE were
performed BY HAND in ELEVEN
HOURS.

THE CLOTH was then given to
Mr. ISAAC WHITE, Tailor, of Newbury,

Whose Son, James White, cut the Coat out and had it
made up within

TWO HOURS AND TWENTY MINUTES,

When the Master Manufacturer, Mr. John Coxeter,
presented it to

Sir John Throckmorton, Bart.

who appeared with it on before an assembly of 5000 spectators
who had come far and near to witness this singular and
unprecedented performance completed in

THIRTEEN HOURS AND TWENTY MINUTES.

COPY of Poster printed by Blacket, Stamp Office, Newbury, Berkshire, in the 19th Century spooled, warped, loomed and wove, the cloth burred, milled, rowed, dyed, dryed, sheared and pressed, and put into the hands of the Tailors, by 4 o'clock that afternoon. At 20 minutes past six o'clock, the coat entirely finished, was presented by Mr Coxeter, to Sir John Throckmorton, who appeared with it on before an assemblage of upwards of 5,000 spectators, who rent the air in acclamations. On the occasion, the 2 sheep were roasted whole on the same day, one of which, with 120 gallons of strong beer, was given to the work people belonging to the Factory; the other to the public, aboard the Prince Regent, a vessel furnished for that purpose by Messrs Slocock and Batten, Newbury.

Bells rang during the day and every demonstration of joy appeared; and thus the experiment hitherto unexampled was compleatly effected, in the short space of 13 hours and 20 mins.

Sir John Throckmorton and nearly 40 gentlemen sat down to a sumptuous dinner provided by Mr Coxeter, on the occasion – The Cloth was a Hunting Kersey; the colour, the admired dark Wellington.

Col. Stead
A. Bacon Esq. ⎬ Stewards
W. Bud Esq.

Mr. R. W. Hiscock ⎬ Inspectors
Mr Lockett

The Reading Mercury and Oxford Gazette
Monday, 1 July, 1811

The fascination of cheap-jacks lies in their rapidity of patter as much as their persuasive arts, as Flora Thompson shows in the passage overleaf. In our local market place we stand, passive and admiring, while the cheap-jacks cajole and berate us, their faces purple with shouting and the cold wind, their arms flailing like windmills. We don't really want anything. We just want to watch. But we feel glad when something is sold.

'*He certainly earns his money,*' *we say to each other as we tear ourselves away.*

One autumn evening, just before dusk, he arrived with his cartload of crockery and tinware and set out his stock on the grass by the roadside before a back-cloth painted with icebergs and penguins and polar bears. Soon he had his naphtha lamps flaring and was clashing his basins together like bells and calling: 'Come buy! Come buy!'

It was the first visit of a cheap-jack to the hamlet and there was great excitement. Men, women and children rushed from the houses and crowded around in the circle of light to listen to his patter and admire his wares. And what bargains he had! The tea-service decorated with fat, full-blown pink roses: twenty-one pieces and not a flaw in any one of them. The Queen had purchased its fellow set for Buckingham Palace, it appeared. The tea-pots, the trays, the nests of dishes and basins, and the set of bedroom china which made everyone blush when he selected the most intimate utensil to rap with his knuckles to show it rang true.

'Two bob!' he shouted. 'Only two bob for this handsome set of jugs. Here's one for your beer and one for your milk and another in case you break one of the other two. Nobody willing to speculate? Then what about this here set of trays, straight from Japan and the peonies hand-painted; or this lot of basins, exact replicas of the one the Princess of Wales supped her gruel from when Prince George was born. Why, damme, they cost me more n'r that. I could get twice the price I'm asking in Banbury tomorrow; but I'll give 'em to you, for you can't call it selling, because I like your faces and me load's heavy for me 'oss. Alarming bargains! Tremendous sacrifices! Come buy! Come buy!'

But there were scarcely any offers. A woman here and there would give threepence for a large pudding-basin or sixpence for a tin saucepan. The children's mother bought a penny nutmeg-grater and a set of wooden spoons for cooking; the innkeeper's wife ran to a dozen tumblers and a ball of string; then there was a long pause during which the vendor kept up a continual stream of jokes and anecdotes which sent his audience into fits of laughter. Once he broke into song:

There was a man in his garden walked
And cut his throat with a lump of chalk;
His wife, she knew not what she did,
She strangled herself with the saucepan lid.
There was a man and a fine young fellow
Who poisoned himself with an umbrella.
Even Joey in his cradle shot himself dead with a
    silver ladle.
When you hear this horrible tale
It makes your faces all turn pale,
Your eyes go green, you're overcome,
So tweedle, tweedle, tweedle twum.

All very fine entertainment, but it brought him no money and he began to suspect that he would draw a blank at Lark Rise.

'Never let it be said,' he implored, 'that this is the poverty-strickenest place on God's earth. Buy something, if only for your own credit's sake. Here!' snatching up a pile of odd plates. 'Good dinner-plates for you. Every one a left-over from a first-class service. Buy one of these and you'll have the satisfaction of knowing you're eating off the same ware as lords and dukes. Only three-halfpence each. Who'll buy? Who'll buy?'

There was a scramble for the plates, for nearly everyone could muster three-halfpence; but every time anything more costly was produced there was a dead silence. Some of the women began to feel uncomfortable. 'Don't be poor and look poor, too' was their motto, and here they were looking poor indeed, for who, with money in their pockets, could have resisted such wonderful bargains.

Then the glorious unexpected happened. The man had brought the pink rose tea-service forward again and was handing one of the cups round. 'You just look at the light through it – and you, ma'am, and you. Ain't it lovely china, thin as an eggshell, practically transparent, and with every one of them roses hand-painted with a brush? You can't let a set like that go out of the place, now can you? I can see all your mouths a-watering. You run home, my dears, and bring out them stockings from under the mattress and the first one to get back shall have it for twelve bob.'

Each woman in turn handled the cup lovingly, then shook her head and passed it on. None of them had stockings of savings hidden away. But, just as the man was receiving back the cup, a little roughly, for he was getting discouraged, a voice spoke up in the background.

'How much did you say, mister? Twelve bob? I'll give you ten.' It was John Price, who, only the night before, had returned from his soldiering in India. A very ordinary sort of chap at most times, for he was a teetotaller and stood no drinks at the inn, as a returned soldier should have done, but now, suddenly he became important. All eyes were upon him. The credit of the hamlet was at stake.

'I'll give you ten bob.'

'Can't be done, matey. Cost me more nor that. But, look see, tell you what I will do. You give me eleven and six, and I'll throw in this handsome silver-gilt vase for your mantelpiece.'

'Done!' The bargain was concluded; the money changed hands, and the reputation of the hamlet was rehabilitated. Willing hands helped John carry the tea-service to his home. Indeed, it was considered an honour to be trusted with a cup. His bride-to-be was still away in service and little knew how many were envying her that night. To have such a lovely service awaiting her return, no cracked or odd pieces, every piece alike and all so lovely; lucky, lucky, Lucy!

Flora Thompson: *Lark Rise*

MR JORROCKS AT NEWMARKET

The sherry had done its business on them both; the Baron who, perhaps, was the most 'cut' of the two, chaunted the Marseillaise hymn of liberty with as much freedom as though he were sitting in the saddle. Thus they proceeded laughing and singing until the Bury pay-gate arrested their progress, when it occurred to the steersman to ask if they were going right. 'Be this the vay to Newmarket races?' inquired Jorrocks of the pike-keeper. The man dived into the small pocket of his white apron for a ticket, and very coolly replied, '*Shell out*, old 'un.' 'How much?' said Jorrocks. 'Tuppence'; which having got, he said, '*Now* then, you may turn, for the Heath be over yonder,' pointing back, 'at least, it was there this morning, I know.' After a volley of abuse for his impudence, Mr Jorrocks, with some difficulty, got the old mare pulled round, for she had a deuced hard mouth of her own, and only a plain snaffle in it; at last, however, with the aid of a boy to beat her with a furze bush, they got her set agoing again, and, retracing their steps, they trotted 'down street,' rose the hill, and entered the spacious, wide-extending flat of Newmarket Heath.

R. S. Surtees: *Jorrocks's Jaunts and Jollities*

MR JORROCKS' PHAETON RIDE

On their turning off the rough pavement on to the quiet smooth macadamised road leading to Waterloo Bridge, his dissertation was interrupted by a loud horse-laugh raised by two or three toll-takers and boys lounging about the gate.

'I say, Tom, twig this 'ere machine,' said one. 'Dash my buttons, I never seed such a thing in all my life.'

'What's to pay,' inquired Jorrocks, pulling up with great dignity, their observations not having penetrated the cloak collar which encircled his ears. 'To pay!' said the toll-taker – 'vy, vot do ye call your consarn?'

'Why, a phaeton,' said Jorrocks. 'My eyes! that's a good un,' said another, 'I say, Jim – he calls this 'ere thing a phe-a-ton!' 'A phe-a-ton! – vy, it's more like a fire-engine,' said Jim. 'Don't be impertinent,' said Jorrocks, who had pulled down his collar to hear what he had to pay – 'but tell me what's to pay?' 'Vy, it's a phe-a-ton drawn by von or more 'orses,' said the toll-taker. 'And containing von or more asses,' said Tom. 'Sixpence-halfpenny, sir.' 'You are a saucy fellow,' said Jorrocks. 'Thank ye, master, you're another,' said the toll-keeper; 'and now that you have had your say, vot do ye ax for your mount?' 'I say, sir, do you belong to the Phoenix? Vy don't you show your badge?' 'I say, Tom, that 'ere fire-engine has been painted by some house-painter, it's never been in the hands of no coach-maker. Do you shave by that 'ere glazed castor of yours?' 'I'm blowed if I wouldn't get you a shilling a week to shove your face in sand, to make moulds for brass knockers.' 'Ay, get away! – make haste, or the fire will be out,' bawled another, as Jorrocks whipped on, and rattled out of hearing.

R. S. Surtees: *Jorrocks's Jaunts and Jollities*

TOWING AND BEING TOWED

Another example of the dangerous want of sympathy between tower and towed was witnessed by George and myself once up near Walton. It was where the tow-path shelves gently down into the water, and we were camping on the opposite bank, noticing things in general. By and by a small boat came in sight, towed through the water at a tremendous pace by a powerful barge horse, on which sat a very small boy. Scattered about the boat, in dreamy and reposeful attitudes, lay five fellows, the man who was steering having a particularly restful appearance.

'I should like to see him pull the wrong line,' murmured

George, as they passed. And at that precise moment the man did it, and the boat rushed up the bank with a noise like the ripping up of forty thousand linen sheets. Two men, a hamper, and three oars immediately left the boat on the larboard side, and reclined on the bank, and one and a half moments afterwards, two other men disembarked from the starboard, and sat down among boat-hooks and sails and carpet-bags and bottles. The last man went on twenty yards further, and then got out on his head.

This seemed to sort of lighten the boat, and it went on much easier, the small boy shouting at the top of his voice, and urging his steed into a gallop. The fellows sat up and stared at one another. It was some seconds before they realised what had happened to them, but, when they did, they began to shout lustily for the boy to stop. He, however, was too much occupied with the horse to hear them, and we watched them flying after him, until the distance hid them from view.

Jerome K. Jerome: *Three Men in a Boat*

Adrian Bell was born in 1901 and became a farmer in Suffolk. He described his agricultural experiences in the three books Corduroy *(1930),* Silver Ley *(1931) and* The Cherry Tree

239

(1932), and since then he has written several more novels in the shapely lucid prose which delights readers.

A Suffolk Meet *has been very much condensed, and comes from* Corduroy.

A SUFFOLK MEET

We mounted and were off. Mr Colville looked a typical hunting farmer with his round face under his bowler hat. He had lent me a bowler, that I might look the part, as I had not brought one, hardly considering it applicable to country life, the possibility of hunting being a fantastic vision in Chelsea.

He rode Jock, the heavyweight, while I perched on the nimble Cantilever.

'Rare good jumper, that mare is,' said Mr Colville. But the news at that time did not thrill me, only suggested a disturbing possibility of the mare springing suddenly from under me. 'She's safe, too.' That was better. 'But don't let other horses get too near her; she might kick. Only in play, of course; but people wouldn't like it.'

240

Apprehension again! Where did I go when she kicked?

A light wind was blowing. The mist had risen early, and the day was cold and clear. Conversation was cut short for the moment because a piece of paper in the road woke up and flapped, and the next I knew was that horse and I were on the top of a steep bank and then on the road again twenty yards ahead. I found I was still on the horse's back.

'I shouldn't let her do that,' said Mr Colville blandly. 'It's just that she's a bit bird-eyed, being fresh out.' He added: 'But I like to see a horse show a bit of spirit.'

I noticed, however, that his was a model of decorum, with complacent ears. (Cantilever's were a-twitch with nervous inquiry). Occasionally Mr Colville would make believe Jock had stumbled, and growl at him. I began to envy him his mount, though certainly Jock had not seemed as docile under me. Mr Colville's extra weight, no doubt. Jock moved with the magisterial surety of an elephant beneath his rider's fourteen stone.

Mr Colville exclaimed: 'I wish I were light enough to ride your mare. I'd show some of them how to go. Now, you're a nice weight; you could ride anything.' He sighed. 'Ah, well, you are only young once. I never cared what I rode one time of day, but I have to be careful now. I'm no light weight to fall.'

The hounds were gathered in front of the 'Rose and Crown' with the huntsmen and whips near by. The small space was packed with cars, horses, and people.

Everybody knew Mr Colville, and I kept alongside him. Cantilever was a-quiver with anticipation, and I had some apprehension in guiding her between shining limousines and the haunches of other horses, especially those with red tape on their tails – a danger sign of which Mr Colville had informed me.

The hounds alone were unaffected by the subdued excitement. They lay about with lolling tongues and sleepy red eyes, and occasionally yawned.

Consultations were in progress between the master and the huntsman, a shrewd old leatherface. There came a short toot of the horn and they were moving off.

241

Mr Colville turned to me. 'What do you think about it? Coming on or not?'

Before I could decide, I found myself swept onward in a crowd of horses. Cantilever was in no mood to retire. I went with the tide and hoped for the best.

'The only thing is,' I said, 'I have never done any jumping.'

'The mare is as safe as a church,' answered Mr Colville. 'All you have to do is to sit back and hold tight. Hug her well with your legs.'

I hoped my legs would be equal to the occasion. I was balanced, I felt, rather than seated.

We entered a field and spread. As soon as their feet touched soft earth, many of the horses tried to canter, and one or two bucked sensationally. I held Cantilever close, for she seemed disposed to give an exhibition of high spirits herself. Mr Colville's mount was magisterial as ever, his only sign of enthusiasm being to lift his legs higher and jog occasionally.

'We shall find here,' said Mr Colville, indicating a wood ahead. 'We always do.'

We stood under the shadow of the trees. The whole hunt seemed to have vanished, and silence reigned. A crowd of pigeons flew out of the wood. Rabbits lolloped silently towards us, paused, and scuttled away. A hare dashed past with a swishing noise through the stubble.

' 'Ark!' whispered Mr Colville, 'is that a 'oller?' – his aitches forsaking him at the moment of excitement.

I listened obediently, for what kind of noise I knew not; but Cantilever continued to champ her bit restlessly. Mr Colville raised his fist at her threateningly, but I saw no means of causing her to desist.

Suddenly a yelping and roaring filled the air, which immediately flashed upon me a childhood memory of the lions waiting to be fed at the Zoo.

'Ah!' said Mr Colville, 'that's the music at last.'

The horses were all of a twitter at the noise, and mad to be off. The horn sounded a rapid note. There was a thunder of hoofs behind, and half a dozen horses went flying past.

'Gone out towards Sedley Willows!' shouted somebody. Earth spattered on me. Next moment we were flying in their wake.

I had made up my mind to follow Mr Colville as best I could, but it was with difficulty I could keep Cantilever from getting ahead. My arms ached; my fingers were numb. The mare made that noise that the Bible translates as 'Ha, ha!' and bounded on. It was downhill, and all were converging towards a single gateway. I could no longer hold Cantilever. I saw disaster ahead, and resigned myself. I understood then the intoxication of the Gadarene swine in rushing down a steep place into the sea. I did not care what happened.

The gateway was a stampede of horses. Somebody in a pink coat went crashing through the hedge to the right with a catastrophic din. Horses squeezed me on either side. Stirrups clanked against mine. Hosts were behind, indicated by fierce panting breath and squelching mud. Cantilever's nose was against the warning red ribbon on another's tail; but that was nothing to me now. Somebody said: 'Big dog fox, going like smoke.' Suddenly the pressure on either side of me relaxed. We were through the gateway.

We dashed through a village street with a terrific clatter. Women stood in doorways, children clung to mothers' skirts; at the inn, mugs paused half-way to mouths. The good news from Ghent to Aix; yes that was it. Cantilever's hoofs between the houses begot echoes of a more heroic purpose than the chasing of a fox.

The fields again; hounds and horsemen streaming into a hollow and up the opposite slope; the whole hunt in a vista. 'The river!' shouts somebody, and we pass a bearded old yokel, lusty in excitement, hat held high, shouting: 'The river, gentlemen, that's where he's gone!'

Now we squelch through a miry farm gateway. I am close behind Mr Colville, and feel wet mud splash on my neck. Through the stackyard we fly. A threshing-machine is at work there; it runs empty. All hands hang idle as we pass, all eyes gaze, mouths are agape. We pass a pen of bullocks. A sow scrambles up and leans its forefeet over the door of its sty; a horse in a stable tries to break out. Chickens fly right and left; a cow prepares to defend its calf.

'Damn good bullocks in that yard. Wonder whose they are,' Mr Colville cries back to me. Always the farmer.

Hounds invade the vicarage garden. The vicar runs out, his sermon forgotten, and watches us into the distance, shading his eyes. Ploughmen hold the heads of their teams, which stamp and whinny with excitement. Six Suffolk colts at grass gallop beside us, then pause, frustrated, as we leave their field behind. Cows gather in groups, angry and afraid. Women and children run from their houses to points of vantage. Cantilever is striding easily a neck behind Jock.

'The river.' I wonder about that.

'We are getting into some hairy country,' said Mr Colville. There were small fields with ragged hedges and ditches. We came to a hedge seven feet high. Half a dozen people were waiting at the only feasible opening. It was awkward; a tree with low boughs growing over a ditch of more than usual width left a kind of hole into which in turn the riders disappeared, crouching. Mr Colville bade me go first. The man before me came off, his horse not getting across and falling sideways on the opposite bank. But he lugged him out and mounted again in a moment. Cantilever looked at it. I bowed myself to her neck and hoped for the best. Twigs thrashed me; we sank; we rose. I opened my eyes, and we were on the opposite side. Cantilever had not tried to jump it, but crept into the ditch and out again. I heard Mr Colville swear lustily somewhere in the hedge as I cantered on between two spinneys. In a minute he came flying past, fuming at Jock, his bowler hat awry and a big dent in it.

'The damned old fool tried to jump it,' he said as I came up with him, 'and hit my head the hell of a crack against the bough.' He looked so like the comic man on the stage, with his hat askew and indignation in his face, that I could not help laughing. I dropped back so that he should not see my mirth, and the more I looked at him the more I laughed. It seemed no end of a joke, especially as I had had a tot from his whisky flask a little before; I could hardly keep on my horse.

However, another unkempt place ahead toned down my amusement.

I urged Cantilever, though she needed no urging. The speed and the mare's eagerness beneath me were exhilarating. Gone were all qualms of my security of seat. I was confident. I felt that I could never fall off, that the mare could never stumble. It was as though I had known her for years. We took place after place without a thought, Cantilever jumping, creeping, and scrambling, I toppling and recovering. I was close behind the pink coat. Where he went I went also. I found that flying an obstacle was not nearly so unseating as jumping it standing. I was congratulating myself, saying: 'You've been a first-rate horseman all these years and not known it.' I began to enjoy the hazards. A hedge ahead. Pink coat was over. Cantilever sprang at it. Next moment her head seemed miles below me and I was flying through the air. I found myself turning a somersault, and as I did so I remember thinking: 'You are coming the deuce of a cropper.' I hit the ground with my shoulder, then stood on my head. I seemed poised thus for ages. It felt undignified; I kept wishing my legs would come down.

As soon as my legs reached earth I made the mistake of jumping up. Many thoughts had been crammed into the space of a second, and Cantilever was only just galloping towards me from the hedge. Had I lain still she would have sprung over me, but I was on my knees, and her hoof hit my side and winded me. I rolled over. Mr Colville, the horse-dealer, and the man in the pink coat were gazing down at me, and I, flat on my back, was gazing up at them, unable to speak or breathe. They were wondering how much I was damaged, but I knew (remembering a football incident at school) that, though at the moment I was dying of suffocation, my breath would suddenly return. I felt an impostor, being so anxiously gazed upon, and longed to tell them to go on with their hunting and that I should be all right in a minute. Strangled words actually escaped me – 'Nothing . . . be all right . . . minute.' They gave advice to one another.

Suddenly my breath returned. Mr Colville was saying something about laying me on a hurdle and a farm-house near. But I jumped up. I felt as right as rain. I found I was clasping the bridle in my hand all this time.

I slipped on the bridle, undented my bowler, and remounted.

*   *   *   *

It was now late afternoon. The smoke of hedgerow fires hung in the air; distances grew hazy.

We found another fox, but I was feeling very stiff and had really had enough.

As we went away after the second fox John Bull shouted: 'It's Cropley this time,' as he galloped by.

John Bull was right – Cropley it was. Cropley was a wood of vast extent, a virtual sanctuary for the fox. Once he gained it, it was almost impossible to get him out again. It was getting dusk, and there was much galloping along shadowy wood rides, hallos and yoicks and toot-tooting of the horn.

At length the horn sounded a long waning note, as though proclaiming truce with the evening, and there was an end.

We jogged homeward under the rising moon.

Mr Colville said to his wife: 'I reckon he'll be so stiff he won't know how to move in the morning.' And I reckoned I should.

I was asleep as soon as I was in bed, and never ceased galloping all night. It ended, I think, by Cantilever leaping the railings of the square in which my home stood. As I remember, we found in Battersea Park.

Adrian Bell: Corduroy

And, as a final fling, here is:

MR JORROCKS' DINNER PARTY

Mr Jorrocks then called upon the company in succession for a toast, a song, or a sentiment. Nimrod gave, 'The Queen and her Staghounds'; Crane gave, 'Champagne to our real friends, and

real pain to our sham friends'; Green sang, 'I'd be a Butterfly';
Mr Stubbs gave, 'Honest Men and Bonnie Lasses'; and Mr
Spiers, like a patriotic printer, gave, 'The Liberty of the Press,'
which he said was like fox-hunting – 'if we have it not, we die'
– all of which Mr Jorrocks applauded as if he had never heard
them before, and drank in bumpers. It was evident that unless tea
was speedily announced, he would soon become –

'O'er the ills of life victorious,'

for he had pocketed his wig, and had been clipping the Queen's
English for some time. After a pause, during which his cheeks
twice changed colour, from red to green and back to red, he
again called for a bumper toast, which he prefaced with the
following speech, or parts of a speech: –

'Gentlemen, – in rising – propose toast about to give – feel
werry – feel werry – (Yorkshireman, "Werry muzzy?") J. –
feel werry – (Mr Spiers "Werry sick?") J. – werry (Crane
"Werry thirsty?") J. – feel werry (Nimrod "Werry wise?")
J. – no; but werry *sensible* – great compliment – eyes of England
upon us – give you the health – Mr H'Apperley Nimrod – three
times three!'

He then attempted to rise for the purpose of marking the
time, but his legs deserted his body, and, after two or three
lurches, down he went with a tremendous thump under the
table. He called first for 'Batsay' then for 'Binjimin,' and, game
to the last, blurted out, 'Lift me up! – tie me in my chair! – fill
my glass!'

R. S. Surtees: *Jorrocks's Jaunts and Jollities*

Andrew Dodds

H. E. Bates has used many settings for his novels and short stories, but my favourite is the country inhabited by Uncle Silas, that little-known district between the rivers Ouse and Nene, where Bedfordshire and Northamptonshire adjoin.

Uncle Silas is a superb character, crusty, crafty and glinting with wicked life despite his years. Here, with the trusting small boy as a foil, we see him with all his fun and foibles.

The Little Fishes *comes from a collection of short stories about Uncle Silas called* Sugar for the Horse, *published by Michael Joseph in 1957.*

H. E. Bates was born at Rushden in Northamptonshire in 1905, and now lives in Kent.

THE LITTLE FISHES

My Uncle Silas was very fond of fishing. It was an occupation that helped to keep him from thinking too much about work and also about how terribly hard it was.

If you went through the bottom of my Uncle Silas's garden, past the gooseberry bushes, the rhubarb and the pig-sties, you came to a path that went alongside a wood where primroses grew so richly in spring that they blotted out the floor of oak and hazel leaves. In summer wild strawberries followed the primroses and by July the meadows beyond the wood were frothy with meadowsweet, red clover and the seed of tall soft grasses.

At the end of the second meadow a little river, narrow in parts and bellying out into black deep pools in others, ran along between willows and alders, occasional clumps of dark high reeds and a few wild crab trees. Some of the pools, in July, would be white with water lilies, and snakes would swim across the light flat leaves in the sun. Moorhens talked to each other behind the reeds and water rats would plop suddenly out of sight under clumps of yellow monkey flower.

Here in this little river, my Uncle Silas used to tell me when I was a boy, 'the damn pike used to be as big as hippopotamassiz.'

'Course they ain't so big now,' he would say. 'Nor yit the tench. Nor yit the perch. Nor yit the—'

'Why aren't they so big?'

'Well, I'm a-talkin' about fifty years agoo. Sixty year agoo. Very near seventy years agoo.'

'If they were so big then,' I said, 'all that time ago, they ought to be even bigger now.'

'Not the ones we catched,' he said. 'They ain't there.'

You couldn't, as you see from this, fox my Uncle Silas very easily, but I was at all times a very inquisitive, persistent little boy.

'How big were the tench?' I said.

'Well, I shall allus recollect one as me and Sammy Twizzle caught,' he said. 'Had to lay it in a pig trough to carry it home.'

'And how big were the perch?'

'Well,' he said, rolling his eye in recollection, in that way he had of bringing the wrinkled lid slowly down over it, very like a fish ancient in craftiness himself, 'I don' know as I can jistly recollect the size o' that one me and Arth Sugars nipped out of a September morning one time. But I do know as I cleaned up the back fin and used it for horse comb for about twenty year.'

'Oh! Uncle Silas,' I would say, 'let's go fishing! Let's go and see if they're still as big as hippopotamassiz!'

But it was not always easy, once my Uncle Silas had settled under the trees at the end of the garden on a hot July afternoon, to persuade him that it was worth walking across two meadows just to see if the fish were as big as they used to be. Nevertheless I was, as I say, a very inquisitive, persistent little boy and finally my Uncle Silas would roll over, take the red handkerchief off his face and grunt:

'If you ain't the biggest whittle-breeches I ever knowed I'll goo t'Hanover. Goo an' git the rod and bring a bit o' dough. They'll be no peace until you do, will they?'

'Shall I bring the rod for you too?'

'*Rod?*' he said. 'For *me*. *Rod?*' He let fall over his eye a tremulous bleary fish-like lid of scorn. 'When me and Sammy Twizzle went a-fishin', all we had to catch 'em with wur we bare hands and a drop o' neck-oil.'

'What's neck-oil?'

'Never you mind,' he said. 'You git the rod and I'll git the neck-oil.'

And presently we would be walking out of the garden, past the wood and across the meadows, I carrying the rod, the dough and perhaps a piece of caraway cake in a paper bag, my Uncle Silas waddling along in his stony-coloured corduroy trousers, carrying the neck-oil.

Sometimes I would be very inquisitive about the neck-oil, which was often pale greenish-yellow, rather the colour of cowslip, or perhaps of parsnips, and sometimes purplish-red, rather the colour of elderberries, or perhaps of blackberries or plums.

On one occasion I noticed that the neck-oil was very light in colour, almost white, or perhaps more accurately like straw-coloured water.

'Is it a new sort of neck-oil you've got?' I said.

'New flavour.'

'What is it made of?'

'Taters.'

'And you've got two bottles today,' I said.

'Must try to git used to the new flavour.'

'And do you think,' I said, 'we shall catch a bigger fish now that you've got a new kind of neck-oil?'

'Shouldn't be a bit surprised, boy,' he said, 'if we don't git one as big as a donkey.'

That afternoon it was very hot and still as we sat under the shade of a big willow, by the side of a pool that seemed to have across it an oiled black skin broken only by minutest winks of sunlight when the leaves of the willow parted softly in gentle turns of air.

'This is the place where me and Sammy tickled that big 'un out,' my Uncle Silas said.

'The one you carried home in a pig trough?'

'That's the one.'

I said how much I too should like to catch one I could take home in a pig trough and my Uncle Silas said:

'Well, you never will if you keep whittlin' and talkin' and ompolodgin' about.' My Uncle Silas was the only man in the world who ever used the word ompolodgin'. It was a very expressive word and when my Uncle Silas accused you of ompolodgin' it was a very serious matter. It meant that you had buttons on your bottom and if you didn't drop it he would damn well ding your ear.

'You gotta sit still and wait and not keep fidgetin' and very like in another half-hour you'll see a big 'un layin' aside o' that log. But not if you keep ompolodgin'! See?'

'Yes, Uncle.'

'That's why I bring the neck-oil,' he said. 'It quiets you down so's you ain't a-whittlin' and a-ompolodgin' all the time.'

'Can I have a drop of neck-oil?'

'When you git thirsty,' my Uncle Silas said, 'there's that there spring in the next medder.'

After this my Uncle Silas took a good steady drink of neck-oil and settled down with his back against the tree. I put a big lump of paste on my hook and dropped it into the pool. The only fish I could see in the pool were shoals of little silver tiddlers that flickered about a huge fallen willow log a yard or two upstream or came to play inquisitively about my little white and scarlet float, making it quiver up and down like the trembling scraps of sunlight across the water.

Sometimes the bread paste got too wet and slipped from the hook and I quietly lifted the rod from the water and put another lump on the hook. I tried almost not to breathe as I did all this and every time I took the rod out of the water I glanced furtively at my Uncle Silas to see if he thought I was ompolodgin'.

Every time I looked at him I could see that he evidently didn't think so. He was always far too busy with the neck-oil.

I suppose we must have sat there for nearly two hours on that hot windless afternoon of July, I not speaking a word and trying not to breathe as I threw my little float across the water, my Uncle Silas never uttering a sound either except for a drowsy grunt or two as he uncorked one bottle of neck-oil or felt to see if the other was safe in his jacket pocket.

All that time there was no sign of a fish as big as a hippopotamus or even of one you could take home in a pig trough and all the time my Uncle kept tasting the flavour of the neck-oil, until at last his head began to fall forward on his chest. Soon all my bread paste was gone and I got so afraid of disturbing my Uncle Silas that I scotched my rod to the fallen log and walked into the next meadow to get myself a drink of water from the spring.

The water was icy cold from the spring and very sweet and good and I wished I had brought myself a bottle, too, so that I could fill it and sit back against a tree, as my Uncle Silas did, and pretend that it was neck-oil.

Ten minutes later, when I got back to the pool, my Uncle Silas was fast asleep by the tree trunk, one bottle empty by his side and the other still in his jacket pocket. There was, I thought, a remarkable expression on his face, a wonderful rosy fogginess about his mouth and nose and eyes.

But what I saw in the pool, as I went to pick my rod from the water, was a still more wonderful thing.

During the afternoon the sun had moved some way round and under the branches of the willow, so that now, at the first touch of evening, there were clear bands of pure yellow light across the pool.

In one of these bands of light, by the fallen log, lay a long lean fish, motionless as a bar of steel, just under the water, basking in the evening sun.

When I woke my Uncle Silas he came to himself with a fumbling start, red eyes only half open, and I thought for a moment that perhaps he would ding my ear for ompolodgin'.

'But it's as big as a hippopotamus,' I said. 'It's as big as the one in the pig trough.'

'Wheer, boy? Wheer?'

When I pointed out the fish, my Uncle Silas could not, at

first, see it lying there by the log. But after another nip of neck-oil he started to focus it correctly.

'By Jingo, that's a big 'un,' he said. 'By Jingo, that's a walloper.'

'What sort is it?'

'Pike,' he said. 'Git me a big lump o' paste and I'll dangle it a-top of his nose.'

'The paste has all gone.'

'Then give us a bit o' caraway and we'll tiddle him up wi' that.'

'I've eaten all the caraway,' I said. 'Besides, you said you and Sammy Twizzle used to catch them with your hands. You said you used to tickle their bellies—'

'Well, that wur—'

'Get him! Get him! Get him!' I said. 'He's as big as a donkey!'

Slowly, and with what I thought was some reluctance, my Uncle Silas heaved himself to his feet. He lifted the bottle from his pocket and took a sip of neck-oil. Then he slapped the cork back with the palm of his hand and put the bottle back in his pocket.

'Now you stan' back,' he said, 'and dammit, don't git ompolodgin'!'

I stood back. My Uncle Silas started to creep along the fallen willow-log on his hands and knees. Below him, in the band of sunlight, I could see the long dark lean pike, basking.

For nearly two minutes my Uncle Silas hovered on the end of the log. Then slowly he balanced himself on one hand and dipped his other into the water. Over the pool it was marvellously, breathlessly still and I knew suddenly that this was how it had been in the good great old days, when my Uncle Silas and Sammy Twizzle had caught the mythical mammoth ones, fifty years before.

'God A'mighty!' my Uncle Silas suddenly yelled. 'I'm a-gooin' over!'

My Uncle Silas was indeed gooin' over. Slowly, like a turning spit, the log started heeling, leaving my Uncle Silas half-slipping, half-dancing at its edge, like a man on a greasy pole.

In terror I shut my eyes. When I opened them and looked again my Uncle Silas was just coming up for air, yelling 'God A'mighty, boy, I believe you ompolodged!'

I thought for a moment he was going to be very angry with me. Instead he started to cackle with crafty, devilish, stentorian laughter, his wet lips dribbling, his eyes more fiery than ever under the dripping water, his right hand triumphant as he snatched it up from the stream.

'Jist managed to catch it, boy,' he yelled, and in triumph he held up the bottle of neck-oil.

And somewhere downstream, startled by his shout, a whole host of little tiddlers jumped from the water, dancing in the evening sun.

H. E. Bates: *Sugar for the Horse*

INDEX OF AUTHORS

Aumonier, Stacey, 131

Bates, H. E., 249
Bell, Adrian, 240
Bell, Julian, 164
Blake, William, 48
Blunden, Edmund, 104, 125, 127, 175, 227
Bridges, Robert, 157

Cambridge Chronicle, 165
Cambridge Coronation Festival, 207
Cane, Melville, 169
Chaucer, Geoffrey, 20, 157, 211
Clare, John, 124
Coatsworth, Elizabeth J., 167
Cornford, Frances, 86, 90, 94
Culpeper, Nicholas, 187, 189, 190, 192

Davies, W. H., 162
De la Mare, Walter, 163
Dolci, Danilo, 122

Eliot, George, 28, 97

Farjeon, Eleanor, 61
Fielding, Henry, 35, 38
Fleming, Marjorie, 120
Frost, Robert, 113, 170

Gaskell, Elizabeth, 106
Gerard, John, 194, 198, 199, 200, 201, 202
Grattan, J. H. G., and Singer, Charles, 185
Goldsmith, Oliver, 27

Hardy, Thomas, 46, 126, 220
Herrick, Robert, 85
Hodgson, Ralph, 58
Horace, 19
Howard, Henry, 155

Jefferies, Richard, 120
Jerome, Jerome K., 121, 214, 239

Keats, John, 57, 118, 158, 171, 219
Kirkup, James, 168

Lee, Charles, 63
Lee, Laurie, 34

Macneice, Louis, 162
Mew, Charlotte, 96
Mitford, Mary Russell, 49, 51, 87, 223

Newbury Weekly News, 43

Old Rhyme, 127
Osborne, Dorothy, 40, 44, 176, 212

Pope, Alexander, 89

Reading Mercury and Oxford Gazette, 231

Scovell, E. J., 115
Shakespeare, William, 106, 123, 158, 160, 168, 170, 184
Singer, Charles and Grattan, J. H. G., 185
Sitwell, Sacheverell, 58
Smith, Bertram, 112
Smollett, Tobias, 42, 55
Surtees, R. S., 237, 246

Thomas, Dylan, 25, 92, 93
Thomas, Edward, 125, 128
Thomas, R. S., 52
Thompson, Flora, 22, 43, 53, 59, 91, 177, 178, 215, 229, 234

Uttley, Alison, 32, 95

Walton, Izaak, 114, 193
White, Gilbert, 111, 116, 182, 183
Woodforde, James, 104, 105, 119, 179, 180, 181, 182, 203, 210, 223, 231
Wordsworth, Dorothy, 21, 26, 119, 159, 161, 218
Wordsworth, William, 160, 163